PARIS SYNDROME

PARIS SYNDROME

Tahir Shah

SECRETUM MUNDI PUBLISHING
LONDON
MMXIV

Secretum Mundi Publishing

3rd Floor, 36 Langham Street, London W1W 7AP, United Kingdom

http://www.secretum-mundi.com/

info@secretum-mundi.com

First published
Secretum Mundi edition, 2014

ISBN 978-1-291-73643-4

*This book is dedicated to the memory
of Takeki Taketani, and to the many people
who showed me such kindness when I lived in Japan.*

In a mad world, only the mad are sane.
Akira Kurosawa

Paris Syndrome: A transient psychological disorder encountered by some individuals visiting or vacationing in Paris, France. It is characterized by a number of psychiatric symptoms such as acute delusional states, hallucinations, feelings of persecution, derealization, depersonalization, anxiety, and also psychosomatic manifestations such as dizziness, tachycardia, sweating, and others. Similar syndromes include Jerusalem Syndrome and Stendhal Syndrome.

1

ON THE MORNING of her fifth birthday, Miki Suzuki sat perched on her grandfather's knee, at the edge of the porch in the family home, a short distance from Sendai.

Giggling and grinning, and tugging at his scraggly beard, she pleaded for her birthday gift.

His eyes narrowing until they were little more than creases in a wrinkled face, the old man said:

'I am going to give you something very special my little plum. A gift that you can never lose – one that will be with you every minute of the day, forever.'

Squirming up closer to her grandfather's face, Miki kissed him gently on the cheek.

'What is it, Ojiichan?'

'It is a story,' he said.

And, before the little girl could utter another word, her grandfather began:

'Once upon a time,' he whispered softly, 'there was a city that was Paradise on Earth. All the women were beautiful and were dressed in the finest gowns, their skin scented with delicate perfumes. And all the men were handsome, like movie stars. The streets were wide and graceful, and were lined with trees abundant with blossom all year round. The sun never stopped shining, and the warm air was filled with butterflies and birdsong.'

Miki tugged at the long hairs of her grandfather's chin, and she laughed.

'I want to go there, Ojiichan!' she cried. 'Will you take me there, please, please, please?!'

The retired old salaryman smoothed a wizened hand over his little granddaughter's cheek.

'One day we will go there together,' he said, 'and will walk the length of the great boulevard hand in hand.'

'But, *when*, Ojiichan? When will you take me?'

Miki's grandfather looked deep into the little girl's eyes.

'When you are a little bit older, my little plum.'

'Tomorrow? I will be older tomorrow.'

'Well, maybe a little after that.'

'Next week?'

'Perhaps.'

Miki stood up on her grandfather's lap, and wrapped her short arms around his neck.

'Do you promise?'

'Of course I do.'

'Ojiichan?'

'Yes, Miki-chan?'

'Will you tell me one last thing?'

'Yes, what is it, Miki-chan?'

'What's the name of the city – the one in the story?'

The retired old salaryman hugged his granddaughter, and pressed his lips to her ear.

'It is called Paris,' he said.

2

TWENTY YEARS PASSED.

Miki grew into an energetic woman, with a frenzied love for life. She had long black hair, an impish face, and did everything at top speed. But, most of all, she was kind in a deep down way, a quality that endeared her to almost everyone she met.

After school, Miki had left the slow suburbs of Sendai, and moved to Tokyo. There, she got a job selling discounted beauty products door to door, for the Angel Flower Beauty Company.

She may have been far from home, but Miki never forgot her grandfather's story, and would turn it around in her mind as she trudged from one apartment building to the next.

And, on some nights when she couldn't sleep in her minuscule apartment, she would fantasize about the place first seeded in her thoughts all those years before.

She would imagine herself strolling through the streets of Paris in late spring, wearing a floral print dress from Dior, with a matching pink parasol.

And all the young men's heads would turn.

The sunlight would be dazzling, gleaming on the serene waters of the Seine. There would be music flowing from the little cafés, and the sound of feet tap-dancing on the sea of cobblestones.

As the years passed, Miki became more and more preoccupied with her fantasy, the fantasy of the French capital. It was a symbol as much as a destination – a symbol of all that was good and right.

She spent every spare moment reading about its secrets and its history, learning of the museums and the architecture, and of the traditions. And the more she learned, the more Miki realized that Paris was a place tied to her destiny, a place in which her own future would be acted out.

It was just a matter of time.

3

Every few months, Miki would leave the urban sprawl of Tokyo behind, and travel back home to Sendai on the Shinkansen.

Sitting at the window, she would stare out, as the bullet train gathered speed, her eyes glued to the blurred landscape of identical concrete homes, their balconies cluttered with rusting bicycles and junk.

And she would find herself dreaming – of Paris's magnificent stone *hôtels particuliers* and of the grandeur conjured by Baron Haussmann a century and a half before.

There was no detail Miki couldn't imagine – from the patina of the roof slates on the Elysée Palace, to the aroma of the creamy cappuccinos served up at Café de Flore. She could visualize the Eiffel Tower illuminated on a chill winter evening, as though she were standing before it, or the great rose window on the Gothic façade of Notre Dame, or the enormous tricolour rippling back and forth in the breeze high above the Grand Palais.

Each time Miki arrived at her family home, her parents were a little older and a little more subdued. They always asked about their daughter's life in Tokyo, and she did her best to make it sound exotic and amusing. Secretly, Miki wished she could tell them the truth – that she detested her job and a life in a city so large that there was hardly a beginning or an end.

She missed her family home in the suburbs of Sendai, but most of all she missed Paris – a place she regarded as her real home, a place she had known only through stories.

The one person who could grasp the infatuation was her beloved ojiichan.

The summer before, he had suffered a stroke. Now he spent his days staring into space, propped up on the futon against goose-down pillows. He couldn't talk, but he could whisper, although he tired after only a minute or two.

Miki had always dreamed of walking arm in arm with him down the Champs-Elysées, from the Arc de Triomphe towards Concorde. She imagined kicking through the autumn leaves with him as they strolled past the posh shops. Most of all, she imagined herself glancing into the old man's eyes as they went.

Deep down, Miki knew there was little hope of her grandfather ever leaving the house, let alone travelling so far as the capital city of France.

Each year, for twenty years, the ojiichan had presented his grand-daughter with another fragment of the same birthday gift.

The story.

Less of an actual tale, it was more of a description – one gleaned from a first-hand memory of a short visit he had made to Paris in the decade after the War.

'I was young then,' he whispered on the afternoon of Miki's twenty-fifth birthday, 'so young and so foolish. I wandered day and night through the cobbled streets, my feet floating, my heart beating as though I had fallen hopelessly in love.'

'In love with Paris?' Miki asked, as she sat on the corner of her grandfather's futon.

'Yes… with Paris, my true love,' Ojiichan sighed, 'the most bewitching of lovers. She casts a magic spell on every man who sets eyes upon her.'

Miki reached out and touched her grandfather's fingers with her own. There were tears welling in her eyes. She could feel the old man's strength draining away, as though he were coming to the end of his story-telling days.

'Tell me something, dearest Ojiichan,' she said, stroking his hand with hers. 'Out of all your experiences in Paris, what was the most wonderful moment of all?'

Her grandfather's eyelids lowered very slowly, and his breathing seemed to shallow, until it was so faint that Miki wondered whether he had expired. His eyes still closed, she felt his hand tremble in hers. And then, in a voice so soft as to be inaudible, he said something.

'I didn't hear, Ojiichan.'

The old man tugged tenderly at his granddaughter's hand. She edged closer, until her ear was an inch from his mouth.

'The coin pouch,' he said. 'It was the moment that I saw the coin pouch.'

Miki didn't understand. Squeezing her ojiichan's hand a little tighter, she coaxed him to tell the tale.

There was silence for a minute or even two.

All of a sudden the old man began to whisper again.

'It was a bright Sunday morning,' he said, 'Paris in spring, and my last day in the French capital. I had been ambling through the Tuileries Gardens, enjoying the calm pace of life, and watching people out walking their dogs, or just relaxing in the sun. There was nothing planned until the evening, and so I decided to do a little exploring. Without looking at my map, I meandered through the quiet back-streets, until I reached the beautiful Avenue Marceau.'

Miki's grandfather took a deep breath, his eyes still closed. Only after another long pause did he continue, his words delivered slowly, one by one:

'I had heard about that street,' he said. 'It was very famous at the time – famous for expensive shops. My guidebook said that it was where royalty, fashion models, and Hollywood stars shopped. I had heard that Emperor Hirohito himself had even visited in 1921, when he travelled to Paris as Crown Prince.'

'What about the coin pouch, Ojiichan?' Miki prompted, worried that her grandfather had lost his train of thought.

'I am coming to that,' he replied pointedly. 'As I said, I was strolling down Avenue Marceau, enjoying the fine weather, and window-shopping. After all it was a Sunday and most of the shops were closed. I can remember every detail – the pigeons flapping about; the sound of a little girl screaming because she had dropped her ice cream; the stiff uniformed police officer on patrol; and the sight of a wealthy woman striding past me, wearing a voluminous green hat.

'And then, suddenly, I found myself peering into the window of a luggage shop. I remember that it stood at Number 78, and that it had two large windows, in which were displayed all manner of fine leather goods. Above them, in discreet lettering mounted on the iron railings, was the name – Louis Vuitton.

'As I stood there, peering into the window, I set eyes on a little coin pouch, crafted from simple brown leather. It was not the grandest thing at all – there were bulky steamer trunks and other far more elaborate items. But that coin pouch was the most exquisite thing I had ever seen.'

'Did you buy it, Ojiichan?' Miki asked in a low voice.

'No, no… as I told you, the shop was closed, and early the next day I had to leave for home. Almost every day which has passed since then, I have thought of the little coin pouch. It may sound silly to you, but seeing it was the high point of an unforgettable visit to Paris. Indeed, in a way it was the high point of my life.'

The old man opened his eyes, allowing the memory to fade. He sighed again and, as he did so, Miki leaned forward and kissed his cheek, as she had done twenty years before.

'Thank you for my birthday gift,' she said lovingly. 'It means more to me than anything I have ever been given.'

'A silly gift,' said the ojiichan with a smile.

Miki sat upright.

Overcome with solemnity and emotion, she pressed her fingertips together as if in prayer. As she did so, she looked into her grandfather's clouded eyes.

'I will go to Paris!' she exclaimed. 'I don't know how, but I will… and I will bring the coin pouch for you dearest Ojiichan – the coin pouch from Louis Vuitton!'

4

THE NEXT DAY, Miki took the bullet train back to Tokyo.

And, the day after that, she was again trying to entice the housewives of overworked salarymen into buying beauty products on the cheap. The winter chill was biting, the city bracing itself against a cold front racing south from Sakhalin.

Miki's studio apartment was more freezing than it had ever been. There was ice on the inside of the windows, and a pool of frozen water on the bathroom floor.

As soon as she got home from work, Miki would put on her pyjamas and clamber into bed. And she would lie there, thinking of her ojiichan, and how she could get the coin pouch for him from Louis Vuitton.

Each afternoon she struggled out into the roaring wind, to give demonstrations in small apartment homes far from the centre of town. The format was always the same, carefully designed at head office in Shinjuku by an army of planners in uniform grey suits. They had trained Miki on a special course, teaching her exactly how to respond to any conceivable situation.

An officious angry man had been appointed as her boss. He was named Kiato Yamato. He had a big red wart in the middle of his forehead, and very rotten teeth, the kind that make children giggle in fear and surprise. Behind his back everyone called him 'Pun-Pun', which is the onomatopoeic sound of someone being angry. No one liked Pun-Pun, not even his wife. But, as with everyone else, she endured him because she was very frightened of him indeed.

During the long and wearisome training course, Pun-Pun had taught Miki to always stress the positive side of the Angel Flower beauty line. This included being excellent value for money, and being easy to use. Over and over he underlined that she was never, ever, on any account to mention the shortcomings of the brand. These included a plethora of adverse effects which had been widely reported in the media – such as the way the cleansing balms caused severe blistering on sensitive skin.

Following Pun-Pun's orders, Miki had learned to wax lyrical about the secret ingredients and the miraculous effects of the much-lauded Angel Flower range. With time and indoctrination, she had learned the right way of selling the lotions, creams and ointments.

This entailed getting as many women as possible clustered together in a small apartment. Friends and neighbours, and even passersby, all were welcomed by 'special invitation', to take part in what was a classic party plan marketing method.

Three days after returning from Miyagi Prefecture, Miki went out to Kasai on the Toyo Line. The journey from her home in Ikebukuro was a long one, but the rewards were great. There wasn't another Angel Flower representative working the patch, and so rich pickings were assured for a diligent saleswoman like herself.

Laden with boxes of samples and gift boxes to sell, Miki made her way to the apartment of a friend. Through a great deal of social networking in the days before, she had lined up a casual coffee morning for a dozen local housewives.

On the dot of 10.45 a.m., the invited women arrived at her friend's two-room flat. Removing their shoes as they entered, they bowed a greeting and filed inside to the sitting-room, where they took their places on the floor.

Once they were assembled, the owner of the apartment, Keiko, welcomed the ladies formally and set about serving green tea. There was a great deal of smiling and anxious laughter. Having been trained how to handle a group meeting and, more importantly, how to turn it into sales, Miki began her routine.

'The Angel Flower beauty range has been brought from Australia,' she said, 'and it is brightening the lives of women just like you across Japan. Our products are different from those of other companies, because they are made with natural ingredients from an ancient formula.' Miki paused. 'A formula that we don't test on animals,' she said.

Kneeling together in the tiny sitting-room, the housewives sipped their tea, and listened attentively. Once Miki was done with her introduction, she opened the oversized lacquered box before her, and handed out little gift packs, one to each of the women.

A wave of enthused cooing rippled through the room.

'Go on, please open them up,' said Miki, as she had been told to do by the training team. 'Try the products, and see how you look.'

With great delight, the housewives tore open the packaging, and began rubbing their skin with the scented lotions and creams.

As Miki watched them, she found herself thinking of her ojiichan strolling through Paris on a Sunday in spring. She imagined the soles of his leather shoes on the gleaming cobbles, and the bright yellow light filtering through the young green leaves of the sycamore trees. The memory may not have been her own, but she wished it were. And the more she wished, the more she felt warm inside, as though she were staring into a painting in which she belonged.

'I will go there,' she whispered.

'Go where?' asked Keiko, as she spooned a pungent-smelling balm onto her cheeks.

'To Paris.'

'*Paris*?!'

'Yes…'

'You're going to Paris?'

Miki nodded. Then she giggled, covering her teeth modestly with a pair of horizontal fingers.

'When?'

'I don't know.'

'Oh,' Keiko replied.

'It's my dream,' said Miki quietly. 'The greatest dream of my life.'

Her friend smiled in a kind way.

'Believe hard enough, and dreams always come true,' she said.

5

THE NEXT DAY, the temperature fell even lower and it began to snow.

But rather than being disheartened by it, Miki found herself enlivened. The pristine mantle of white gave a sense of serenity to Tokyo's bleak cityscape. With her morning sales sessions cancelled because of the weather, Miki arranged to meet her best friend, Ichiko, in Shinjuku.

Ichiko worked for Angel Flower as well. A little shorter than Miki, she had unusually round eyes, a feature that gained her the attention of a great many young men. She, too, spent her life crisscrossing the suburbs, desperately trying to get impecunious housewives to take advantage of discounted beauty products.

Arriving early, Miki slipped into Kinokuniya, the cavernous bookshop on Shinjuku Dori, on the south side of the station. Once inside, she made a beeline for the section where the coffee table books were sold.

A clerk with gelled-back hair stepped forward and asked whether he could be of help. Nodding her head in thanks, Miki smiled and, in the shrill voice of formal enquiry, she said:

'Do you have a big colourful book about Paris?'

The sales clerk touched a finger to his upper lip. He tilted his head on one side, then the other.

'Yes,' he said abruptly, 'I think we have just what you are looking for.'

His hands caressing their way through the forest of vertical spines, he withdrew a large square-shaped volume. Prominent on the front was a photograph of the Eiffel Tower.

'Are you going there?' he said, passing Miki the book.

'Yes!'

'When?'

'Not sure. But soon, I hope.'

'I went there once,' said the clerk, combing a hand back through his shiny hair.

Miki gasped.

'What was it like?'

'It was like a daydream.'

Clutching the volume to her chest, Miki sighed.

'I want to go there very badly,' she said.

'Well, when you do, you must go to a little museum. It's called Musée Nissim de Camondo.'

'*Nissim de Camondo?*'

'Yes… Camondo.'

'I will remember.'

The clerk asked Miki if she was going to buy the book.

Her enthused expression melted.

'I think that I will just look at it today,' she said. 'Because it will help me to get a little closer to the daydream of my own.'

Once the clerk had gone off to help someone else, Miki flicked through the pages. Each spread was packed with wonders – immense boulevards and prim little cafés, chic couples strolling arm in arm, and grand stone buildings.

As she stood there, the large volume held between her hands, Miki began to cry. She couldn't help it. The thought of a place so perfect in every way, and the notion of her own ojiichan being a bridge between her and Paris, was too much to take.

Half an hour later, she was sitting with Ichiko in Starbucks, each of them slurping hot chocolate with whipped cream on the top.

Ichiko pulled out a little gift bag.

'For your birthday,' she said.

Miki clapped her hands fast and emitted a short squeal of delight.

'You remembered!'

'Of course I did.'

'What is it?'

'Open it and see.'

Miki tore away the gold and blue packaging and found herself holding a French phrase book. She began sobbing again.

'How did you know?!' she exclaimed, wiping her eyes.

'About what?'

'About my love for French... about my love for Paris?'

'I am your best friend,' Ichiko replied. 'I know everything about you.'

Miki sipped her chocolate.

'Then, do you know that I am going to Paris?' she said.

'When?'

'Everyone asks me that. And the answer is – *I don't know*. But I have to go there. You see, I've made a promise.'

'Who to?'

'To my ojiichan.'

'What is it… your promise?'

'To bring him a little coin pouch from Louis Vuitton.'

Ichiko frowned.

'There's a Louis Vuitton in Ginza,' she said. 'You could get the coin pouch there.'

Miki dried away her tears.

'It wouldn't be the same,' she said.

6

THE NEXT WEEK, the Angel Flower Beauty Company was in the news again.

A housewife from Fukuoka went on television denouncing the firm's cactus cleansing lotion, claiming it had given her a painful rash and swelling on her face. The rash had gone septic and she had been left looking as though exposed to a chemical weapon rather than having been treated with a beauty product.

The firm's leadership went into crisis management. The chairman called an emergency meeting for the top executives. A beefy, round-headed barrel of a man, he was feared by all – even more than Pun-Pun – not because he was cruel or angry, but because he was so mysterious.

No one knew anything about him. They didn't even know his name.

After outlining the situation, the chairman pledged funds for a special publicity campaign. Then, with a grunt, he asked for suggestions on how to boost sales.

One of the executives suggested giving away samples at subway stations. Another had the idea of getting a celebrity to champion the brand. Then a young manager from Sapporo raised his hand.

Pun-Pun looked at him with characteristic ire, wondering how such a lowly executive had got into the meeting.

'What do you want?' he snapped.

'Excuse me, but I have an idea, sir.'

'What idea?'

'To hold a competition.'

'What?!'

'We will put special tickets inside our products for our customers to win, and the woman in our own workforce who sells the most products will…'

'*Will what?*'

'Will go on an amazing journey!'

Yamato slapped his hands together and dismissed the idea as utterly preposterous. He was about to reprimand the young executive, when the chairman cleared his throat.

'A splendid idea!' he roared.

There was complete silence while the leader ruminated.

'But where would they go, on this vacation?'

'On a cruise, sir!' a voice called out.

'It's been done already.'

'What about New York?' suggested an executive from the Osaka office.

Again, the chairman wagged an index finger, left and then right.

'Our products have been banned in America,' he said awkwardly.

The young executive who had come up with the idea rose to his feet.

'They will go to Paris!' he exclaimed.

7

THAT EVENING, MIKI got home and immediately climbed into bed, huddling beneath half a dozen blankets.

The ice on the inside of the windows was twice as thick as it had been the evening before. She didn't have enough money to buy a heater, let alone to run it. But, having grown up with her grandfather's tales of post-War economizing, Miki was content to make do without the luxuries that others took for granted – luxuries like heat.

Her salary was entirely based on a commission from sales. In recent weeks, the slew of negative press reports featuring the Angel Flower brand had done nothing to help Miki afford a heater, let alone buy a long-haul air ticket.

Despite this, just before turning in for the night, she caught her neighbour's WiFi signal and went online to check prices of flights from Narita airport to Paris.

Tickets started at 100,000 yen.

With hotels and other incidentals, it was a trip way beyond a saleswoman's means.

Closing her old laptop, Miki switched off the light and laid her head on the pillow. And, then, before lulling herself to sleep, as she did each night with silent landscapes of Paris, she said a prayer.

She prayed to her ancestors, that they hear her wish and transport her magically from the cramped studio in Ikebukuro to the sprawling boulevards of the French capital. And she prayed that she would find true love and happiness in the city of her dreams.

'It's not only because I want to go there,' Miki whispered to the ancestors, 'but to get the coin pouch for my dear ojiichan.'

8

At the end of the week, Angel Flower announced a new product line, a range of creams called Blue Onyx, made with aged shark liver oil. The line was hoped to act as an added diversion from the recent tempest of bad publicity.

The entire sales force was given a special briefing in the company's assembly hall on the many merits of Blue Onyx. The chairman of the firm himself made an appearance to wish the saleswomen the best of luck. Addressing them from the stage, he gave thanks for all the work they did in the good name of Angel Flower. And then, before sending them off to sell the new range, he asked for one last minute of their attention.

'I have an announcement,' he said in a distant voice, as Pun-Pun, his much-maligned henchman, stepped forward from the shadows.

A wave of murmuring swept through the room. At least half of the sales force imagined they were about to be laid off. After all, it was no secret that Angel Flower was in serious financial trouble.

But the chairman's sour expression warmed.

'Here at Angel Flower, we are dedicated to making lives more pleasurable,' he said. 'Each day, women across Japan use our cosmetics and, as a result, they find happiness and escape. Even though they might be here in Tokyo, or in Osaka or even in Hokkaido, they can apply our creams to their skin, and imagine they are walking down the Champs-Elysées.'

The chairman buttoned the jacket of his charcoal suit as he scanned the hundreds of female faces below him.

'I am proud to announce a competition,' he said. 'Three members of the public who find winning tickets in our special gift packs will be taken on a journey of a lifetime! And, with them, will go the one member of our own sales force who outperforms all the rest in the next thirty days.'

Lowering his head as if to stress his humility, the chairman paused. 'And where will these lucky people go?' he boomed.

The sales force looked up at their leader, a vacant expression on every face.

'Well, I shall tell you,' he thundered. 'They shall go to Paris!'

A cheer ripped through the hall as the all-female sales force celebrated the thought that one of them – one in six hundred and twenty-two – would be selected to represent Angel Flower in the French capital.

On the far right side of the hall, Miki Suzuki stood still as a statue. She couldn't speak, or even make a sound. She was too excited and too terrified. Even when her friend Ichiko hurried up to her, she just stood there, paralysed.

'Did you hear what he said?!' she cried. 'They're sending someone to Paris!'

All of a sudden, Miki thrust her arms up over her head and gave the loudest scream of her life.

'I'm going to win! I'm going to win!' she shouted over and over. 'I just know it for sure that I am going to win!'

9

FOR THE NEXT three weeks, Miki worked harder than she had ever imagined possible.

Each morning she left home in darkness, returning late at night. Taking trains further and further away from Ikebukuro, she reached housewives who had never before been offered the affordable and interesting products of Angel Flower. Some showed curiosity, while others slammed the door – having heard about the firm's shortcomings on the national news.

Every night when she finally got home, Miki rubbed her feet, cooked up a little fish and rice, and counted the money she had made for the company. Before going to bed, she would get her products ready for the next morning, and would pray to her ancestors to give her a little more strength to carry on. So preoccupied was she with the competition, that she forgot all about the cold.

The days passed, and Miki sold more and more cosmetics.

Whereas, before, she would only need to have her stock replenished every month, she was now getting restocked twice a week. Even the hard-hearted Pun-Pun managed to raise an eyebrow when he saw her sales sheet.

But Miki wasn't the only member of the sales force breaking records.

Noemi, whose name meant 'little laugh', was the most celebrated saleswoman in the entire company and had been for years. She was pretty, funny, popular, and was practically perfect in every way. And these assets did wonders when selling to the legions of housewives on whose doors she knocked.

As a way of increasing the sense of competition, Angel Flower's top sales totals were sent by SMS to everyone at noon each day. It was the one moment that Miki dreaded more than any other. And, even though looking at the numbers made her sick to the pit of her stomach, she forced herself to go through them one by one.

At the end of the first week, Noemi had sold 342 gift packs. The next closest sales figure was 212. As for Miki, she had only sold 199, and that was by almost killing herself through overwork.

Undeterred, with holes in her shoes from walking, and hardly able to breathe from a severe chest cold, she carried on – each day travelling further and further from home.

At the end of the second week, Miki's best friend found her lying in bed, with a fever and badly swollen feet.

'You have to stop this!' she ordered. 'In any case, Noemi is sure to win. She has sold more gift packs than anyone. I heard she's already been out shopping for the dress she'll wear in Paris.'

Miki scrunched up her fists and held them to her eyes.

'I hate her! I hate her! I hate her!' she yelled. 'I have to be the one who goes to Paris. It *has* to be me!'

Ichiko shrugged.

'Well, if you are going to beat her, you will have to think of a clever plan,' she said.

'What kind of plan?'

'Something that housewives can't resist.'

10

BY THE THIRD week, all three of the special tickets had been discovered by lucky customers. The winners were featured on TV, shown jumping up and down with excitement. The lavish details of the trip were broadcast, and the Blue Onyx line of cosmetics got plenty of free publicity.

Meanwhile, each morning Miki scraped herself out of bed and carried on selling door to door, at mothers' meetings and coffee mornings as she had always done. The problem was that each rendezvous took time because the housewives loved to gossip.

It was a vicious circle.

You couldn't get them to buy until they had been given a sufficient opportunity to gossip. And, the longer you let them gossip, the less time there was to move on to the next group of housewives.

Another drawback was that, like all the saleswomen, Miki had to carry her stock of gift packs around with her. They were heavy and bulky, and she could never carry quite enough to satisfy demand.

Losing hope, she sank into a terrible depression, and for three days she stayed in bed.

'I can't win!' she moaned to Ichiko on the phone. 'I'll never beat Noemi. You even told me so yourself!'

'Well, you won't beat her by not trying,' her friend replied.

'But what's the point?' asked Miki. 'I've given up trying to get to Paris. I'll just go to Louis Vuitton in Ginza and use my credit card to buy Ojiichan the coin pouch from there.'

'It won't be the same,' Ichiko said sternly, as she hung up.

Miki tossed the telephone onto her bed and burst into tears.

She couldn't remember ever being so unhappy. Shuffling into her minuscule kitchen area, she opened the cupboard. At the back was an extremely large bar of extra-dark chocolate. She had been saving it for a moment of inconsolable melancholy, a moment that had at last come.

Taking it out, she pulled off the gold wrapper and ate it all.

Then, feeling sick, she flopped back down on her futon and turned on the TV.

She watched the news – a stream of misery from Japan and then the world. But, after that, just before signing off, the anchor told the cheery story of a homeless man in Ueno Park, who had become something of a celebrity merely for being different. People brought him food and blankets, and applauded him.

And they loved him.

All he did was to stand there in rain and shine – on one leg, greeting everyone who passed.

Miki screwed up her face. It was the stupidest thing she had ever heard or seen.

But it gave her an idea.

11

THE NEXT MORNING, Miki took her suitcase filled with Blue Onyx gift packs over to Shiba Park. Selecting a spot where a lot of people passed, she closed her eyes and wished. She wished and she wished, and she wished and she wished. Then, taking out a white sheet of card and a black marker, she wrote a neat sign in *kanji*. It read:

MUST GO ON AN EXPENSIVE JOURNEY
TO FULFIL A FAMILY DUTY.
MY ONLY HOPE IS IF YOU TAKE ONE
OF MY GIFT BOXES FOR FREE.
DONATIONS ARE WELCOME.

For half an hour Miki stood beside the open suitcase.

It was so cold that everyone who passed was in such a hurry to get to work, that no one bothered to read the sign. Or, if they did, they didn't give it a second thought. Miki felt her fingers and her toes getting colder and colder. She stamped up and down to get her blood circulating, but it didn't do anything to warm her up.

Three hours went by, and she hadn't sold – or even given away – any of her gift packs. She began cursing herself for being so stupid. The homeless man on the TV had done so well because people felt sorry for him.

And no one felt sorry for Miki.

Just as she was about to pack up her case filled with Angel Flower gift packs and head for home, something especially unpleasant occurred.

It began to snow.

But, rather than rushing away, Miki stayed standing there. She wasn't quite sure herself why she didn't move. It was as though someone was calling to her to be patient, to hold her ground.

The snow began falling more heavily.

Great crisp flakes of it covered Miki, her suitcase, and the edges of her sign. Rather than feeling colder though, she felt her fingers and toes warming, as if something magical was happening.

Then, spontaneously, she began to laugh – a laugh inspired by hopelessness.

And, at that moment, a student approached where Miki was standing. He was dressed in a thick blue duffel coat like Paddington Bear. Although he didn't say anything, he took out his phone and clicked a picture of the sign, the bag filled with gift packs, and Miki, laughing.

Five minutes later, he had uploaded it on Mixi, Japan's number one social media site.

Ten minutes after that, people began to arrive.

At first it was a handful of ladies who worked in offices nearby. Having seen the Mixi post, they had been touched enough to come out and help a young woman trying to fulfil a family duty. Then, as they took pictures and shared them with their friends, more and more women started to turn up.

By lunchtime, dozens had come.

And, by mid afternoon, the dozens had become hundreds.

They lined up, neat and orderly in the cold, pledging donations in return for an Angel Flower gift pack from the Blue Onyx range.

At three o'clock, Miki called headquarters and ordered an emergency supply.

'How many gift packs do you need?' the sales officer had asked.

'As many as you can spare. It's an emergency!'

Within the hour, six hundred gift packs were delivered. But they were quickly gone.

Some women gave five times the money that one gift pack normally cost, but took only one. Bowing reverently, they offered words of encouragement, and told Miki how well she was doing. A great many of the women brought hot soup and cocoa, mittens and scarves.

And, all the while, the snow fell.

By early evening, a thousand women were lining up. They spilled out from the spot where Miki was standing, around and around in a great human spiral. The snow was deep now, but the more heavily it came down, the more women arrived.

And the more Angel Flower gift packs they bought.

At 8.30 p.m., Miki phoned the head office again to request another emergency delivery of stock. This time the call was put through to Pun-Pun, who was still crouched over his desk. When he heard where Miki wanted the gift packs delivered to, he bristled with anger, and ordered her to stop wasting company time. He was about to hang up the phone, when one of the executives held up a hand.

'Request that you look at Mixi, sir,' he said.

Again, more extra stock was rushed to Miki. As soon as it arrived it was handed out, with the donations amounting to many times the value of the stock.

By the time the park was closed for the night, Miki had distributed all the cartons. But, better still, she had become a celebrity in her own right. Three local TV crews had lit up the frozen air with their floodlights, their reporters telling Miki's tale to millions of viewers watching at home.

The next day, Miki stood out in Shiba Park again, as the commuters filed silently through to work. But, before she could get back into position, women started to arrive. They were armed with banknotes, blankets, and soup. Each of them wanted to be touched by the myth – the myth of Miki Suzuki and her family duty.

By the end of the week, Angel Flower executives had drawn up an entire sales strategy based on the idea of donations in return for goods. Henceforth, they declared, all their products would be given away for free – in exchange for a minimum recommended donation.

All across Japan sales teams were suddenly studying Miki Suzuki's business model.

In boardrooms, from Kagoshima in the south to Sapporo in the north, experts discussed the model, poring over its simple genius. Social media tapped the youth market, spreading the message like wildfire, while donating for a cause had touched the hearts of ordinary Japanese.

As for Miki, she was frozen to the bone, but elated like she had never been before.

On the Saturday evening, Ichiko brought her best friend a pot of noodle soup.

'I have to tell you something,' she said, as Miki slurped the meal.

'What is it?'

'It is Pun-Pun.'

'What about him?'

'He hates you.'

'Why?'

'Because he wants Noemi to go to Paris.'

'I do not understand.'

Ichiko rolled her eyes.

'Didn't you know?' she said. 'They're having an affair.'

Miki balked.

'But everyone hates him – even his wife.'

'Noemi doesn't. She loves him, especially the huge red wart on his forehead.'

12

On Sunday morning Miki went back to the Kinokuniya bookshop in Ginza.

She found the coffee table book about Paris, and took it to the counter. It was expensive, many times what she could afford, but she needed it. The book's pages represented far more than the French capital. To her, they signified the love for a grandfather, and the dream that was somehow keeping her alive.

The clerk with gelled hair who had helped her the previous time, welcomed her again. He looked down at the book, held between her hands.

'I saw you on television,' he said bashfully.

Miki nodded.

'Shiba Park is very cold,' she replied.

'I am your fan, on Mixi,' the clerk said with a grin.

'Thank you!'

'Do you know now when you are going to Paris?'

'I still haven't been chosen to go,' Miki said, blinking.

The sales clerk held an index finger in the air and whispered an apology. He picked up a white telephone on the counter, dialled the number 3, and spoke hesitantly into the receiver.

Then, giving thanks, he put the phone down and turned back to his customer.

'My boss has asked me to give you the book,' he said. 'It is a small gift from us all at Kinokuniya.'

Miki couldn't believe it.

Ducking her head subserviently, she thanked the sales clerk.

'I'm not worthy of your kindness,' she said.

The clerk held up his finger a second time.

'If you get to Paris,' he said… '*When* you get to Paris… please don't forget to go to the Camondo Museum.'

Clasping her hands together, Miki Suzuki bowed deeply, and apologized for having been a nuisance.

'I promise with all my heart,' she said.

13

THE NEXT DAY, Miki was called to the thirty-ninth floor, where the legions of high-ranking all-male executives were found.

Few of the saleswomen had ever been up there before. There were rumours that the men ran riot in the corridors, treating any women who happened to venture up by mistake, with shameless abandon.

A secretary had once confided that a drunken manager up there had flashed at her, before passing out. Another woman, a cleaning lady, said that the executives were into every imaginable fetish, from smelling soiled schoolgirl *Burusera* uniforms, to *Bukakke* sessions, to lusting after young women in knee-length socks.

The very thought of the thirty-ninth floor filled Miki with dread.

'Maybe they will abuse me!' she confided to Ichiko, as she stood waiting for the elevator.

'I'm sure they won't.'

'Then, perhaps they will fire me.'

'Why would they?'

'Because I have brought shame on the company.'

'Nonsense!'

Miki began to shake.

'I should resign,' she said.

'Don't be silly!'

The elevator doors opened. Ichiko pushed Miki in, pressed the button, and wished her best friend luck.

As the elevator rose up through the floors packed with number-crunching fetish-lusting executives, Miki found herself trembling all the more. She had enjoyed the limelight of Shiba Park, but hadn't meant to stick out. All she had wanted was to get to Paris, so that she could buy her ojiichan a coin pouch.

The doors opened and, before she knew it, Miki was standing in a large open-plan office packed with cheap prefab desks. Behind each one was a grey-suited executive. There was something utterly uniform about them, as though they were the same man cloned over and over.

Pun-Pun hurried up and pointed at a wooden door at the end of the room.

'The chairman wants to see you!' he barked, angrily. 'Make sure that you are courteous with him! And remember that you are only a humble saleswoman! Do you understand?'

Miki let out a whimper and lowered her head. She shuffled on towards the lacquered wooden door in slow motion, as if heading for the guillotine.

The door opened electronically as Miki approached it and, timorously, she stepped inside.

A moment later, she was standing before the chairman's desk, too fearful to look up.

'Are you Miss Suzuki?!' the chairman growled.

Miki didn't dare look at the face from which the voice came.

'I am sorry. Please forgive me!'

'Please tell me why you went to Shiba Park.'

'I... I... I wanted to sell the Blue Onyx gift packs so that I could win the trip to Paris.'

'How many did you sell?'

'Three thousand two hundred and thirty, sir.'

The chairman thumped his desk. Miki's eyes jerked up. They caught contact for a brief moment, before making landfall on the floor again.

'And why do you want to go to Paris?'

'Because Paris is the most beautiful place in the world,' Miki said, sniffling. 'The women are all like models from a fashion magazine, and the streets are filled with flowers and soft music.'

'*Music?*' the chairman said, frowning.

'From loudspeakers. There are loudspeakers hidden all around. You can't see them, but you can hear the music.'

'And what is playing through the loudspeakers?'

Miki allowed her gaze to rise slowly upwards. Her line of sight climbed from the rug, up over the drawers of the mahogany desk, taking in the chairman's chest, his thick neck, chin, and nose.

Eventually, she found herself looking timidly into his eyes.

'Bach,' she said very quietly. 'I think the music is Bach.'

14

THE NEXT AFTERNOON, the chairman summoned the entire workforce of the Angel Flower Beauty Company to the assembly hall at 4 p.m. precisely. Five minutes before the appointed hour, the saleswomen filed in silently. Seating themselves at the back, they kept space for the grey-suited executives, who took their places in the front rows.

Once the entire hall was filled to capacity, the company chairman strode in. Bowing to the audience, he took his seat at a table, arranged squarely in the middle of the stage.

After a short pause to collect his thoughts, he said:

'As I am sure you know, three members of the public have now won their places to go as guests of Angel Flower to Paris!'

A cheer rang through the hall.

The chairman held up a hand, requesting silence.

'And, as promised, the saleswoman who has sold the most gift packs will join them – on a lifetime adventure to Paris.'

There was another cheer.

Then, as it subsided, the chairman took an envelope from Pun-Pun, who had stepped onto the stage. He opened it, squinted at the name, and said:

'On behalf of the entire company, I am proud to announce that Noemi Watanabe-san has sold more gift packs than anyone else!'

This time, there was no cheer.

Instead, a wave of tut-tutting swept from the back of the room. It moved gradually forward, through the ranks of saleswomen, and on into the rows of grey-suited executives.

Way at the back, too short to be seen, Miki Suzuki hid her face in her hands, and she wept. Her best friend, Ichiko, muttered words of consolation. As she did so, the tut-tutting got all the louder. It became so deafening that the chairman raised both hands. He exchanged urgent whispers with Pun-Pun. The two men appeared to be in disagreement.

All of a sudden, the chairman thumped the table with his hand.

The assembly hall fell silent.

'I understand,' the chairman said, 'that according to the rules of the competition, our gift packs were supposed to be sold. In the much-publicized case of Miss Miki Suzuki, this was not done. Miss Suzuki gave her gift packs away, in return for donations. Yes, it is true that the donations exceeded the retail price of the gift packs but,' the chairman said, as his cheeks blushed, 'at Angel Flower, we all play by the rules of the game.'

Through the assembly hall swept a raucous wave of hostile grumbling, the like of which was unknown at the firm.

Never in his long career had the chairman ever witnessed such a thing. He held up both hands again but, still, the clamour continued. Standing at the edge of the stage, Pun-Pun called for silence. Only after another full minute of noise did the outburst begin to abate.

The chairman dipped his head in a tense bow.

'Nothing is more important at the Angel Flower Beauty Company,' he said, 'than keeping everyone content – even if it means bending the rules. And so, through an executive decision, it has been decided that we shall be sending not one – but *two* – saleswomen to France: Noemi Watanabe-san *and* Miki Suzuki-san!'

The assembly hall erupted in cheers.

Huddled at the back, her face still hidden by hands, Miki felt as though she were about to pass out. With her friends patting her on the back, she jumped up, and ran through the hall.

'I'm going to Paris!' she cried over and over. 'I am going to Paris for my ojiichan!'

15

OVER THE NEXT three weeks, Miki prepared for the journey.

Using up all her remaining holiday time, she devoted herself to getting ready for Paris. This entailed buying suitable clothes and studying French, poring over photographs and maps, and learning the ins and outs of Parisian etiquette.

Unfortunately, the commission on sales was made after a three-month delay, meaning that Miki lived in an eternal state of cash flow misery. So, having secured a bank loan, she bought a new wardrobe, and paid for French lessons with a gentleman from Okinawa. He was named Mr. Saito, and he lived in the former fishing village of Hayama, in Kanagawa Prefecture.

Saito-san had been recommended to Miki by the niece of a friend. Dressed in a cravat and tweed suit, he was elderly and suave, and was the only man Miki could find who knew not only French, but the all-important etiquette as well.

Each afternoon, she went to and fro from Ikebukuro to Saito-san's home. It was a tedious journey, one that involved two trains and a bus. But the commuting time gave her a chance to read about Paris, and to build on her already extensive knowledge.

After a thorough session of French conversation, Saito-san would explain the complicated and often bizarre subject of French customs.

'French people shake hands all the time,' he said, 'and friends kiss once on either cheek when they meet. Even complete strangers kiss, when introduced by a mutual friend.'

'Strangers kiss?' Miki asked, confused.

'Yes, that's right. I know it seems strange, but it's just the way things are in Paris.'

Saito-san wagged a finger towards his student.

'You must remember that politeness is golden,' he said. 'But it's not the kind of politeness that we have here in Japan. Indeed, sometimes it seems ruder than it does polite. But that's not the only thing that is strange.'

With Miki listening attentively and taking notes, her teacher opened a textbook and pointed to what looked like a small toilet.

'Do you know what that is?' he asked.

Miki sucked air in noisily through her back teeth.

'Not sure,' she said.

Saito-san looked at her like a wise old cat, one that had been tried and tested by the rigours of international travel.

'It is called a *bee-day*,' he said.

'What's it for?'

'For washing your bottom.'

'Ah, I see,' Miki said, her brow furrowed with interest.

'But they are not like our state-of-the-art toilets which dry you as well.'

'I do not understand, Mr. Saito.'

'They are low tech and smelly. And...'

'*And...?*'

'And they spread disease!'

Miki let out a shriek and clutched her cheeks.

'Oh, there is so much I have to still learn about Paris! How will I ever master it all in time?'

Again, Saito-san wagged his finger.

'It will take you many years to know Paris as I do,' he said. 'And so don't try and master in a few days what has taken me a lifetime to learn!'

Miki ducked her head subserviently, as she had done in the chairman's office.

'I could never hope to know Paris like you, Saito-san,' she said.

The teacher smiled, and pinched thumb and forefinger to his wispy moustache.

'The last thing I will teach you today,' he replied, 'is that the French smell different from us. They have a *gaijin* smell, but it's worse than that.'

'Worse than other *gaijin?*'

'Yes, much much worse!'

Miki grimaced.

'Why is that, Saito-san?'

'It's because they don't use deodorant,' he said.

16

As THE FINAL week before the journey counted down, Miki found she couldn't sleep at night.

She sat propped upright in bed, with a fraught expression tight over her face, the blankets pulled up tight to her neck. When she did manage to doze off, most of her dreams were nightmares of the most fearful kind.

She dreamt that she would forget, just when she needed it most, all the French etiquette that Saito-san had taught her: that she would use the wrong fork or spoon in a restaurant, and that everyone would look round at her and jeer. And, she dreamt that people would laugh at her, too, because she would use the wrong words; or that they would consider her stupid ugly or, even worse – stupid *and* ugly.

Three days before she was due to leave, Miki wrote a letter to the chairman of Angel Flower. Phrased in the most formal language she could muster, she thanked the company for all it had done for her. Then she explained that she did not deserve the privilege of going and, sobbing as she wrote the words, she withdrew from the journey to Paris.

On her way to deliver the letter by hand, she met up with her best friend at a Doutor Coffee Shop in Harajuku.

Ichiko expected Miki to be rapturous with excitement.

'How are your preparations going?!' she asked enthusiastically.

Miki raised her cappuccino to her lips, but put it down before taking a sip.

'I'm not going to Paris,' she said.

Ichiko winced.

'What?! Tell me, has that evil Pun-Pun refused to let you go? If he has, I will throw my shoe at him!'

'No, no. It's not like that!'

'Then?'

'I am not going because I am not worthy of the honour.'

Ichiko looked hard across at her friend, sitting there all crumpled up and forlorn. She slapped her hand down on the table-top.

The people at the next table turned at the noise.

'*Sumimasen!* Excuse me!' she said, embarrassed. Leaning forward, she craned her neck low. 'You *must* go to Paris on this trip!'

'But why?'

'Because you are not going just for yourself.'

'I don't understand.'

Her eyes burning, Ichiko jabbed a finger in the air.

'You are going to Paris for all of us,' she said, 'for all of us saleswomen of Japan who could never hope for such a journey!'

17

ABOARD A ROLLERCOASTER of emotion, Miki took a deep breath and drained her cappuccino.

She was awash with excitement again.

Tearing up the letter to the chairman, she went shopping for more outfits and accessories, the kind that were worthy of a Japanese tourist.

She bought a Burberry hat and matching scarf, a Burberry belt, and even Burberry shoes. After that, she bought the Dior print dress that she had always dreamed of owning, a matching parasol, and a pair of Prada sunglasses. And she bought the most expensive camera imaginable at an electronics shop in Akihabara.

The day before she was due to leave, Miki was invited on NHK's breakfast television show, *Good Morning Nippon*. The press office of the Angel Flower Beauty Company had leaked the story that their celebrated saleswoman – the one made famous in snowy Shiba Park – was about to embark on the journey of a lifetime, as a guest of the company.

All dressed up in her new clothes, Miki arrived at the TV studio as the rest of Tokyo slept. She was taken into a make-up room and had a thick slimy foundation smoothed over her face. And, blinking from the bright lights, she was led to the sofa, where the presenter was waiting for her. A slim good-looking man with a square jaw, he smiled a great deal, as though his career depended on it.

'So, your journey to Paris began in the snows of Shiba Park,' he said, smiling.

'Yes,' Miki replied, terrified.

'And what are you hoping to find in the French capital?'

Miki thought hard for a moment, sucking the air in through her teeth.

'Love, beauty and tranquillity,' she said spontaneously, although it sounded like a line she had rehearsed.

The presenter smiled, glanced at the camera and then at his notes.

'That's a lot to find on one journey!' he laughed.

Miki apologized. She had not meant to boast.

'I am very grateful to all the ladies who helped me when I was standing out in Shiba Park,' she said. 'It is because of them that I am going to Paris.'

A minute later, Miki had been replaced on the sofa by a leading film director. He had come to talk about his new project, a horror movie in which the men played the women, and the women played the men. A junior assistant led Miki down a long snaking corridor and, before she knew it, she was back on the street outside the NHK studio.

It wasn't yet 7 a.m.

All of a sudden, she was hit with a kind of euphoria. Standing there, her heart racing, her eyes wide open with exhilaration, she screamed. She couldn't stop herself. She must have screamed for a minute and a half, until her throat was sore and her lungs were stinging.

She was going to Paris – the dream she had wished for since she was five years old. It was a dream that had coaxed her to sleep each night for twenty years, a dream that had been both tormentor and friend.

And now at last it was really happening.

Taking the Yamanote Line back to Ikebukuro, Miki felt the euphoria coming on again. It welled up from her toes, through her feet, up her ankles and shins, legs and up into her abdomen. As it coursed northward towards her head, she began to sweat uncontrollably.

Loosening her thick winter coat, she began fanning herself with her hand, taking quick deep breaths. The subway carriage was packed with salarymen on their way to work. All on auto-pilot, they were lost in their own worlds.

Suddenly, unable to control herself, Miki started to jump up and down and to scream, just like she had done outside the NHK studio.

'I'm going to Paris tomorrow!' she yelled. '*Paris! Paris! Paris!*'

No one in the carriage turned. They had all seen it before – a saleswoman driven to the point of hysteria by the pressures of stress and overwork.

Miki pulled out a perfectly pressed handkerchief and dabbed her forehead. As she did so, a lady sitting near to her leaned forward a fraction. Without making eye contact, she said:

'Paris is a very beautiful place in spring.'

18

EARLY IN THE afternoon, Miki was summoned back to the thirty-ninth floor.

She was less nervous this time. Or, rather, she was less nervous of being in the presence of Angel Flower's executives, while still petrified at the thought of finally going to Paris.

Without delay, she was ushered into a conference room.

Inside, next to the window, Pun-Pun was standing with Noemi. They were close, as if they had been even closer a moment before. Miki was not certain, but she thought she saw a smudge of lipstick on Pun-Pun's left cheek. Noemi turned sharply as she entered, her face overlaid with a mask of jealousy and hate.

'Sit down in silence and wait for the chairman!' Pun-Pun snapped.

Miki did as she was told. She felt like crying, but managed to control herself.

A minute passed, then the door swung open wide.

The chairman entered with another man, who was introduced as Mr. Nakamura. Dressed in a cheap blue blazer, tan trousers, and low-quality slip-on shoes, he didn't look like an executive or a businessman. He seemed eager to exude an air of low self-worth, as though he were insignificant.

'Mr. Nakamura is from Paradise Tours, the tour company that is taking us to Paris,' the chairman explained.

Miki flinched.

'I shall be joining the group,' the chairman announced, 'as will Mr. Yamato. We will be the chaperones.'

Pun-Pun looked up from his seat. He glanced over at Noemi, who giggled and pressed a hand to her hair. The arrangement had clearly been devised to give them a little romantic time together – in the city of love.

The chairman looked at his wristwatch.

'Mr. Nakamura is now going to give us a short presentation about the visit to Paris,' he said.

The tour leader stood up.

'I shall have the honour of taking you to Paris tomorrow,' he said unctuously. 'It is my hope that you will be very satisfied with the service offered by Paradise Tours.'

The lights dimmed, and Mr. Nakamura began a well-practised PowerPoint presentation.

'We shall stay for one week in the city where hearts beat a little faster,' he said, 'and where style is a work of art.'

The first slide flashed up.

It showed the Eiffel Tower against a blue sky, and was followed by the Arc de Triomphe, the Louvre, and by scenes of casual café life.

'This is the Paris of our dreams,' Mr. Nakamura said, running through a memorized script. 'It's the Paris we have all heard of, and have longed to know. But,' he said, his voice lowering, 'there is another side of this city that I am going to reveal to you. *The city of secrets.*'

The next slide came into view.

It showed a toilet. A French toilet.

'This is what will await you in your room.' The slide changed. 'And this is a picture of a *bidet*. On no account are you to use it as a toilet as well.'

Miki watched the slides, but was bored by them. She had learned all she needed to know from Mr. Saito, and from all the years obsessing about the French capital.

When Nakamura-san was finished with the presentation, he opened his briefcase and took out a stack of low-grade plastic gift pouches. He passed them around. Receiving hers timidly, Miki opened it up.

Inside, there was a French phrasebook and a map of Paris, three cheap ballpoint pens, and a sticker of the Eiffel Tower, with the slogan, 'Paradise Tours Towers Above the Rest!'

Mr. Nakamura bowed deeply, and praised the wise choice of engaging his firm. He was escorted back outside by the chairman. When he had left, Pun-Pun went to the door and closed it.

Miki looked up. She had been hoping to leave as well.

Looming over her like a cobra about to strike, Pun-Pun slapped his hands together, as Noemi looked on from the other side of the room.

'I am not happy that you are coming to Paris!' he said venomously. 'You cheated in the competition, and have brought shame on us all!'

Cringing, Miki whimpered as though mortally wounded. She forced herself to look up at her boss. He was so close that Miki could see the individual hairs sprouting from the mole on his chin.

'Yamato-san?' she said very softly, as he loomed.

'What is it, you vile little girl?'

'I think I should tell you something.'

'What?!'

Miki swallowed.

'Excuse me, sir,' she said, 'but you have red lipstick on your cheek.'

19

AT NARITA AIRPORT next morning, Miki called her family.

Her mother told her three times to take care. It was her daughter's first time out of Japan, and she was fearful that something terrible might happen. Then the telephone was passed to the ojiichan.

Although frail, he managed to wish his granddaughter well. As soon as she heard his voice, Miki started to cry.

'I will not let you down, dear Ojiichan!' she said.

'Your dream is about to come true, as mine did for me so many years ago.'

Miki sniffed, then wiped away her tears.

'It was your story, your gift, that made my journey possible,' she said quietly.

'Promise to think of me when you are there,' the old man whispered.

'Yes, yes, I will. I promise! It will be as though we are walking through Paris together, arm in arm!'

20

TEN MINUTES LATER, Miki was standing at the check-in desk with Pun-Pun, Noemi, the chairman of Angel Flower, and the tour leader. Another round of gift pouches was passed out. Everyone took them obediently, too polite to refuse.

A few minutes after that, the three women who had won the trip in the competition arrived. They were all housewives – two from Tokyo, and the third from Osaka. The beauty firm had rolled out the red carpet, bringing them to the airport in a limousine.

Mr. Nakamura distributed the boarding cards and led the group down the air bridge to the plane. Miki noticed that her card was blue, and all the rest were gold, except for the one which the tour leader had kept for himself.

The reason for the different coloured boarding passes became apparent when they got on board. Everyone, except Miki and Mr. Nakamura, was in Business Class, while they were given seats in Economy, at the rear of the aircraft.

As Miki shuffled back through Business, Noemi slipped her a poisonous grin.

'Enjoy the hospitality in the back!' she hissed.

Miki didn't reply. She was depressed at being treated differently, but she had not expected to travel Business Class. In any case, the journey was not what was important to her – it was the destination that mattered.

21

AT ROISSY CHARLES de Gaulle, the luggage was loaded into the back of a black Mercedes minibus, as the Paradise Tours group took their seats inside. After many hours of good sleep and pampering, they were all relaxed and in buoyant spirits.

Miki was the only one who was exhausted.

She hadn't managed to sleep, because Mr. Nakamura had passed out in the next seat, resting his head on her shoulder as he snored. Her jaws were aching from chewing her way through several inedible meals, and her back was aching from sitting rigid in a seat that didn't recline.

Despite the discomforts, Miki was more excited than she had ever been. Whipping out the new camera, she took pictures of everyone and everything. She had photographed the airport's arrivals building and the luggage carousel. And now that she was actually outside, she took endless shots of the bus, the driver, and the road into Paris.

The Mercedes minibus rolled through the suburbs and, as it did so, Mr. Nakamura drew attention to the solid French infrastructure, and pointed out each Japanese car they passed.

'French people rely on Japanese high technology,' he said smugly, 'and they like our cars as well. They think we are Number One!'

The housewife from Osaka asked how many times the tour guide had been to Paris. It was Mr. Nakamura's dream question. Merely thinking of the answer made him blush.

'I have been here fifty-two times,' he replied. 'All of them in the humble service of Paradise Tours. I am honoured to be a servant of the company.'

The vehicle turned onto the Périphérique, and found itself mired in gridlocked traffic. Eventually, it began inching forward at a snail's pace. As it did so, Miki and the others had the chance to scrutinize the graffiti. It seemed to cover every surface of the outside world like a second skin.

Miki took many photographs of it.

Unlike the others in her group, she found the graffiti strangely beautiful, and was excited at seeing a side of Paris of which she had not heard before.

As the minibus steered a path around the Porte Maillot roundabout, there was yet more gridlock. All of a sudden, a man with a ragged beard and tatty clothes was seen tearing through the traffic, weaving his way fast between the cars.

Clutched to his chest was a woman's handbag.

The members of the Paradise Tours group appeared worried.

'He is a thief!' exclaimed the chairman.

Mr. Nakamura gasped, then touched a hand to his head.

'No, no, he is not a thief,' he replied quickly. 'I think he is helping a woman who has dropped her handbag. He is rushing it back to her as quickly as he can.'

'Ohhhh,' the others declared in unison.

'That is good,' Miki said. 'He is a good man.'

22

EVENTUALLY, THE TOUR bus reached the Four Seasons George V, and the luggage was unloaded.

Mr. Nakamura led the way inside.

The winning housewives cooed with anticipation as they entered, marvelling at the sumptuous furnishings and the immense bouquets of flowers poised on small tables with gold fittings.

Following behind them came the chairman, and then Pun-Pun and his beloved Noemi. Miki went in last. She was feeling fragile, and needed sleep. But, having finally arrived at the one place on the planet she had spent her life thinking about, she felt a little overcome by it all.

The sense of culture shock was compounded a thousand times when she caught her first glimpse of the George V's lobby. The crystal chandeliers, the marble, and antique furniture were too much to take in. Sobbing into her handkerchief, she said a prayer of thanks to her ancestors.

A steward stepped forward with a polished salver upon which the room keys were laid out. There were six of them.

Each of the housewives took theirs, then the chairman, Pun-Pun, and Noemi.

Miki reached forward to the salver, to take her key.

But there was none left.

Regarding her with a dismissive glance, her superior shooed her away.

'There's no space for you here,' he said heatedly, 'and so you are staying somewhere else.'

The tour guide forced a smile.

'It is a nice hotel,' Mr. Nakamura said reassuringly. 'I am booked there too.'

'I am not staying at the Four Seasons George V?' Miki said, crestfallen.

'No,' Mr. Nakamura replied. 'We are going to be around the corner at the Belle Rose Travel Lodge.'

As the others from the group went up to their luxurious rooms, Miki followed the tour guide round the corner to their meagre accommodation. The Belle Rose would perhaps have seemed a little less miserable had Miki not been dazzled first with the rare excesses of the George V.

The foyer was a mirror of herself – tired, unloved, and in desperate need of pampering. The walls were peppered in curiously shaped patches of damp, and marks where suitcases had struck them very hard. The concierge was watching TV and wouldn't look up, even when the duty manager called him to help with the bags. The carpeting stank of stale cigarettes, and the elevator had broken down a year before. But no one could bother enough to get it repaired.

So Miki and Mr. Nakamura ascended the five flights, hauling their suitcases behind them.

As soon as she got into her room, Miki opened the window, hoping to get rid of the stench of cigarettes. But no amount of fresh spring air could lessen it. The curtains were stained with what looked like dried blood, and there was an outgrowth of fungus on the bathroom wall. The plastic bath was masked in a cobweb of cracks, and had been patched half a dozen times. As for the toilet, it was stained sludge-brown and stank of raw sewage. Thankfully, there was no *bidet*.

Miki sat on the bed, and slipped down into the crater just left of centre. She thought of all the years of anticipation, all the hype and the hope that had preceded that very moment. The first mention of Paris by her ojiichan, his birthday gifts of detail, and the years she had devoted to a meticulous study of the French capital.

Peering around the room slowly, taking in its deficiencies, Miki began to laugh. She laughed and she laughed, and she laughed and she laughed, unable to control herself. How silly she was to care about an unimportant hotel room, she thought. After all, her ojiichan had always told her that the real wonders of Paris were to be found outside in the streets, not in the confines of a building – however sordid or grand.

23

AT THREE O'CLOCK, the group assembled in the Paradise Tours bus.

The trio of housewives had all taken long bubble baths, and smelled of ginger and lotus blossom. The chairman had resorted to drinking half the contents of the minibar. He stank of single malt whisky and was hunched against the vehicle's window. Pun-Pun and Noemi were sitting in silence very close to each other. And, despite the less than opulent accommodation of the Belle Rose Travel Lodge, Miki was in a jubilant frame of mind.

She was sitting in the front seat, between Mr. Nakamura and the driver. Her eyes were bright with wonder, her enormous camera slung around her neck.

'This is the first day, and so I expect you are very tired,' the tour leader said. 'But I am going to show you a little piece of the magic – the magic that is Paris!'

The housewives applauded, and Miki followed suit. The chairman gagged into his paisley handkerchief. As for the love-birds, they were too busy with each other to have heard.

The minibus pulled away from the kerb, and was soon driving down the Champs-Elysées in the direction of Concorde. It was a bright afternoon, intense sunshine breaking through the young green leaves of the horse-chestnut trees. Couples were out strolling, arm in arm, miniature dogs on prim leather leashes, children skipping, everyone and everything touched by a sense of *bonheur*.

On one corner, a florist was selling red roses.

Miki watched as a handsome young man rushed up and bought a great bouquet of them. And, turning to his girlfriend, he presented the flowers, crouched on one knee. A stone's throw away, a wealthy woman was walking towards a pink Rolls-Royce. Coutured in a full sable coat with matching hat, she was attended by three retainers, each of them laden with mountains of shopping, all of it from designer stores.

'It's so beautiful!' Miki shouted out, unable to control herself. 'I will never forget any of it!'

She turned to the tour leader.

'I am hoping to visit Louis Vuitton,' she said. 'Do you know where I can find it?'

Mr. Nakamura patted the air in front of him with his hand.

'There will be plenty of time for shopping,' he replied. 'Plenty of time for the designer shops. But today we will just drive around a little and see what wonders lie in store for us.'

Miki thanked Nakamura-san but, secretly, she wished she could have been able to go straight to Louis Vuitton and buy the coin pouch for her ojiichan. Making the purchase was inextricably linked to her visit, and was the one thing she regarded as more important than anything else. After all, it had been her grandfather's story of his own visit that had led to her obsession.

The minibus rattled over the cobbles, as the tour leader pointed out the sights, and offered smatterings of history and detail.

They passed the Arc de Triomphe and Place de la Concorde, the Louvre with its great glass pyramid, and the ancient sanctuary of

Notre Dame. Then on past the Musée d'Orsay, the Pompidou Centre, and to the Eiffel Tower.

Miki watched it all through her camera's viewfinder. Wildly over-excited, she kept squealing, her hands and face trembling through sheer delight. She told Mr. Nakamura about her grandfather's visit to Paris, and about her dream of walking with him arm in arm. He thanked her for telling him the story and, once again, promised that Louis Vuitton would be on the agenda at least once during their stay.

Halfway through the ride, the vehicle slowed, and pulled over next to a slim ribbon of parkland lined with chestnut trees. Located just beside the Seine, between the Grand Palais and Pont Alexandre, it was a little oasis of tranquillity. Mr. Nakamura invited his group to get down and stretch their legs.

One by one they climbed out of the bus.

As soon as her feet touched the grass, Miki started taking pictures.

'My grandfather would have liked this,' she said quietly. No one was listening to her. Or if they were, they pretended they hadn't heard.

The tour leader took out a neatly furled umbrella and, raising it before him like a cheerleader's baton, he led the way, walking down the path. As if following the Pied Piper of Hamelin, the others fell into line, with Miki at the rear.

All of a sudden, a handsome Parisian man hurried towards them.

He was dressed in a tweed jacket, a woollen scarf knotted around his neck. In one hand he was holding a bunch of pink roses. They had long stems and seemed to be damp with dew. Impulsively, offering greeting to the group, he presented each of the women with a flower.

'Welcome to my city!' he said in faultless Japanese, 'I hope you have the most wonderful time in Paris, and that your heart sings like a caged bird before you leave!'

Then he vanished – gone as quickly as he had come.

'How kind he was,' said Miki dreamily, as she sniffed her rose. 'I think he was very generous and kind.'

They carried on a little further, crossing over to the park area outside the Petit Palais. And, soon, they came to a group of elderly men playing a game of pétanque. Each of them was dressed impeccably in a blazer, beret and cravat. Taking it in turns, they tossed their boules with good humour, concentration and skill.

Mr. Nakamura suggested they watch for a moment or two.

Suddenly, the old men invited the tour group to join them in their game. No one thought it unusual that the gentlemen all spoke a smattering of Japanese, or that they had singled the Paradise Tours group out from all the other passing tours.

'This is a very rare honour,' said Mr. Nakamura proudly. 'Please take a shot at throwing a ball.'

One at a time, the members of the group had a go, with the housewives trying their luck first. There was much laughter and delight, even though none of them got close to the jack. Miki managed the best shot, and was cheered by the men. She photographed them all, so that she could tell her ojiichan about them when she next visited the family home.

Thanking the pétanque players, Mr. Nakamura produced a packet of wet-wipes and passed them around to his group. It was almost as though he had known they would encounter the friendly boules players on their spontaneous stroll.

They turned the corner and found the Mercedes tour bus waiting for them near the statue of Winston Churchill. In the shadow of the great Englishman, a street-seller was selling baseball caps. Embroidered across the front were the flags of France and Japan. As soon as he saw the group from Paradise Tours, the street-seller sprinted up and handed everyone a cap for free. Then, in Japanese, he called:

'I hope you have enjoyed your first day in Paris!'

Everyone in the group gave thanks, cheered, and took photos of the man.

'How did he know it was our first day?' said Miki, as she clambered aboard.

Mr. Nakamura smiled uneasily.

'He must have been guessing,' he said.

24

AT THE END of the first day, the chairman of Angel Flower invited the group to dine at the George V's legendary restaurant, Le Cinq.

Even though she was not staying at the hotel with the others, Miki was invited as well. She went back to the Belle Rose to change for dinner. Once back in her room, she began trembling again. She was petrified about making a mistake, and equally fearful about how she would look. Unpacking her clothes on her bed, she took out her Dior sundress and smoothed a hand over the creases.

An hour later, she was standing at the bar in the George V, waiting for the others to arrive. Self-conscious and nervous in her new high heels, she dared not order a drink. She didn't know what to have and, besides, it looked very expensive. The bar was panelled in dark wood, with fine oriental carpets laid over the parquet. There was understated lighting, and a faint scent of polish from the leather chairs.

As she stood there, desperate to be invisible, an elegant man in a pinstripe suit walked up to the bar and ordered a martini. He had a gentle face, a dark Gallic complexion, and wore a gold signet ring on the little finger of his right hand. With care, he gave the barman exact instructions on how he wished the drink to be prepared, hinting at a meticulous nature.

He smiled at Miki, his forehead creasing slightly as though he was sincere. Paralysed with trepidation and dread, she nodded a greeting, then opened her handbag and rooted about, as though she were terribly busy.

'Could I invite you for a martini, Mademoiselle?' the man asked in Japanese.

'*You... you... you* speak...'

'*Japanese?*' he replied, smiling again. 'Yes, I lived in Tokyo for three years. I was with the French embassy there.'

Bowing his head a fraction, he introduced himself – Comte Hugo de Montfried. He reached out and kissed the back of Miki's hand.

Melting, she gasped, sighed, and begged forgiveness.

'Why do you apologize?' he asked.

'Because... because I am so... so ugly.'

Rounding her shoulders inwards, Miki stared limply at the floor.

'On the contrary, I think you are very beautiful,' the Comte replied.

At that moment, Pun-Pun strode into the bar.

'There you are!' he wailed. 'We have been waiting for you in reception. Hurry up!'

Miki blinked thanks to the Frenchman for his compliment, and followed her superior out to where the group was assembled.

They filed through into Le Cinq, each of them awed by the palatial surroundings.

On one side of the room a pianist was playing Handel's *Water Music* on an Erard grand, the candlelight reflected in the black lacquer. The walls were adorned in gold detailing, the furnishings as sumptuous as any Miki had imagined, let alone ever seen. There was a fragrance of wild lilies, and the gentle sound of distant conversation mixing with the music.

The *maître d'hôtel* escorted the group to their table, set beside a lovely window that looked out onto the courtyard. A flurry of waiters hurried from nowhere, pulling out the chairs, flapping starched napkins open, and offering their welcome.

A lump in her throat, Miki sat down beside one of the housewives. She felt light-headed as though she were about to pass out. Struggling to stay calm, she took in the vast array of cutlery and crystal, the miniature candles and the rose petals arranged in tiny glass bowls. She said a prayer to her ancestors, then wished aloud her ojiichan was there.

He was the one man she knew who deserved it.

A sommelier approached, a silver tastevin hanging around his neck on a chain. Having consulted the chairman, he went away, returning a few minutes later with a vintage bottle of Nuits-Saint-Georges. With great care and appropriate skill, the sommelier opened the wine. He sniffed the cork once and then again, before pouring a few drops of the blood-coloured liquid into his tastevin. Only after much swilling, inhaling, and holding it to the light, did he take a discreet taste.

'*Impeccable!*' he said.

The wine was decanted, and only then was a little poured into each glass.

After a suitable pause, the chairman thanked the housewives for honouring the humble employees of Angel Flower with their presence. He gave a toast and, one by one, the guests sipped their Burgundy. None of them liked wine very much, but they each applauded its taste for fear of sticking out.

Two hours later, after a meal that featured black truffles from Alsace and fillet of wild venison slow-cooked in grenadine sauce, pistachio soufflé and a platter of cheese from the hillside villages above Beaune, the group from Paradise Tours were unable to move.

'It's rich food,' said the chairman, his eyes straining to focus.

'Very good,' the trio of housewives affirmed, speaking as one.

'It was the best meal of my life,' Miki said.

Once the chairman had signed the bill, the *maître d'hôtel* glided up to the table, exuding thanks in superlatives. One by one, the members of the Angel Flower group gave thanks and bowed. Then, falling in line behind the chairman, they followed him like ducklings behind their mother, back out to the lobby.

Secretly, they were all wishing they had eaten Japanese food instead.

25

ALL THAT NIGHT, Miki dreamed of Comte Hugo de Montfried.

Over and over she replayed the moment when his lips touched the back of her hand, and the moment when he had declared that she was beautiful. Having slipped down into the middle of her bed, she swooned, clutching a pillow to her chest.

The Comte was the first person she thought of next morning. As she sat taking an early coffee with Mr. Nakamura, she was still imagining the gentleman whispering sweet nothings in her ear. Plucking up courage, she told her secret to the tour leader. Tilting his head sideways, he sucked air through his back teeth.

'He is a Comte, which means he is a member of the aristocracy,' he said, as if an authority on the landed gentry. 'I am sure he has a chateau and a wealthy family.'

'He wore a ring on his little finger,' Miki added, hoping to supply useful information.

'Ah yes,' Nakamura-san added, 'the gold ring... the ring is a signal that he is very very rich.'

26

AFTER BREAKFAST, THE full group met in the lobby of the George V.

The rest of the party had slept more deeply than on any other night of their lives, all except for Pun-Pun and Noemi – who both looked worn out.

'Today we are going to see the enchanting sights of Paris,' Mr. Nakamura said, once they were outside. 'We will go beneath the curtain that shrouds the city, and find the real Paris, a magical realm hidden from most tourists.'

Miki was the first one onto the bus.

More usually, she would have abided by protocol and gone last, but she had had enough of decorum.

'The *real* Paris!' she cried. 'We are going to see the *real* Paris!'

'I am sure that's what every tourist is told,' Pun-Pun grumbled from the back.

'No, no, sir,' Miki corrected bravely. 'I am sure Nakamura-san is the expert in this area. He has been to Paris so many times.'

'Our first stop will be the Louvre Museum,' said the tour leader, buckling up his seatbelt. 'It is a palace that changes the way you see the world!'

The Mercedes minibus rolled down the Champs-Elysées' cobbles towards Place de la Concorde. Outside, the air was balmy, infused with the scent of spring. As the vehicle picked up speed, Miki gazed out at the beauty and swooned again, her mind entertained by a fantasy of the Count.

Mr. Nakamura pointed out Hôtel de Crillon and, beside it, the American embassy. Then he drew attention to the great obelisk from Luxor, presented to the people of France by Sultan Mehmet Ali. He reeled off a list of facts and figures that were hardly heard, let alone remembered.

The minibus turned onto Rue de Rivoli, and then sped towards the Louvre.

As it neared the celebrated museum, the driver threw on the brakes. Heading towards them fast, and with placards held high in anger, was a protest.

Mr. Nakamura barked something quickly to the driver, who threw the vehicle into reverse. Spinning the steering wheel through his hands, he took a side street, and skirted around to the Louvre another way.

'Who were they?' the chairman asked uneasily.

'Ordinary people declaring their affection for the President,' said the tour leader. 'They love him like children love their father.'

'But they looked angry,' Miki blurted subversively.

Mr. Nakamura let out a frivolous laugh.

'Here in France,' he said, 'people may look angry, but inside, they are dancing with delight!'

The minibus parked, and the tourists were led through into the great courtyard, where the morning light was dazzling on Pei's glass pyramid. Miki took pictures of the architecture and the fountains, of the other tourists, and even the sky. She was so excited that, for a moment, she completely forgot about Louis Vuitton and the promise to her much-loved ojiichan.

All she wanted to do was to get inside – and track down the *Mona Lisa*.

'We will see it a little later,' said Mr. Nakamura reassuringly, as he led his group through halls, each one crammed with Chinese tourists.

They trooped past the Egyptian mummies, and the antiquities from Classical Rome, Etrusca and Greece. Then on through ancient Mesopotamia and the Levant, past Italian marbles of the Renaissance, and masterpieces of the Dutch School. And, at last, pushing upstream against the current, and exhausted from anticipation, they reached the room where the *Mona Lisa* was kept.

There were so many tourists swarming inside that it took a half an hour to get anywhere near Leonardo's masterpiece. As she was swept past it, Miki managed to snap three blurred shots.

Then Pun-Pun elbowed her out of the way.

Defying the force of physics, he managed to root himself and Noemi to the parquet for a split second, before a tidal wave of Chinese washed them back towards the margins of the room.

As Mr. Nakamura led his group back to the minibus, he straightened his tie and apologized for all the crowds.

'Other tourists are not so cultured and polite as we Japanese,' he said pessimistically. He was referring to the Chinese, who had invaded Paris like a conquering army. 'Perhaps one day they will learn some manners,' he said.

27

BACK AT THE George V, the chairman of the Angel Flower Beauty Company called the front desk in horror.

The safe in his room had been opened, and its entire contents stolen.

Downstairs, the duty manager enquired what valuables the chairman had lost. He gave a list, which included cash, credit cards and diamond cuff-links.

The security chief arrived. In his hand was the duty book. Even before he was introduced to the chairman, he seemed shamefaced and submissive.

'Did you not call for your room safe to be opened at three o'clock, sir?' he enquired anxiously.

The chairman shook his head.

'I was at the Louvre,' he replied.

'*Mon dieu!*' the chief of security exclaimed. 'It has happened again!'

'What has happened again?' the chairman enquired.

'The Chinese.'

'I do not understand.'

The chairman was led into a private salon by the duty manager, where the ruse was explained.

'They come into the hotel, and wait in the corridor,' he said. 'Then, pretending that they cannot find their key, they approach a housemaid. Assuming that they are the bona fide Japanese client, she lets them in at once. Once inside, they call for the security team, insisting that they have forgotten the passcode for the safe, and...'

'*Voila!*' the chief of security said.

'They are doing the same trick in leading hotels across Paris,' the duty manager added. 'And they catch us out each time.'

28

NOT WANTING TO panic the housewives, or to unsettle the rest of his group, the chairman accepted the hotel's generous compensation, and agreed to forget the matter.

He didn't even mention it to Mr. Nakamura, when he arrived next morning for the visit to Montmartre. It was an embarrassment, one which might have cast a shadow over what had so far been an enjoyable trip.

Her feet swollen from walking miles through the Louvre the day before, Miki sat at the front of the bus, camera at the ready. She was eager to cram as much into each day as possible and, for this reason, she had made a list over breakfast.

Gleaned from her guidebook, entitled *A Thousand and One Parisian Delights*, her own inventory ran to well over three hundred entries – ranging from visiting Le Marais, to touring the dank twisting labyrinth of the Paris catacombs. The highlights were scribbled over twenty sheets of paper in a small intense script.

'I am going to see all these things,' she told Mr. Nakamura, as he took his place beside her on the bus. 'Every last one.'

The tour guide smiled, and sucked air in through his teeth – suggesting anxiety.

'That looks like a great many places,' he said, sucking air again.

'I will cross them off with my red pen as I see them,' Miki explained.

'Sometimes it is not easy to see *every* tourist sight,' Nakamura-san said in a firm statement, one that didn't mean to judge his customer's plan.

'Well, I am going to see them all. We have five days. That is sixty-nine sights a day. Then I will be finished.'

'Maybe we will have difficulty,' said the guide obliquely. 'But we will do our best.'

The minibus set off towards Montmartre.

As it bumbled over the cobbles, Miki took a stream of photos. They weren't of the imposing buildings or the beautiful people, but of the details. Back in Hayama, Saito-san had advised his student to view Paris through the lens of detail. It had sounded very nice but, now that Miki was actually there, she wondered whether she had understood.

She photographed dozens of street names, ceramic white lettering on backgrounds of royal blue. And she took pictures of antique-shop windows with opulent displays of furniture baroque, and photos of advertising boards and hoardings, and street musicians, and painted shutters, Métro signs, and warm baguettes nestled under arms, and café chalkboard menus, and row upon row of identical Vélib' cycles.

As the minibus rolled up towards Sacré-Coeur, Miki sensed a new feeling in her stomach, a new feeling that had just formed.

It wasn't the same euphoria of the arrival, so much as a fresh sensation, one of curious nationalistic pride. Miki may have been Japanese, but she was feeling patriotic in a way that she had never known. The strange thing was that it wasn't patriotism for her own homeland – but for France.

The sight of the tricolour fluttering in the wind made her tight-chested from a sense of duty. In the same way, Haussmann's stone buildings now filled her with elation – a sense that she was part of the grandest tradition ever spawned by human culture.

Laying the camera down on her lap, Miki began to tremble. The trembles turned into shaking, as though she were frozen to the bone.

Seated beside her on the bus, Mr. Nakamura lowered his head.

'Are you feeling cold?' he asked warily.

Miki didn't reply at first. Her jaw was shaking so much that when she did finally speak, the words were unclear.

'It's… it's… it's so, so, so *be-au-ti-ful*,' she said.

The tour leader looked into Miki's eyes and he saw something he had seen many times before – the obsession, the obsession for Paris.

29

AFTER TOURING THE Basilica of Sacré-Coeur, the group was ushered on to a street market in the Place du Tertre.

The square was filled with artists and their works, a blizzard of vibrant colours, Gauloises smoke and laughter. The kind of Parisian scene that adorns postcards and chocolate boxes, it was played out in blinding sunshine. The trees were chameleon-green, and the sky the brightest shade of blue. But, best of all, was the abiding sense of *bonheur*.

Miki and the others followed Nakamura-san as he led them to the far corner of Place du Tertre.

A handsome young artist was crouched there on a flimsy stool. His hair was covered in a black beret, his torso in a striped blue and white sweater. In his right hand was a palette, dabbed with random splotches of paint and, in his left, was a brush.

Spotting the tour leader, the artist jumped up, gushed greetings in good Japanese, and insisted that the three housewives sit. After pulling out a row of stools, he picked up his box of crayons and got down to work.

Giggling, the housewives perched on the stools like crows on a fence, and the artist began to sketch.

A short while later, three impressive portraits were completed.

The artist presented them, insisting they were gifts. Even when pressed by the chairman, he refused all payment. Then, folding away his easel and supplies, he shepherded the tour group towards a narrow little house on the north side of the square.

'Please come to my home and be my guests for tea,' he said, again in Japanese.

The chairman motioned to Nakamura-san.

'We cannot be an inconvenience,' he said.

The tour leader waved the concern aside, and grinned.

'This is an example of real Parisian hospitality,' he replied. 'And it would be regarded as rude not to accept.'

Within a minute or two, the group had filed into the artist's home, and were seated in his sitting-room. They were all quite uncomfortable at having kept on their shoes, although aware that French homes did not follow Japanese tradition.

The little salon had exposed wooden beams running the length of the ceiling. Three of the walls were obscured by oil paintings and sketches of Parisian landmarks; the fourth was hidden beneath an embroidered tapestry from Caen. From upstairs were coming the muffled strains of music.

Before anyone could ask about it, a pair of oversized feet thumped across floorboards. Then there was the sound of someone heavy charging down the stairs.

A large man entered.

He was dressed identically to the artist, in a beret and a striped blue and white sweater. In his hands was an accordion.

Spontaneously, he began to play and, as the music filled the house and poured out onto the street, the artist stepped forward and took Miki's hand. As the housewives, the chairman, Pun-Pun, Noemi and Mr. Nakamura looked on, they danced.

A week before, Miki might have been fearful of making such an example of herself in public, and in the company of her superiors – not least the chairman himself. But something inside her had altered. She felt released and carefree, as though Paris had been a key turned in a lock, liberating her from the judgement and the expectations of others.

The music grew faster, and faster, reaching a climax.

As it did so, the soles of Miki's sensible shoes skipped over the cold stone slabs. And all the while, the others looked on – tense and surprised. Noemi nudged Pun-Pun discreetly, furious that he had not pulled her up to dance as well.

All of a sudden, the music stopped.

Panting, her skin gleaming with perspiration, Miki returned to the default position of her chair. Her nostrils were flared and filled with the smell of *gaijin*, the artist's sweat. And her heart was racing with the raw and unbridled affection of a teenager's first love. Had it not been for the Comte she had met at the bar of the George V, Miki felt certain she would have fallen in love.

The musician went through into a back room.

While he was gone, a pretty young woman came in with a tray of tea and pastries. Like the artist, she spoke Japanese. The chairman asked whether she was a native Parisian.

She seemed anxious, her smile vanishing.

'We are all from Arles,' the artist said, answering for his friend. 'From the town where Vincent Van Gogh lived.'

'Ohhhhh,' said everyone politely, nodding their heads.

The woman smiled again, passed out the pastries and poured the tea, as though she was familiar with Japanese etiquette.

Then she went out of the room and broke into a loud argument with the musician in the kitchen. The guests pretended that they couldn't hear, until the squabble got so raucous that the artist strode out of the room to break it up. Within a moment or two, he was also in the fray, yelling at the top of his voice.

'They are excitable because they are all artists,' said Nakamura-san apologetically.

'Excitable like Vincent Van Gogh,' the chairman replied.

The group from Paradise Tours sipped their tea, each of them wishing they were not in the little house. As they squirmed in their seats, the disagreement got even louder, with the artist's voice rising above the others.

Miki suddenly screwed up her face.

'They are not speaking French,' she said.

'It sounds like… like Polish,' Pun-Pun added.

'We should be going now,' said Mr. Nakamura tautly, as he glanced at his watch. 'There is so much more to see.'

30

THROUGH THE AFTERNOON, the group toured the famous sights of the French capital.

And, all day long they were welcomed where other tourists were shut out and shunned. But, more pleasing still, was the fact that the visitors from Paradise Tours were treated like VIPs.

They were invited through side entrances at public buildings, or beckoned forward past snaking lines of tourists. Lavished with little gifts, they were received with such demonstrations of respect that they felt like superstars.

Nothing was too much trouble for the clients of Paradise Tours.

At the Musée d'Orsay, a young man stepped up and presented each member of the group with a free coffee table book in Japanese. It showcased the highlights of the collection. At the Arc de Triomphe, a blind man gave them all expensive-looking fridge magnets as gifts. And, on the Bateau Mouche, a young woman introduced herself, before presenting them all with free tickets to the Lido evening spectacular. Like everyone else who had approached them, she spoke Japanese.

The chairman answered for them all:

'We cannot accept such a valuable gift,' he said.

The woman's face erupted into a broad smile. Nimbly, she stepped backwards so that she could bow all the deeper. When her body was vertical once again, she declared formally:

'You honour me by accepting.'

31

Freed from her characteristic sense of inferiority, Miki found herself at the front of the group.

Unlike the others, she already knew each tourist sight they visited inside and out. Reeling off extraneous information and snippets of history, gleaned from years of obsession, she was as versed in *la culture française* as even Nakamura-san.

Whenever anyone singled the group out with kindness, she thanked them in French – then reminded the others that the Gallic way was one of equality and fraternity between all.

Pushed to the back, Pun-Pun and Noemi regarded Miki with increasing resentment. They took every opportunity to remind the chairman that she had cheated in the rules of the competition. But, instead of agreeing with them, he found himself warming to the enthusiastic charms of Miki Suzuki-san.

At the end of the day, when the Mercedes minibus returned to the George V, he stepped over to the reception desk and whispered something to the manager. Still embarrassed by the Chinese thievery, the manager wiped the perspiration from his brow, nodded thoughtfully, and presented the chairman with a salver.

Upon it was a large brass key.

A moment later, the key was in Miki's hand.

'There was a mistake,' the chairman said. 'And now I am pleased to tell you that you shall be staying with us all, at the George V.'

32

THE MANAGER CLICKED his fingers and, within seconds, a bellboy was hastening Miki's belongings from the squalid confines of the Belle Rose Travel Lodge to the extravagant grandeur of the George V. So eager was the hotel to redeem itself in the chairman's affections, that the new room was upgraded to the Empire Suite.

Once her suitcase had been brought up, Miki danced around the apartment in a parody of *The Sound of Music*. Then she got down on her hands and knees and rubbed her hands over the carpet. After that, she ran into the bathroom and smelled the soaps, and the miniature bouquet of flowers. And, after dancing a little more, she fell face down on the bed and burst into tears.

That night, while tucked up in a corner of the colossal imperial-size bed, Miki giggled and sobbed alternately until she eventually fell asleep.

She dreamt of the rickety old family home in the suburbs of Sendai, and of her parents. They were the kind of people who never stuck their heads above the parapet of life. As far as they were concerned, the only way to live was to lie low and hope that misfortune stayed away.

As it always did, Miki's dream turned to her ojiichan.

She dreamed of him all suited and bright, his reflection shining in the window of Louis Vuitton. And she dreamed of herself passing him in the street – he in 1951, and she in her own time.

The dream began to melt away, the edges blurring, but Miki forced it to keep going. After all, it was a dream, and she was the dreamer – she could dream anything she liked.

The street came into focus again, and Miki picked out the details. She could see a woman in the background in long gloves, hat and heels; a nanny out with an iron perambulator; and Citroën's latest grey monsters of steel juddering by over cobblestones.

Turning, Miki followed her ojiichan.

He walked briskly, his small feet moving with distinct purpose, as though he were late for a pressing appointment. Every few seconds he glanced at his wristwatch and quickened his step all the more.

Making his way through Place Vendôme, he strode fast up Rue de la Paix and on along Avenue Montaigne. Miki's ojiichan crossed the street, ran a hand back through his hair, bought a newspaper, and took a seat on the pavement outside a café.

It was crowded with people – the men in dark suits, and the women in hats and gloves. There was a sense of propriety, as though everyone was following the same script.

Miki watched as her grandfather lit a cigarette, crossed his legs, and sipped a *café noir*. He seemed content, if a little anxious. Taking a document out from his inside pocket, he folded it twice, and slipped it into the newspaper that was lying on the corner of the table.

At that moment, a woman arrived.

She was no ordinary woman. Her long slim form was clothed in a yellow sundress, a matching hat pinned to her hair. She was French, so very French, her complexion alabaster white, her lips painted fire engine red.

Kissing Ojiichan on both cheeks, she sat down across from him, and stared deep into his eyes. He made a joke and she laughed, her perfect white teeth glinting in the sun.

Miki wondered who the woman was and, as she did so, something strange happened. Her ojiichan picked up the newspaper and presented it to her with both hands. The woman kissed him again.

But this time she kissed him on the mouth.

A moment later she was gone.

33

THE NEXT MORNING, an antique cloisonné mantel clock struck eight times, waking Miki from her slumber.

Breathing in sharply, she focused on the nightstand, her gaze moving up slowly over the curtains, the dresser, and onto the chandelier. Her back warmed with pleasure and with fear, as she remembered where she was.

And, as she lay there, the dream slipped back into her mind. She replayed the moment in the café once and then again, the moment of the handover. Frowning, she wondered what her grandfather's secret had been.

There was a knock at the door.

A steward entered, easing a trolley before him through the vestibule and into the spacious salon. It was laden with warm croissants and little pots of jam, a plate of scrambled eggs, fresh cut fruit, orange juice, coffee and toast.

'I am in Paradise,' Miki said in French.

'*Oui, Mademoiselle*,' the steward replied, 'the Paradise of the George V.'

When the steward had left, Miki sat on the corner of the bed. Clenching her fists, she pulled them up under her chin and began hyperventilating. The delicious food, the luxurious room, the sunshine, and the fact that she was in Paris, were leading to an alchemical reaction, the likes of which she had not experienced before.

Faster and faster she breathed.

And, as she did so, her body began shaking like a crack addict going cold turkey.

Suddenly, it reached a critical threshold.

Sliding off the bed, Miki fainted and fell to the floor.

34

IT WAS PUN-PUN who discovered her lying at the foot of the imperial-size bed.

Furious that she had been invited into the hallowed corridors of the George V, he had arrived to give the order that she swap her suite with the chairman's standard room.

The steward had left the door ajar, and Pun-Pun barged in.

'What are you doing lying there!' he growled.

Confused and dazed, Miki struggled to open her eyes and make sense of what had happened. The blurred elegance of the room was replaced by Pun-Pun's distorted face leering close, the wart like a big red mountain on a wide plateau.

'Get up at once!' he ordered. 'And how dare you behave so badly! You have disgraced the good name of Angel Flower!'

Miki started to cry. She struggled up, fell down again, and strained to stand a second time.

'I am so sorry,' she said. 'I think I fainted.'

Her superior clapped his hands, more out of rage than out of anything else.

'If I could have my way, I would make sure you were sent home to Tokyo this morning!'

'I promise to behave,' Miki said in a soft voice. 'Please let me stay. This is my dream, a dream I have longed to come true my entire life.'

'You are to swap this suite with the chairman's modest room!' Pun-Pun hissed. 'As soon as you have done that, you are to go downstairs. I will give you five minutes. And...' he spat, as he stormed out, 'be sure that I shall tell the chairman of your embarrassing behaviour!'

35

RUSHING DOWN TO the lobby, Miki found that the rest of the tour group was not yet there.

In her hand she clutched the wad of pages inscribed with the list, the places she was so desperate to see. Out of the three hundred and forty-five names, only nine had been crossed off.

As Miki riffled through the pages, Mr. Nakamura arrived.

'Good morning,' he said.

Miki looked up.

'Good morning, Nakamura-san.'

'We have a busy day planned. There is still much to see.'

Miki held up her list.

'I am frightened that I will not be able to get to it all in time!'

Mr. Nakamura leaned back on his heels.

'Sometimes it is best to keep something for the next trip,' he said.

'Oh, but I do not know if I will ever be able to come back to Paris,' Miki explained. 'You see I do not have a job that pays well. I am not rich like other people, and I do not work in the travel business.'

The tour leader smiled very gently, the kind smile of someone who genuinely cared.

'Perhaps you should think of getting a job as a tour guide like me,' he said. 'Then you could come to Paris often.'

Until that moment, Miki had been downhearted – the result of Pun-Pun reprimanding her yet again. But it was as though a light switch had been suddenly flicked on, and the world was illuminated for the first time.

Miki raised her head slowly. Her face was vacant at first but, gradually, it came to life, as if an artist had pencilled in an expression of utter delight.

'Yes! Yes! Yes!' Miki exclaimed. 'That is it! That is the best idea I have ever heard! Yes! I will become a tour guide and I will marry Comte Hugo-san!'

The duty manager looked up from his desk. Miki froze. She apologized for speaking so loudly.

And then the chairman arrived. After him came the others.

'I heard you fell,' he said tenderly. 'Are you alright?'

Miki began trembling. She bobbed her head low, indicating subservience.

'I am so sorry, sir,' she moaned. 'I was just tired, tired from all the excitement. I promise to behave.'

'Do you want to see a doctor?'

'No, sir. I am well. Again, I am sorry to have caused an embarrassment to Angel Flower.'

Mr. Nakamura stepped forward and gave everyone yet another plastic pouch bearing the name and logo of Paradise Tours.

'Today is the most important day of all,' he explained. 'Because we are going to travel back in time, and visit the Cathedral of Notre Dame. And we will meet some more real French people.'

'Will we go shopping, too?' enquired Miki in a whisper.

'Yes! We will go shopping on the Champs-Elysées!'

The trio of housewives tittered with merriment and, when they had finished cooing, Noemi clapped her hands.

'Champs-Elysées! Champs-Elysées! I want to go to Champs-Elysées!'

Miki got a flash of her dream, of her ojiichan kissing the woman with bright red lips. She blushed, and then thought of the coin pouch, and of Louis Vuitton, the headquarters of which were located on the Champs-Elysées.

At last she would be able to fulfil her promise. She was touched by a sense of destiny. Unable to stop herself, Miki jumped up and down like a schoolchild in a sweet shop.

The thought of going to Louis Vuitton at last, and the newly conceived idea of getting a job as a tour guide, had filled her with the kind of joy that she had never known. What could be more perfect a job than devoting one's life to showing Paris to other Japanese?

Mr. Nakamura bowed to the group.

'If you are ready, we can go now,' he said. 'The minibus is waiting for us.'

One by one, the visitors stepped through the wrought iron and glass doors, into the sunshine.

As they walked over to the Mercedes minibus, a posse of paparazzi jumped out from nowhere. With cameras clicking and flashguns flaring, they clustered around the group from Paradise Tours.

'They must have the wrong people,' said Pun-Pun anxiously.

'We are not celebrities,' the chairman tried to explain.

But then one of the photographers held up a sign. It bore a short slogan in *hiragana*, which read:

PARIS LOVES ANGEL FLOWER!

Mr. Nakamura herded his group into the bus.

Once they were in their seats, everyone fussed and clucked at the thought that they were regarded as celebrities, and were being hounded by actual paparazzi.

'Maybe they will put the pictures in a magazine,' said Noemi, hopefully.

'Maybe we will be very famous!' Miki said in a loud voice.

'Oh, but you *are* all famous,' Nakamura-san replied, as he gave an inconspicuous thumbs-up to the photographers. 'Didn't you see – the people of Paris love Angel Flower?!'

36

TAKING A DETOUR on the way to Notre Dame, the minibus trundled down Rue de Longchamp. As it did so, Mr. Nakamura said something to the driver in French. The vehicle slowed, then pulled over outside a plain stone-fronted building.

'Welcome to the most famous pastry shop in France!' the tour leader declared, 'the Pâtisserie des Rêves! It is where all your dreams will come true!'

The group trooped down off the minibus and filed into the shop, while Mr. Nakamura placed an order for seven pastries.

'We will taste the choux cream,' he said, 'the very best choux cream in the world!'

'Choux cream!' the housewives cooed in a single voice. 'We love choux cream! It is very very good!'

'It's my favourite!' said Noemi ecstatically.

'Mine too,' added Miki.

The pastries were passed across the counter to Mr. Nakamura. Bowing, he served them to the members of his group, and then went out to the minibus to make a telephone call.

One at a time, the tourists sank their teeth into the cakes.

And, one by one their expressions soured.

'It is a little too sweet,' said one of the housewives, bashfully.

'And a little moist,' mumbled another.

'Mine is very rich,' the chairman said.

'I cannot finish this,' whispered Pun-Pun. 'It is making me feel sick.'

'The choux cream in Tokyo is much better than this!' Noemi grumbled.

Then all at once, the group condemned the pastries as miserable imitations of the real thing. After all, choux cream is well-regarded as a Japanese delicacy, one unmatched by anyone else – even by the French, who invented it.

More normally, Miki would have fallen into line and condemned the pastries as well. But she felt a sudden pang of Gallic patriotism in her stomach, patriotism tinged with an overdose of fresh cream. Stuffing the pastry into her mouth, she chewed for a moment, swallowed, then shook her fists frantically, and yelled:

'That was perfect, so perfect! I love Paris! *Vive la France!*'

37

A LITTLE LATER, having taken in the solemn wonders of Notre Dame, the Angel Flower tour group was led by Mr. Nakamura out of the cathedral and into the sunlight.

Squinting, shading eyes with hands, they felt the warmth on their faces.

'It is a very old building,' said one of the housewives.

'It is beautiful,' said another.

'Very big,' said the third.

Noemi was about to make a comment, when Pun-Pun pointed to a homeless man lying on a park bench. He was dressed in endless layers of soiled clothing, with many bags of worthless possessions in a heap beside him.

As they watched, the man got up, pulled down his trousers, and pooed on the grass.

'He should be arrested,' said Pun-Pun angrily.

'It's a disgrace,' said Noemi.

Miki took a step forward and put her hands over her mouth. She didn't approve of the man, but disliked the fact that others were criticizing him. So she waved her hands, as if calling everyone else to listen.

'He is ill, a poor ill man,' she said stridently, 'and that is why we must all feel sorry for him.'

Pun-Pun shook his head in disbelief.

'That man is shameful and there is only one thing for such a shameful man – *prison*.'

'He will get nice food in prison,' Noemi said.

'And a proper bed,' one of the housewives chirped.

'Good clothing as well, clothing which is clean,' said another.

'No!' shouted Miki, her hands now gripped into fists. 'This is Paris, where everyone has rights! *Liberté, Égalité, Fraternité*. Everyone has the right to behave as they like!'

The chairman pointed at the homeless man.

'Does *he* have the right to behave like *that*?' he asked.

Miki's fists waved all the harder.

'Yes! Yes!' she yelled. 'It's his human right... his *French* right!'

38

AFTER THE OUTBURST at Notre Dame and at the pâtisserie, Mr. Nakamura was becoming worried. He had been watching Miki's obsession for the French capital grow in momentum, and he feared that it was about to disrupt the harmony of the group.

Taking the Angel Flower's leader aside, he said:

'Perhaps it would be best for Miki to rest at the hotel for a little while, until she is feeling better.'

The chairman agreed, and the minibus made a beeline back to the George V, where Miki was off-loaded.

'We are all going to take a siesta,' Nakamura-san lied. 'It is a tradition in France. After all, we will be staying up late tonight, for the floor show at the Lido.'

Clutching her camera to her chest, Miki let out a pained squeal.

'But I want to go to Louis Vuitton,' she said. 'You told us that we would go shopping!'

'There will be plenty of time for that,' the tour leader replied in a reassuring voice. 'I promise that you will leave Paris laden with bags!' He smiled, dipped his head a little, and said: 'Sometimes the city can be overwhelming, because there is so much to do and there is never enough time.'

'But I want to see *everything*,' Miki announced, holding up her crumpled list. 'And we are moving very slowly. I wish we could move faster, much much faster. And I don't want to be laden with shopping. All I want to buy is a coin pouch from Louis Vuitton.'

The tour leader gave a secret signal to the others, and they all went inside. As soon as Miki had been chaperoned up to her new room, the group hurried back down to the minibus.

'She should be sent back to Tokyo immediately,' said Pun-Pun. 'She is a shame on the good reputation of Angel Flower!'

'She is just a little tired,' the chairman replied. 'Young women are like that. All silly and excitable.'

The minibus sped away. A moment or two later it was pulling up outside Louis Vuitton.

Meanwhile, up in her room, Miki lay on the queen-sized bed and tried to sleep. She wanted to be obedient and, although she had little affection for Angel Flower, she appreciated that the firm had brought her to Paris.

All of a sudden she remembered something.

The Musée Nissim de Camondo.

She had promised the kind clerk in the Kinokuniya bookshop that she would visit it. Snatching the list of sights from her nightstand, Miki thumbed through it until she came to the museum.

She gasped, then choked.

And, without knowing quite why, she ran to the door and put on her shoes.

Gripped with panic, a raw terrible panic, she felt as if iron doors were closing all around her.

In a fluster, Miki fled from the room and down to the lobby, then out onto the street. She was dazed and fearful, uncertain of whether to laugh or cry, or whether to follow orders and go back upstairs and rest.

The doorman asked if he could help her with directions.

Miki tapped a finger to the Nissim de Camondo on her list.

'This one. I would like to go to this one.'

'Walk up to the Champs-Elysées,' the doorman said courteously, 'and then straight over, and on for a kilometre or so until you reach Rue de Monceau.'

Bowing, thanking, apologizing, Miki set off at a fast pace.

By the time she crossed the main thoroughfare, she was jogging. And, within a block or two more, she was sprinting. Unsure why she felt it so important to reach the museum right then, it was as though something deep down inside was willing her on.

Had Miki looked to her left as she reached the Champs-Elysées, she would have seen Louis Vuitton's flagship store, the one place she had curiously forgotten. And, had she gone inside, she would have met the members of her own tour group, who were shuffling around the displays in a state of timorous awe.

As she ran down Rue Washington, Miki saw a huge heap of litter piled up on the side of the street. A cluster of homeless men were rooting through it with their dogs, spreading it around in their hunt for food.

Miki frowned in surprise.

Saito-san had never mentioned garbage or the homeless, and neither was ever shown in the coffee table books featuring the highlights of the French capital.

Forcing the thought out of her head, Miki kept on running.

Within a few minutes she reached number 63 Rue de Monceau, and the imposing stone façade of the Musée Nissim de Camondo.

Set over four storeys in a splendid villa, the museum reeked of aristocratic grandeur and private affluence.

Cautiously, Miki bought an entrance ticket and went inside on tiptoes.

The simple exterior gave no clue to the excesses of what lay within. The central hallway was floored in black and white mosaics, and adorned with sculptures and potted plants. A glorious sweeping stone staircase rose up to the first floor, an exquisite wrought iron handrail echoing the curve of the stairs.

There were lovely statues and medieval tapestries, giant portraits of imperious-looking aristocrats, and the very finest furniture. There were crystal chandeliers, too, and faded photographs, fauteuils, and bookcases filled with volumes bound in matching red morocco.

Miki closed her eyes and breathed in the smell.

It was a *gaijin* smell, one she had not experienced before. Tinged with musk and dust, it made her think of the pictures she had seen in the coffee table book from Kinokuniya. It was the Paris she had dreamed of, the one that squared so perfectly with the memories of her ojiichan.

Walking softly through the house, Miki felt unworthy and awkward, and wished she had not left the hotel. Still on tiptoes, she made her way through the grand public salons and then up into the private apartments. The grandeur and the luxury were so impressive that Miki felt dizzy.

She feared that she might faint again.

Stepping through into the library, illuminated by the incandescent sunshine of early spring, she steadied herself on the doorframe, and slowed her breathing. The room was a picture of elegance, the walls adorned in oak shelves, each of them arranged with antique leatherbound books.

There was a sense of mystery, as though magic was at work.

Calming herself, Miki paced slowly over the parquet until she reached the first window. She turned her back on the room and stared out at the sun breaking through the trees.

A minute passed, perhaps two.

Miki didn't move. She couldn't. It was as though something was rooting her to that spot, just as she had been drawn to visit the museum right then by some inexplicable force.

All of a sudden, a voice startled her.

'Good afternoon, *Mademoiselle*.'

Miki swivelled around.

A tall, suave gentleman was standing two yards away. He was dressed in a cream linen suit, with a red rose pinned to his buttonhole.

'You do not remember me from the bar of the George V?' he asked in Japanese.

'Yes, um, er, yes!' Miki froze like a rabbit caught in blinding headlights.

'The fact that I find you here at Nissim de Camondo, and in the library of all places, suggests what I had already surmised was true – that you are a young lady of impeccable taste.'

Miki blushed, and choked, and apologized more sincerely than she had ever apologized before.

'I am sorry to disturb you,' she said after a roll call of apology.

'But it was I who approached you,' replied the Comte with a smile. He bowed his head a little, as he had learned to do while stationed in Tokyo. 'I should not want to be overly forward,' he said, 'but I wonder whether you would do me the honour of dining with me tonight at the Interalliée.'

Miki clutched her hands to her chest. She apologized again, choked a little more, and gushed an acceptance.

'You are very kind,' she said.

'How did you know that?' the Count said. 'After all, you have just met me.'

'Because...'

'*Because...?*'

'Because you have very clean shoes,' Miki said.

39

LESS THAN A minute after the Comte Hugo de Montfried kissed her hand and excused himself until the evening, Miki was overcome with a sense of absolute terror.

She had accepted the aristocrat's invitation to dine even though the tour group was expecting her to join them for the much-publicized spectacular at the Lido on the Champs-Elysées.

Miki ran out from the Nissim de Camondo Museum in a state of frenzied hysteria. The chance meeting with the count had been the miracle she had wished for, a miracle undoubtedly sent by her ancestors. It was testament that they approved of her obsession with Paris, and of her wish to marry a French aristocrat.

Her head spinning, Miki could think of nothing but her love for her darling Hugo. Chanting his name over and over in her mind, she imagined every detail of his face. Ready to follow him to the end of the earth, she would serve him until breath left her chest.

As she shuffled down the street, she thought of the house they would share together on the edge of a brook, a vase of chrysanthemums in the hallway, and delicate touches of Japan all around. And, she thought of the children they would have and raise together, little clones of their father – tall, stylish, and exceedingly kind.

Struggling to regain her composure, Miki glanced around hesitantly and spotted greenery nearby – the Parc Monceau. Hurrying over to it, she found herself in a little oasis of tranquillity. It reminded her of a park she had visited as a child near Sendai, taken there by her grandfather in the years before illness took hold.

She sat down on one of the slatted wooden benches, and tried to think straight about that evening. The best solution she could come up with was to tell a lie, to say that she was feeling unwell, and then slip out for the dinner once the others had left for the Lido.

No, no, she thought – that could not work.

Nakamura-san had said that the show began at 9 p.m., but the Count had arranged to arrive at the hotel an hour before that.

Forcing her face into her hands, Miki began to weep.

Her heart was beating fast from love, just as it was pounding from fear of infuriating the chairman of the mighty Angel Flower. Miki may have been regarded as a rebel by Pun-Pun and by her nemesis, Noemi, but she really didn't want to stick out.

The idea of displeasing anyone at all was miserable, but she was ready and willing to endure any amount of condemnation if it meant she might spend an evening in the company of her beloved aristocrat.

Again, she strained to think.

The Comte de Montfried had said he would pass by the George V for a drink in the bar before taking Miki to his club, the Cercle de l'Union Interalliée, on Rue du Faubourg Saint-Honoré. Mr. Saito had once told her of it, explaining that it was where all the debutantes were introduced into society at lavish balls. There was no better address in all Paris.

Suddenly, Miki's attention veered from the predicament of the evening, to the list of places still to visit. Thumbing through the pages fast, she felt sick in her stomach at seeing so many hundreds of names still to be crossed out.

Shaking, she crumpled the paper in her hands. Then she let out a squeal of angst, disappointment, horror and pain, and she stamped her feet up and down.

At that moment a man approached her.

In his hand was a gold ring.

'I think you dropped this,' he said in French.

Miki understood what he meant more from his body language than from his words, which were masked in a thick accent. She shook her head politely.

'No, no, so sorry but it is not mine.'

The man insisted.

'But I am certain it *is* yours,' he replied.

Again, Miki's head shook and, again, the man insisted.

'It is a very pretty ring,' she said.

'So take it, please take it. I won't tell anyone.'

Not wanting to upset the stranger, Miki took the ring and put it on her finger. Still swooning for her comte, she imagined it was a wedding ring, sealing their commitment to one another.

'Thank you,' she said. 'You are a very kind man.'

Smoothing out the sheets of paper, she pretended to be busy with her list, in the hope that the stranger would go away.

But he did not.

Instead, he dawdled there, as if waiting for something.

'Will you give me some money?' he asked.

Miki didn't understand. She put her head on its side and sucked in air through her teeth.

'Give?' she said.

'Money,' the man said. 'I want money for the ring.' He rubbed his thumb and forefinger together and jerked up his chin aggressively.

'*Money?*'

'Yes!'

Again, Miki sucked air. She tried to take the ring off her finger so that she could return it.

But it wouldn't come off. It was stuck.

Worried that she had strayed into a realm of Parisian life for which she had not been prepared, she opened her purse and took out ten euros. She passed it to the man.

He took the money, but still he loitered.

'You must give me more than that!' he shouted. 'I want one hundred euros!'

'*One hundred?*'

'Yes! Give it to me now or I will go to the police!'

Miki let out another shriek and began to cry again. She apologized and bowed, and cried all the more.

'Please, I do not want the ring,' she said, begging.

'Then give it back to me!'

'But as you see it is stuck on my finger.'

The man stepped closer until his shadow fell over Miki and the bench – it was cold and haunting, and seemed to smell very bad. His face muscles twisted into a menacing snarl, and he flexed his fingers as though he were about to attack.

Jumping up, Miki ran.

And the stranger ran after her.

Tearing through Parc Monceau she hurried over to the pond. And the man ran after her, calling out for money or his ring.

Miki's small feet paced fast through a group of ducks and between young mothers out with their prams. She was screaming, pages from her list fluttering away behind her.

The assailant suddenly pulled back. But Miki was too frightened to stop. She sprinted on, out of Parc Monceau, to the main road and on into a labyrinth of smaller streets.

Only after another twenty minutes of running did she dare to look around. The stranger wasn't there. He was long gone, but his ring was still on Miki's hand, and it was so tight that the finger was swollen. She stopped in a doorway and tried desperately to pull it off, sucking at it, twisting it, jerking it.

Nothing worked.

All the tugging had added to the pressure, and the finger was now turning blue.

Spotting a café across the street, Miki went in and asked the waiter if she could use the toilet. She was in urgent need of a tap, so that she could hold the finger under cold water to stop the swelling.

'Toilets are for customers only,' the waiter said in an uncompromising voice. 'You have to order something to drink!' He motioned the act of holding a cup to his lips.

Miki pointed to her finger and screwed up her face, indicating great pain. The waiter pointed at a sign. It showed a toilet with a red cross scrawled across it. Miki ordered a cappuccino and, leaving her handbag on the chair, she went into the toilet to soothe her badly throbbing finger in cold water.

She stayed there for twenty minutes, gently turning the ring round and round, until the skin was less sore.

Then, with all her strength, she gripped the band of gold and eased it over the knuckle.

Suddenly, it slipped off, leaving her bruised ring finger the colour of blue-black ink.

Thanking her ancestors for delivering her from agony, Miki went back into the café to enjoy her cappuccino. It had been sunny when she went into the toilet, but rain was now lashing against the windows.

Miki weaved her way between the tables until she got to where her cup of coffee was waiting. She sat down, sipped the cold coffee, and reached for her handbag.

But it was gone.

Leaping up, Miki rushed over to the waiter, who was serving another customer.

'Please! Please!' she exclaimed.

'You will have to wait until I have finished with this gentleman,' the waiter responded.

'But, my handbag! My handbag has been stolen!'

The waiter turned. He screwed up his face and shrugged.

'Well, I do not have it,' he said.

'But it has been stolen!' Miki declared, repeating herself.

The waiter shrugged a second time.

'You should have taken it with you,' he said, pointing to a sign of a handbag with a big red cross laid over it.

Miki stamped her feet and waved her fists.

'*Quoi?*' asked the waiter, with upturned hands.

'Police. Please get the police!'

The waiter smiled distantly and shook his head. Then he removed a cloth from his apron and began wiping down a table, as if the idea of a theft was deeply uninteresting.

Miki went back to the table where her cappuccino was still waiting. Pressing a hand to her forehead, she closed her eyes. The suave silhouette of Hugo de Montfried came instantly to mind.

I am sure he will help me, she thought.

But, then she remembered the chairman and Pun-Pun, and the other members of the Angel Flower tour group. What was she doing in a café alone without their permission? She reprimanded herself for sneaking away. The theft of her handbag was surely punishment for not doing as she had been told.

And now she would have to admit to the chairman that she had lost her passport, wallet, and all her identification. But worse – much worse – was the fact that the Comte de Montfried's business card had been in the bag as well. Its loss meant that she would never see him again – unless, that is, she managed to elude the others, and meet him for the date.

Miki slumped down on the chair.

After much whimpering she struggled to make a plan. Her head was telling her to retreat to the safety of the George V and to plead with the chairman, begging him to show mercy for her foolishness. But Miki's gut was telling her to sort the problem out for herself.

Placing the gold ring on the table-top beside the cold cappuccino, she cursed. How could she have been so stupid as to take something of such value from a stranger? It was certain to lead to trouble.

As she sat there, trying to work out what to do, the waiter strode up, cloth in hand.

'Do you want a fresh coffee?' he asked.

'I don't have any money,' said Miki. 'I have been robbed and I do not know what to do.'

The waiter's already sour expression soured all the more.

'You have to pay for your coffee,' he said.

'But I don't have any money. All I have is this valuable gold ring. It was given to me by a stranger and it was the start of all my problems.'

Snatching the ring with his claw-like nails, the waiter observed it for a fleeting moment.

'That's not valuable,' he said. 'It's rubbish. Not worth a *centime!*'

Miki put her head in her hands and sobbed.

'You Chinese are all the same,' the waiter barked, 'and you cause too much trouble in our city. You must go now. Get out! *Go! Go! Go!*'

'But it's raining hard.'

The waiter pointed at the door.

'Get out!' he yelled.

40

FOR AN HOUR Miki trudged through the downpour.

She had not been prepared for rain and her sundress was quickly soaked. On an especially high kerb she tripped and the heel came off her shoe, forcing her to limp on through puddles as wide as she was tall.

Three or four times she tried hailing a taxi, but as soon as the cab drivers heard where she wanted to go, they sped away. One of them had shouted: 'They don't accept Chinese hookers at the George V!'

All of a sudden, Miki spotted a little sushi restaurant tucked away on the corner where two narrow streets met. Her eyes lit up. Someone there was sure to take pity on a fellow Japanese. Miki hobbled over to the restaurant, and pulled the door open.

A large woman was standing behind the counter.

She had a thick muscular neck and a face that didn't look very Japanese. Greeting the woman, Miki bowed and apologized. She was about to explain, when she felt it necessary to bow again, and apologize one last time before speaking.

And so she did.

Done with pleasantries, she ducked her head down and, feebly, she said:

'I have been robbed and am in need of a little help.'

The woman rapped her knuckles down on the counter aggressively. 'I don't speak Japanese,' she said in French. 'I speak Mandarin!'

'You are not Japanese?' Miki asked, confused.

'*Hah*! No! We are from Beijing!'

'But this is a sushi restaurant, and sushi is Japanese.'

The waitress slammed her fist down.

'I cannot help you! If you have money, you can eat. If you do not have money, you must go or I will call the police!'

Whimpering and weeping, Miki pulled the door open and limped back out into the rain.

Her tears were instantly washed away by the downpour.

Then it began to get dark. Still Miki trudged on, desperately hoping to find the way back to the George V. One sympathetic shopkeeper did give her directions, but she was so confused that she mixed up her left and right and strayed miles out of the way.

Another hour of hobbling, and Miki was far from the centre of Paris. She found herself in an ugly, deprived area. There were children sword-fighting with sticks in the rain, and car alarms sounding, drug addicts shooting up in doorways, stray dogs and high-rise blocks of flats.

A car pulled up slow and kerb-crawled alongside Miki as she walked. The driver wound down the passenger window.

'*Combien?*' he asked quickly.

'*Combien?*'

'*Oui.*'

'I do not understand. How much for what?'

'For everything?'

Miki still didn't understand, but she knew the man was not a gentleman. He had a big frothy beard and the end of a cigarette screwed into the corner of his mouth.

She limped away at double speed, as the car drove on.

Then the rain grew heavier, and began falling in sheets. Soaking, and frozen to the bone, Miki sought refuge in the doorway of a boarded-up tenement building. She was shaking and moaning, and was about to collapse when a figure jumped out.

He had a knife in his hand.

Jerking it to Miki's throat, he bawled:

'Give me your money – *all* your money!'

'I... I... I do not have money. I was already robbed,' said Miki, stammering in French.

'Give it to me or I'll cut your throat!' the man demanded, as he increased his grip on her neck. The blade was pressed right up to her jugular. She could feel the steel, cold and hard.

Miki got a flash of her grandfather, dancing over the cobblestones, and then of the family home near Sendai, the afternoon sun streaming in through the kitchen window. She struggled to free herself, but the knife pressed all the harder – so much so that Miki feared she was about to die.

Just then, the silhouette of another man turned the corner and began approaching. He was out walking his dog, a pit-bull. Flustered, the assailant clouted his victim on the side of her head with the hilt of the knife, and vanished into the shadows.

Miki fell to the ground without the faintest sound.

Not wanting to be associated with the attack, the man with the pit-pull moved briskly on. For more than an hour, Miki lay there in the rain, her face pressed down into the filth.

Then, by chance, a police patrol spotted the huddled figure of a woman lying on the ground. It had been called to deal with a case of domestic battery in a tenement block nearby.

Forty minutes later, Miki was lying on a bed in a corridor at the local hospital. The passageway was illuminated with strip-lighting, and stank of industrial disinfectant. There was a constant rush of medical personnel, a sense of despondency and gloom.

Another forty minutes passed, and a doctor with a clipboard strolled up and shone a torch into Miki's eyes. He was young and inexperienced, and hadn't slept in days. Explaining what had happened in French, Miki started to sob uncontrollably.

'You will stay here for the night and we will give you a CAT-scan just in case,' the doctor said. 'After that you should be well enough to go home.' He paused. 'Where is your home?' he asked.

'The George V Hotel,' Miki said.

The doctor rubbed a hand down over his tired eyes.

'God knows what you're doing in this hell-hole then,' he said.

'I was robbed,' Miki replied. 'And then I was attacked.'

'You're lucky to be alive. This is a dangerous part of the city. Don't you know that?'

'I have to go to Louis Vuitton,' Miki answered, her concentration drifting.

'*Louis?*'

'*Vuitton*... I have to buy a coin pouch for my ojiichan.'

41

SHORTLY BEFORE NOON the next day, Miki was discharged with a bandage wrapped tight around her head.

She looked like a soldier home from war. A vacant expression in her eyes, she shuffled forwards with a sense of helplessness. Before she could leave the hospital, she was told to go to the business office and settle the bill for her treatment. The severe woman in charge there asked for her Carte Vitale, so that health insurance would pay.

'I am a tourist,' Miki said. 'I do not have French health insurance.'

The administrator's index finger moved over to a large desktop calculator and punched in many numbers. She peered at the display.

'You owe us six hundred and twenty euros,' she said in a stern voice.

'But I was robbed and I do not have any money,' Miki said.

The administrator's expression didn't waver.

'We will give you three days to pay. You will have to leave your passport with us, until we receive the money.'

'But my passport was stolen in the café, when I was trying to take the gold ring off my finger,' Miki said, holding up her hand.

The woman frowned, narrowed her eyes, and mumbled something to her colleague.

'Excuse me,' said Miki. 'I did not hear you.'

Standing tall, the administrator replied:

'I said that you Chinese are all the same. You are thieves!'

42

LATER THAT AFTERNOON, Miki arrived at the George V, the cost of the taxi having been added to her hospital bill, a bill she could not pay. Her head was still bandaged, her clothes dishevelled, and her shoe still missing its heel.

The doorman was about to turn her away, assuming she was an illegal immigrant out begging, when he recognized her and opened the door.

Making a beeline for the reception desk, Miki asked whether Comte Hugo de Montfried had left her a message.

The duty clerk enquired her name.

She gave it.

He shook his head.

'I am afraid not,' he said. 'But it appears, *Mademoiselle*, that you are no longer staying with us here at the George V.'

Miki winced.

'But I am from the Angel Flower Beauty Company,' she said, 'and I am with several other people.'

'Yes, I know,' the clerk replied. 'But they left for Mont St. Michel this morning.' He fished about on the desk and picked up an envelope. 'No message from a comte,' he said, 'but this from your colleague.'

Miki opened the letter, expecting sympathy and an explanation. At once she recognized the small angry script of her superior, Pun-Pun.

The letter read:

Miki Suzuki, you have brought shame on the good name of Angel Flower and are a continued disgrace to the company. The chairman is shocked that you left the hotel when instructed not to do so. The entire firm condemns you in the strongest terms and it has been decided that you are to be fired with immediate effect. Your aeroplane ticket back to Narita is enclosed.

Yamato

Touching a hand to her bandage, Miki lowered her head in shame.

She didn't have the energy to feel resentment towards Pun-Pun, just sorrow that her dream had ended in such despair. The Paris of her grandfather's rose-tinted memories was not the Paris that she had found.

With a click of the duty clerk's fingers, Miki's suitcase was wheeled out from the storeroom. It had been packed hastily by a maid. Tossed in at random, clothing was poking out from the sides.

Having wheeled the case outside, the doorman asked Miki if she needed a taxi.

'I do not have anywhere to go,' she said. 'My passport and my money were stolen.'

'You should go to your embassy,' the doorman said. He looked up the address. 'It's on Avenue Hoche – it's very close, up near Parc Monceau.'

Miki grimaced.

'Yes, I know Monceau,' she replied through gritted teeth, before setting off with her wheelie case.

43

ON THE WAY to the embassy, Miki came to a public telephone.

Remarkably, it hadn't been vandalized like all the others. Suddenly, she had an idea – she would call her parents and ask them to send her a little money. It was an emergency after all.

Giving the number to the international operator, Miki waited for her mother to accept the call. But instead of a woman's voice, she heard an old man on the line. He seemed bewildered and fussed.

'Ojiichan!' she cried out. 'Dear Ojiichan, it's Miki!'

The frail voice seemed to strengthen a little, as though buoyed by good news.

'Miki-chan!' he said, wheezing. 'How is your journey? How is my beloved Paris?'

Miki's eyes were streaming with tears, her face muscles exhausted from weeping.

'Paris,' she said. 'It is… it is… it is *wonderful!*'

The ojiichan let out a muffled laugh as though he knew it was wonderful and had no need to ask.

'I told you,' he said. 'I told you that it was Paradise on Earth!'

The line went dead, and Miki stood there, the receiver in her hand, her cheeks lined with fresh tears.

Calmly, she bowed to the receiver and, with both hands, placed it back on the telephone.

Gripping the handle of the suitcase, she was about to wheel it forward, when half a dozen girls approached her. They were in their early teens, and were far less prim than other Parisian children she had seen.

The oldest girl held up a paper.

She asked Miki if she would sign her petition. Miki didn't really understand but, before she could refuse, a pen was in her hand, and her hand was on the paper.

The girl asked where Miki was from.

'From Japan,' she said, adding: 'I have been robbed and so I am going to my embassy.'

'There are a lot of thieves in Paris,' said the girl. 'They look for tourists like you and then they attack them.'

'They are not good people,' Miki replied. 'A man gave me a gold ring and then he chased me, demanding money. And the ring was not gold, and it got stuck on my finger.'

The oldest girl turned to her friends and said something fast. It didn't sound like French.

'Are you from Paris?' Miki asked.

'No, no, from Bucharest – from Romania.'

Miki put her head on the side and sucked in air through her back teeth.

'Oh,' she said. 'Romania.'

'We are Romany,' the girl explained. 'We came to Paris to make money.'

'You do not go to school?'

The girl shook her head.

'We have to earn money because our families are poor,' she said.

Miki thanked the girls for their conversation and wished them luck with their petition.

Then, bowing, she reached out to grasp the handle of the wheelie case.

But the case was gone.

44

AT THE JAPANESE embassy, a security officer waved his hand forcefully through the air above his head.

A great brute of a man from Brittany, he disliked the Japanese very much indeed. Having taken the job because nothing else had been on offer, he took delight in doing all in his power to bring misery to the people he was supposed to be assisting. And the easiest way to bring misery was to be of no help at all.

'The embassy is closed for the weekend,' he said curtly.

Miki looked at her wristwatch.

'But it is one minute past five,' she replied.

The guard shrugged.

'I am following orders from the Japanese staff inside,' he explained.

'But I have been robbed,' Miki said. 'My passport has been stolen, and my money, too, and all my clothes as well. And the heel has come off my shoe...'

Stepping back, the guard looked at Miki's feet. He sniffed.

'The embassy will open on Monday morning, at 9 a.m.,' he said.

'Is there an emergency number I can call?'

'No.'

'Are you sure?'

'Yes. Quite sure.'

Miki closed her eyes.

She made out the silhouette of a man walking towards her through blinding light. Long before she had seen his face, she had smelled his cologne. It was gentle on the nose, like Provençal lavender. She smiled and, as she did so, Comte Hugo de Montfried took her hand and pressed his lips to its knuckles. 'I will never leave you,' he said.

The security guard coughed hard and the daydream vanished.

Opening her eyes, Miki walked over to the grand wrought iron gates that led into Parc Monceau.

She sat down on the first bench she could find, and thought of all the gift packs she had distributed for Angel Flower, in frozen Shiba Park. Then she thought of the kind young sales clerk at the Kinokuniya bookshop, and her best friend, Ichiko, and of her parents. And, lastly, she thought of her ojiichan.

Miki had been attacked and robbed, but she never wanted her beloved grandfather to know of her distress. It was the rose-tinted memories of Paris that were keeping him alive.

As she sat there, reflecting on the trials and tribulations of the day, Miki spotted a group of girls prancing boisterously through the park. At least two of them were wearing pretty floral sundresses, dresses that were overly familiar to her eyes.

Her blood suddenly fortified with adrenalin, Miki leapt up and ran over to confront the girls.

'Give me back my luggage!' she cried out.

Whooping and whistling, the girls surrounded Miki and started pushing her back and forth. They taunted her, pulling at her hair. Then they got her on the ground and began to kick her. Her arms thrashing, she tried to fight back, but she was no match for a Romanian girl gang.

Eventually tiring of the attack, the teenagers drifted away, leaving Miki covered in dirt, her dress shredded from the brawl. She lay there for a long while, passersby avoiding eye contact, assuming that she was a drug addict who had strayed in from the suburbs.

Picking herself up, Miki staggered back to the slatted wooden bench. Her mind was so befuddled that she was unable to process a single memory or thought.

While she sat there quietly and blank-faced, a man approached her. In his hand was a gold ring.

'I think you dropped this,' he said.

Miki looked up and found herself staring into the eyes of a face she had recently known. Without thinking, she pulled off her shoe, the one missing its heel, and she battered the man in a whirlwind of screaming and rage.

Pleading with her to stop, he fled, the gold ring gripped tight in his fist.

45

WHEN THE MAN was gone, Miki stood there, shoe in hand, a look of utter indignation on her face. To the joggers, and the young mothers out with their pushchairs and their prams, she must have seemed no different than a few moments before – before the man with the gold ring had appeared.

But something deep down in Miki's psyche had changed.

Gone was the feeble, stooping, apologetic, self-excusing young woman – replaced in an instant by a dark, a wrathful alter ego.

Miki's pupils of her eyes were dilated, the muscles around her mouth taut. Her fingers were gnarled and ferocious, and her back was craned forward like a bird of prey preparing to strike.

With one shoe on, and the other still clutched in her hand, Miki roamed through Parc Monceau. She was to report much later that she had no memory of her actions after attacking the conman with the ring.

Weaving a haphazard path through the park, she came to a homeless man standing on a flowerbed. His trousers and underwear were down around his ankles, and he was peeing.

Horrified and angry, Miki jerked forward.

A moment later, she was attacking him, striking him again and again with her shoe. After that, she moved on to a nanny out with a toddler. First, she reprimanded the woman for dropping a piece of litter little bigger than a snowflake. And then, in an act that was to horrify the nation, she took the child's ice cream and stuffed it into her mouth.

As if suddenly aware of geography, Miki strolled down to the Champs-Elysées. Picking the left shoe from her foot, she tossed it away, along with the other. And, taking a deep breath, she stuck her hands up above her head and ran in a crazed zigzag along the wide pavement, screaming at everyone she passed.

Parisians are not unused to acts of insanity.

Most of them simply walked on, or pretended that Miki wasn't there. One or two elderly tourists barked back at her. But, by the time they could do anything, she was long gone, her bare feet tramping fast over the smooth flagstones.

Eventually, after zigzagging back and forth through the crowds – screaming, ranting, bawling – Miki reached an imposing building, fashioned from light grey stone. Way up on the roof was a flagpole and, below it, a great golden monogram set against a background of burnished bronze.

The legend of LV.

Her arms flailing, and her mouth yapping insults and vitriol, Miki ran straight in through the main door.

Once inside, she jumped from one display to the next, shouting ferocious exclamations and expletives.

The immaculate customers and the legions of prim serving staff stopped and watched.

Running through the body of the shop, Miki began howling like a wolf. Then, as the security guards closed in, she lowered her hands and, very calmly, she went up to the nearest sales counter and said:

'I would like to see your coin pouches, please.'

Flustered, the sales clerk pulled out a display drawer. Across from him, a pair of burly security guards were moving forward, as if in slow motion.

As the first coin pouch was removed and held up, Miki turned around. Lifting up the hem of her dress, she pulled down her knickers, bent down, and mooned at the sales clerk.

46

THE EVENING NEWS featured a reconstruction of Miki's outburst, using a Chinese actress and indistinct video footage taken from security cameras on the Champs-Elysées.

Outside the flagship Louis Vuitton store, six satellite trucks were positioned at the kerb. Nearby, a clutch of reporters with microphones in hand were doing their best to describe what had taken place.

By late evening, at least two channels had put investigative reporters on the case. They hoped to draw in extraneous elements, and thereby satiate the public demand for more information on what had become known as *'l'attaque LV'*.

The great interest led to the reporters tracking down the homeless man from Parc Monceau. He was interviewed, and given a hot meal and bones for his dogs. And, realizing that he might do well from the attention, the man with the gold ring, also battered by Miki's shoe, came forward and got his fifteen minutes of fame.

That evening, a late-night news programme assembled a panel of experts who discussed the state of tourism, and what it meant for France. Another channel debated the philosophy of anger. A third devoted a full hour of prime time to examining the cultural significance of mooning.

Meanwhile, there was still very little information about the attacker herself. Undeterred by the lack of details, most of the news channels simply made it all up.

One station went so far as to hire an artist to draw the assailant from eyewitness statements. Curiously, it showed a woman six foot two, with huge powerful hands, a thick neck, and a lantern jaw.

All through the night, scant fragments of information were released by the police. And, next morning, Louis Vuitton's security unit released CCTV footage of the moment the attacker ran in through the doors. Within minutes, Miki's face had been captured from the video and beamed all across the world.

Sitting in a hotel room in the shadows of Mont St. Michel, the chairman of Angel Flower was clipping his toenails, wishing he were back in Japan. Brushing the clippings onto the floor, he picked up the TV remote control and flicked on the TV, in the hope of tracking down a little free porn.

To his astonishment, the face of his former employee filled the screen. It was rather blurred, but there was no doubt that it was Miki Suzuki – the woman who had become synonymous with offering gift packs for free in Shiba Park.

Pulling on his trousers, the chairman knocked at the next room.

Once he had pushed Noemi into the bathroom, Pun-Pun opened the door.

'The television,' the chairman said.

'Yes.'

'You must look!'

'Yes.'

'Miki Suzuki. She is on television!'

47

IN A DANK police cell two floors underground, Miki sat motionless on a cheap plastic chair. She was wizened and limp, her long black hair matted with dirt, her eyes ringed in dark circles.

Closing them once again, she pictured a river wending its way through a meadow, its banks shaded by weeping willows, its waters glistening lightly in the late summer sun. Her mind's eye caught sight of two hands holding each other tight. The first was small and delicate, the second strong and powerful, with perfectly manicured nails.

Her imagination panning backwards, Miki saw herself with the Comte de Montfried. She was dressed in a pretty taffeta frock, and he was in a suit cut from starched navy-blue linen. Pausing, he looked into her eyes, then picked away a strand of stray hair hanging over her face.

Miki smiled, her lips parting, as they readied themselves for his.

There was the *clunk* of steel on steel, and the cell door opened.

A gendarme entered.

He had a cold expression, and a brusque manner, as though his time would be better used catching dangerous criminals.

But Miki didn't notice the officer.

She was still in the meadow with the count.

'Put your hands in front of you,' the gendarme ordered, as he swung handcuffs into place. In all his years at the Commissariat Central on Rue Bonaparte, he had never encountered such bird-like wrists.

Miki did as she was told.

A moment later, she was shuffling forwards in advance of the gendarme. They went up two flights of stairs, the walls scuffed and unpainted, the neon strip-light giving an unearthly quality to the lines of cells they passed.

Up on ground level, the officer opened the door to an interrogation room, and Miki's bare feet shuffled in. It was small, square and painted slate grey. There was a table, a couple of plastic garden chairs, and a faint stench of excrement. Miki might have been concerned about the surroundings, but she was past caring about anything.

Sitting down, she rested her cuffed wrists on her lap, and put her ankles together. The soles of her bare feet could feel the raised pattern of the linoleum floor tiles. Again, Miki's mind slipped back to the riverbank.

There were swallows in the air.

She leaned back a fraction, breathed in deep, and smelled the scent of nature. Her ears were filled with the sound of water trickling gently over pebbles, her spine warmed by the balmy sense of sunlight filtered through the bows of a majestic willow tree.

The gendarme sat down on the other side of the table.

'Which part of China are you from?' he asked angrily.

Miki didn't look at her questioner. Her eyes were fixed on the middle distance, for it was there that she could see the meadow and the riverbank.

'I am from outside Sendai, in Miyagi Prefecture,' she replied in a rather absent voice.

'Is that near Beijing?'

'No. Sendai is *not* near Beijing.'

'Why were you attacking people in Parc Monceau?'

'Because the ring got stuck on my finger,' Miki said.

'*The ring?*'

'The gold ring… I mean the gold ring which was not gold.'

The officer frowned. He lit a cigarette and placed it on the edge of the table, with the burning end poking over the side.

'Why did you attack Louis Vuitton?'

Miki smoothed a fingertip to her left eyebrow. She smiled, her smile erupting into a giggle, the giggle into a laugh.

'Because I wanted to buy a coin pouch for my ojiichan,' she said.

'But you didn't have any money.'

'Yes. No money.'

'And your passport?'

'Gone,' said Miki, almost without caring. 'All is gone.'

48

THREE HOURS OF interrogation followed, in which the officer extracted a few basic details from the detainee, but no more than that.

He managed to establish certain key facts – that she was not Chinese but Japanese, that she was called Miki Suzuki, and that she had been staying at the George V Hotel.

After being photographed against a blank wall, holding a number, her wrists still cuffed, Miki was sent back to the cell to wait while the duty officer tried to make contact with the Japanese embassy. Unfortunately for her, the number on file at the Commissariat Central was missing a digit, and so it didn't work.

The detainee's mugshot was leaked to the press, who were desperate for any information about the woman it had nicknamed 'La Psycho Thriller'.

Within minutes, the picture had been broadcast all over the world, and had graced every news site on the web.

By mid morning all the surveillance footage from the store had been leaked as well.

Instantly, it went viral on YouTube, with a local French rap star using it to launch his latest hit. As for the mugshot, it was doctored by a prominent internet artist, who added Marilyn Monroe's hair and lips, vampire fangs, and a tiara made from crushed emeralds.

Within a day of her arrest, Miki was regarded as one of the most recognizable people on the planet, although no one really knew anything about her – anywhere, that is, except in Japan.

49

SWITCHING ON THEIR old television in time for the lunchtime news, Miki's parents sat back and sipped their green tea. They watched the world news every day, even though they had little time for Middle Eastern wars, African famines, or global warming.

Snoring in the corner was Miki's grandfather. He had no interest in television, and regarded anything happening outside the family home as nonsense.

The only exception was Paris.

Miki's father took off his glasses, wiped them with the corner of his handkerchief, and stuck them back on his face. He coughed, sipped his tea, and looked at the picture which was being flashed on the screen along with an image of the Eiffel Tower.

'She's pretty,' he said. 'She looks Japanese.'

'How can she be Japanese?' his wife said. 'It says she is in Paris.'

'Well, there are Japanese in Paris.'

There was a pause – a long one.

The elderly couple sipped their tea.

'Miki is Japanese and she is in Paris,' said the father.

The mother squinted at the picture, which was being shown a second time, followed by the CCTV footage from Louis Vuitton.

'That *is* Miki,' she said.

50

THE DAY AFTER the arrest of La Psycho Thriller, *Le Monde* carried a lead story about the rampage on its front page.

An editorial inside the newspaper claimed that Far East extremists were targeting the French capital. Such attacks were, it gushed, a price that had to be paid, in return for the export of French fashion goods to China and beyond.

The story of Miki Suzuki divided French society.

Some said she ought to be deported for behaving so shamefully to an innocent homeless man, and for running riot in such a prestigious French store as Louis Vuitton. But an exactly equal number declared that Miki Suzuki should be applauded for standing up against the extremes of society – the derelict takers and purveyors to the super-rich.

51

SITTING AT THE desk of his surgery in the eighteenth arrondissement, the leading psychiatrist Dr. Georges Mesmer finished the editorial in *Le Monde* and laid the newspaper on his desk.

Well-dressed and precise in manner, he was the kind of man who considered even the smallest question before answering. Some of those who encountered him regarded Mesmer as a bore, because he was not prone to drama of any kind.

Squaring the newspaper, he touched a knuckle to his mouth, and thought for a moment. It was surprising to him that the case of the Japanese woman's outburst at Louis Vuitton was attracting such attention.

At the same time, the case seemed very familiar indeed.

Exactly five years before, Dr. Mesmer had been asked by the police to contribute an expert analysis. The patient was a Japanese woman of retirement age who had been found babbling nonsense and flapping her arms up and down in the public toilets near the Arc de Triomphe.

A year later, a young Japanese man was discovered near the Pompidou Centre. He had taken off his suit, turned it inside out, put it on again, and was hopping around on one foot.

The following year, five more isolated cases were brought to the psychiatrist's attention – all of them Japanese tourists in a state of hysteria.

Each case had been reported to the police. And, each time, it was agreed that Dr. Mesmer would be permitted to take charge of the patient. In return, he guaranteed that they would pose no more harm to decent society.

An expert in Japanese culture, and with a keen interest in cross-cultural matters, Mesmer was perfectly placed to make certain deductions. Having carried out a detailed examination of each patient, he had concluded that they were all suffering from the same condition – a condition that was known as *Paris Syndrome.*

Manifesting itself in many ways, the hysterical state frequently included hallucinations and feelings of perceived persecution, aggression and anxiety, dizzy spells, nausea, and acute delusions.

Secret figures collected by the Japanese embassy found that, each year, approximately forty of their citizens were believed to be affected by the condition. Although in private there was a sense of national embarrassment at the condition, diplomats maintained in public that there was no such thing as Paris Syndrome.

Despite the diplomatic denials, victims kept coming to light.

Obsessing about the French capital, they found themselves unable to cope with the language barrier, the breakneck pace of their tours, the beauty, the dirt, the rich food, the strong wine, the rudeness of the café waiters, and the sense that Paris was not at all how they imagined it would be.

During the previous five years, Dr. Mesmer had published sixteen papers on the condition, which he regarded as an offshoot of Stendhal Syndrome. Although received warmly by his profession, the studies had not broken out from the limited world of academia.

Until that moment, no examples of Japanese tourists running amok had ever been featured on television or in the French national press.

Picking the telephone from his desk, Mesmer asked his secretary to connect him with the officer dealing with Miki Suzuki's case. A few minutes later he found himself talking to the officer in charge. Mesmer introduced himself, exchanged pleasantries, and asked for permission to make a cursory evaluation of the patient.

'She is obviously quite insane,' the gendarme-in-charge explained.

'Insanity is my area of expertise,' the psychiatrist replied confidently. 'Then, doctor, I suggest you come down to the Commissariat at once.'

52

MR. NAKAMURA DID not usually listen to the news when he was outside Japan.

Concentrating on the needs of his tour group was demanding enough already, without having his head filled with the tribulations and misdemeanours of others. But, by chance, he received an email from a colleague at the Paradise Tours headquarters in Tokyo. She had sent a link to everyone she knew. Nakamura-san clicked on it, and found himself watching footage on YouTube of a Japanese woman running around Louis Vuitton, then mooning.

The blurred footage had been put to rap music.

The tour leader screwed up his eyes and, slowly, a look of panic descended like a veil over his face. His cheeks turned from pale white to light blue as they drained of their blood. Then he felt acid in his stomach, as though he had been informed that his entire family had just been hacked to death by bandits.

Knocking a knuckle to the chairman's door, he jabbed a finger to the display on his iPhone.

'There is something that is not good,' he said.

'I have seen the television,' said the chairman coldly, the edges of his mouth taut. 'It is an embarrassment.'

'We must go and help Miki-san,' said Nakamura. 'She must be very sad. I do not know what has happened.'

At that moment, Pun-Pun entered the chairman's room.

There was a smudge of fuchsia lipstick on his collar. But the others did not notice. Or, if they did, they were too preoccupied to care.

'We will *not* help her,' said Pun-Pun in a fractious voice. 'She could bring adverse attention to Angel Flower, the kind of attention that we do not need.'

'Our competitors will make a lot of this,' the chairman replied.

'But she looks in need of our help,' Nakamura-san repeated. 'I think we would be advised to assist her.'

Pun-Pun and the chairman of Angel Flower exchanged a glance. Neither said another word, but they had made a decision telepathically.

It was to abandon Miki Suzuki, and to forget that she had ever worked for the firm.

53

THE CELL DOOR was opened by the same gendarme as before.

He escorted Miki up to the interrogation room, but this time she was trussed up in ankle fetters as well as handcuffs.

Still barefoot, she struggled up the grim stone stairs. As she moved forward, she sang to herself – a lullaby that her mother used to sing, a lullaby about a soldier returning from war. Her body may have been in the bowels of a Parisian police station, but her mind was lost in an apocalyptic landscape of destruction.

Once upstairs, the officer steered Miki towards the interrogation room. He had heard from colleagues that the media was camped outside the Commissariat, but he didn't care. As far as he was concerned, the detainee wasn't Japanese, but was a Chinese troublemaker in disguise, the kind that ought to be punished, then routed from French soil.

Miki sat on the same plastic chair as before, ankles together and hands in her lap. As soon as he had directed her to the seat, the gendarme exited. He went through to the next room, where Dr. Mesmer was in conversation with Inspector Maurice du Lac, the operations director. Together they looked through the two-way mirror, observing the detainee in silence.

Miki had stopped singing, and was now howling as she had done at Louis Vuitton. Her arm muscles began twitching forcefully, as though she were in shock. And, leant on its side, her head jerked and convulsed, her mouth drooling.

The psychiatrist watched attentively for five minutes without a single word. From time to time he adjusted his position to get a better view. Only after what seemed like an age to Inspector du Lac, did Dr. Mesmer utter anything at all.

'I've seen it many times before,' he said without emotion. 'I would know it anywhere.'

'Know what anywhere, doctor?'

'Paris Syndrome.'

The Inspector narrowed his eyes. He looked at the doctor quickly and then, gradually, his focus dissolved from the psychiatrist's face, through the glass and into the interrogation room.

C'est quoi – le syndrome de Paris? What is it – Paris Syndrome?'

Dr. Mesmer gave a sigh. He disliked having to explain psychological science to laymen, even to members of the emergency services. Doing so was to trivialize what was a complex matter of mental health.

'A severe psychological condition,' he said, 'one that manifests itself in varying ways, but one that tends to affect the same target group each time.'

'*Target group?*'

The doctor looked at the police chief squarely.

'Japanese,' he said. 'And most notably, Japanese who come to Paris.' He paused, then sighed yet again. 'The city makes them go crazy. It's as simple as that.'

'But why?'

'For all sorts of reasons,' Mesmer said. 'For years, and even decades, they dream of coming here. They read about our capital and idealize it, learn of it in their media, and watch movies set against its backdrop. And, all the while, their expectations are ramped up and up – layer upon layer, detail upon detail – until they reach a kind of breaking point.'

Dr. Mesmer took a step closer to the window, until his face was an inch from the two-way glass. He watched Miki as she sat there, her cheeks twitching, her lips trembling as though plugged into the electrical grid.

'They can picture the window boxes on Rue de la Paix,' he said, 'and the taste of an espresso at Les Deux Magots. They can imagine the jewels in the windows of Harry Winston, and smell the scent of the breeze on the Seine. But then...'

'*Then?*'

'Then they come here and... and the trauma is too great!'

Inspector du Lac frowned.

'But, doctor, I do not understand. How could visiting Paris be traumatic?'

Mesmer pressed a hand to his jaw and clicked his neck to the right. He wasn't in the mood for covering such rudimentary ground.

'It's traumatic because suddenly – *instantly* – the dream-world fantasy collides with reality – like a freight train smashing into a car stranded on railway tracks in the dead of night.'

'*Mais Paris... c'est magnifique!*' the officer exclaimed, his words charged with Gallic pride. 'You know it as well as I.'

Clicking his neck to the left, Mesmer forced a smile.

'Yes and no,' he replied.

'*Quoi?*'

'Yes it is glorious, but it is horrific as well. Let me explain. To understand Paris Syndrome, you have to understand the Japanese psyche. I am acquainted with it well because I have lived there – spent five years studying Japanese language in Yokohama when I was young. And what an education that was! The Japanese like things to be perfect, and they love their idea of *kata*, form… as far as they are concerned everything from chewing gum to crossing the street should be done in a particular way – according to a rigid and unwavering form. So they come to Paris and the rule-book of their well-ordered world is ripped up. Here in Paris everyone's breaking the rules.'

'But of course they are!' the Inspector blurted. 'We are French and we don't want to follow someone else's rules… we don't even want to follow our own!'

'*Exactly.* And so, picture it – the Japanese tourists arrive abounding with anticipation after a long flight. They haven't slept and, like children before Christmas, they are very excited. They arrive and find themselves eating unfamiliar food – fatty food that their livers can't process, and wine, which they are not used to, either. And, although they think they know Paris, there's a secret ingredient that hits them between the eyes. And it floors them – every time.'

Inspector du Lac screwed up his face, then wiped a hand down over his long nose.

'What is it – this secret ingredient?'

'Parisians,' Dr. Mesmer replied. 'To the sensibilities of the overly polite Japanese, the Parisians appear impolite, uncouth, noisy, lecherous, uncaring, hostile and…'

'*And?*'

'And *so* much more. The list never ends.'

'So this woman, *that* woman, she is suffering from the affliction – from Paris Syndrome?'

The psychiatrist nodded with slow confidence.

'I am certain of it.'

'But what is the treatment?'

Dr. Mesmer cleared his throat. Then he rubbed his eyes.

'The only known remedy is to leave Paris and never to return,' he said.

54

THE CHAIRMAN OF the Angel Flower Beauty Company spent an entire morning on the telephone with his lawyers.

Meanwhile, on the hour, every hour, the grainy video footage of Miki running amok at Louis Vuitton was being played on Japanese TV. Although her identity had not yet been determined, it was only a matter of time. The leading executives at Angel Flower knew she would soon be recognized as Miki Suzuki, the girl who had caused a sensation in Shiba Park.

In anticipation, the legal team drafted a statement and kept it ready. The document explained that Miki Suzuki had used a complex web of deceit to dupe the ingenuous, law-abiding executives of Angel Flower. She was, the statement went on, not only deranged but also calculating and duplicitous – an evil-doer of the most shocking and heinous nature.

Offering his contribution, Pun-Pun suggested that Angel Flower press charges against Miki Suzuki, for bringing their good reputation into disrepute.

'I knew she was going to be trouble,' he said. 'I could tell by the way she walks.'

'And how is that… her walking?'

'Like a spider,' Pun-Pun said quickly. 'Haven't you noticed for yourself?'

The chairman didn't reply at once. He thought for a moment. Then, sucking air through his back teeth, he said:

'You are right, Yamato-san. She is the spider who has caught us all in her web.'

55

FOR THIRTY MINUTES Dr. Mesmer observed Miki through the two-way mirror, making meticulous notes in illegible script.

He believed in piecing together the evidence and the clues, layer upon layer, and only then moving in for an initial interview. Having filled seventeen and a half pages of his notebook with tight black lettering, he cleared his throat and gestured to the Inspector.

'I am ready now,' he said.

'Shall I have your meeting recorded?'

Mesmer touched the end of his Mont Blanc to his upper lip.

'I think not,' he replied. 'But if you could leave me alone with the patient, I would be grateful.'

Five minutes later, the psychiatrist was locked inside the interrogation room with Miki. He had asked that her hands and ankles be unfastened, and that she be given a bottle of mineral water.

Seated across from her, on an identical plastic garden chair, Mesmer avoided eye contact. A long and distinguished career in the field of psychiatry had taught him that looking into the eyes of a patient too early was distinctly inadvisable.

Doing so had the effect of eliciting extreme reactions.

Only after an extended silence did the psychiatrist say anything at all.

'The cherry blossom in spring is more beautiful in Sendai than anywhere else I have seen,' he declared in Japanese, his tone flat but assertive.

Miki wasn't listening.

She was too busy pouring the water over her head. When she was finished, she got down on the floor and lay on her back, her limbs shuddering. From her mouth came a curious clicking sound, like that of a dolphin wanting to communicate.

'The blossom. It's so calming,' Mesmer said.

Again, Miki took no notice. It was as though she were quite alone, imagining herself swimming fast through deep water.

The doctor stood up, walked around the table, and offered a hand. Miki didn't take it, not at first, as she was swishing around, her eyes closed tight. Then, all of a sudden, she opened them, blinked hard, and allowed herself to be pulled from the waves by the psychiatrist's hand.

He guided her back to the plastic chair, before taking his own seat once again. Miki sat with a straight back, her chin up, eyes focused on a distant point in mid air, halfway across the room.

'Are you a fish?' Mesmer asked.

Miki frowned.

'No,' she said, although not immediately. 'No I am not.'

'Then what are you?'

'I am a princess,' she replied.

'*A princess?*'

'Indeed, yes.'

'And what kind of princess are you?'

Again, Miki frowned, this time in a callous, condescending way.

'A princess from the Imperial Court,' she said.

'Ah. I see.'

Then Miki Suzuki inspected her fingernails. Not because she needed to, but because it filled the silence with an action worthy of her position. Without lifting the nib from the page, the doctor scribbled a line of text in his notebook. He slipped the book away, and said:

'What is your name, Your Highness?'

'It is Princess Tsune.'

'And who is your father?'

Miki balked, as though anyone could be ignorant of such rudimentary information.

'His Imperial Majesty Emperor Meiji, of course.'

'And the year? What is the year?'

'It is Meiji-41.'

Dr. Mesmer calculated.

'That would be, what… 1909?'

Princess Tsune gave half a shrug.

'I suppose,' she said.

'Well, I am pleased to make your acquaintance, Your Highness,' the psychiatrist whispered, lowering his head subserviently.

Princess Tsune looked away. She sniffed, then stroked a hand gently down the front of her dress, as though it were a sable coat.

'Where is my carriage?' she asked. 'I have been waiting an hour and longer. I demand to be returned to the palace grounds at once.'

'I shall see to it,' Mesmer replied.

Then, standing to his feet, he bowed deeply and walked backwards to the door.

56

Despite several attempts, Inspector du Lac and his staff were unable to reach anyone at the Japanese embassy, as it was the weekend.

Taking pity on the detainee, the Inspector took the decision to release her to Dr. Mesmer immediately. As he saw it, Miki Suzuki would pose less of a threat to herself – and to others – if she were in the care of experts.

An unmarked police car was used for the journey to the asylum.

It had special blue lights mounted into the grille at the front. But unless they were switched on, no one would have known they were there.

Dr. Mesmer sat in the back with Miki, the doors centrally locked, Inspector du Lac in the front. The windows were smoked glass, the smell of the seats an unusual blend of plastic and clinical detergent.

The vehicle moved northward at speed through Paris.

Having recently come from an anti-narcotics unit, the officer at the wheel knew every shortcut in town. As he zigzagged his way towards Montmartre, his mind was replaying the wild nights hunting Romanian drug lords in the *banlieues*.

Mesmer looked over at Miki.

'We are taking you to a little hospital, *my* hospital,' he said. 'It's where we will treat you.'

The detainee didn't react. She was all furled up in a ball, her cuffed wrists pulled tight over her chest. Her eyes were open, focussing down towards the beige plastic seat in front.

As the squad car rumbled down a narrow side street, Miki's left eye shifted fitfully to the side, to gain focus on the world outside.

Her right eye didn't move.

Hunching herself forward, she began sucking the back of the driver's headrest. Dr. Mesmer looked on in some alarm, curious at the behaviour.

'We will take good care of you,' he said tenderly. 'We will feed you nice food. What would you like for dinner... something delicious?'

'I want a big meaty bone,' said Miki. 'One with plenty of marrow and juice.'

57

THE ASYLUM WAS located in Rue Ravignan, a short distance from the Basilique du Sacré Coeur.

The street was cobbled, quiet, and enjoyed sweeping views of the capital below. The hospital's building had once been a private house. It had been donated to the psychiatric sciences almost a century before by a wealthy banker whose only son had succumbed to lunacy, having been shell-shocked in the trenches during the Great War.

Rising four storeys high, it resembled a Swiss chalet more than it did an asylum for the mentally disordered. Perched at the corner of the street, it was constructed from tan-coloured stone. The front of the house was adorned with elegant wrought iron *balcons*, bright red geraniums in window boxes, and vines. And, stretching behind in a profusion of emerald-green was an extensive walled garden.

The police car came to a stop outside, and Dr. Mesmer expressed encouragement to his patient. Opening the door, he ran round and opened hers. Then, before inviting Miki to descend onto the pavement, he asked that the handcuffs be removed.

From the front seat, Inspector du Lac passed him the key.

'She is your responsibility now, doctor,' he said rather sternly.

Mesmer sniffed as he turned the miniature key in the first lock.

'I promise you that this young lady shall give you no more trouble,' he said.

58

IN THEIR FAMILY home near Sendai, Mrs. Suzuki had spent all afternoon trying to get information about her daughter. It was now evening and she hadn't made any progress at all.

On calling the Angel Flower Beauty Company, she was told that the firm no longer employed a Miki Suzuki from Sendai. And, when she telephoned the Home Office in Tokyo, she had been advised that her daughter would be extended the rights of any Japanese citizen abroad.

'Please can you tell me where Miki is now?' the mother had asked, in her most courteous voice.

Straining to maintain a façade of solemnity, the official had replied:

'We understand that your daughter is currently in the custody of the French government.'

Adrift on a sea of emotion, Mrs. Suzuki managed to remain utterly composed.

'Is Miki a prisoner?' she enquired timidly.

The official did not answer.

Mumbling something indistinct, he put the telephone receiver down.

59

At the hospital, new patients were always kept in their own room, at least until they had been assessed by the doctor and his assistant, Nurse Polk.

Miki was taken to room 14, which was located at the back of the house on the second floor, with a pleasant view over the garden.

The walls were painted lavender, the windows barred, and the electrical sockets sealed. There were no sharp edges, no loose cables, and no furniture except for a simple metal-framed bed, a wooden desk and matching chair.

On the wall, positioned beside the light switch, was a red alarm button.

Nurse Polk pointed to it as she was showing the newest patient around. She was slim and compact, dressed in starched white, her face as pale as it was thin, camouflaged against her uniform. Moving with miniature footsteps, her pint-sized feet were squeezed into off-white clogs, fingers fluttering intently at her sides.

'You only press this button if there is a serious emergency,' she said. 'Do you understand that?'

Miki did not reply. She stepped over to the window and looked out at the garden. Down on the lawn, dressed in matching white, a pair of patients was exercising.

One of them were wearing his shoes on his hands.

At that moment, Dr. Mesmer arrived. He asked Miki if she would like a chat with him downstairs.

'I am waiting for my carriage,' she replied. 'See to it that it comes at once!'

'*Your carriage?*'

'To take me to the opera.'

The nurse rolled her eyes, then smiled.

'And what dress will you be wearing tonight?' she asked.

Brushing a hand gently down her blouse, Miki glanced at the back of her hand.

'The new crimson one,' she said.

Forty minutes later she was led through into Dr. Mesmer's surgery, now dressed in the standard-issue white. She had been weighed, measured, and given a rudimentary examination by Nurse Polk.

The doctor motioned to a chaise longue, upholstered in white vinyl.

'Please make yourself comfortable,' he said.

Miki shuffled into the room, her ankles never straying more than an inch or two ahead of one another. Trundling over to the chair, she lowered herself onto it in her own time.

'My carriage did not come,' she said with irritation.

'I heard that the opera was cancelled this evening,' Mesmer responded. He was seated opposite, notebook in hand.

'But I did not allow it.'

'Princess Tsune, have you ever been to Paris?' the doctor asked.

'*Paris?*'

'The French capital.'

The princess smoothed a strand of stray hair from her face.

'No, never,' she said.

'Have you heard of it?'

'Oh, yes, I have heard that the gowns are very well made.'

'What else?'

'That the trees are bright green in the spring, like in Kyoto.'

'Have you ever heard of the people – the Parisians?'

Miki was about to say something, in the high-pitched voice of Princess Tsune. But, all of a sudden, her expression soured. The colour of her face changed, too. It went plum-red.

Dr. Mesmer looked on, as the most astonishing transformation occurred.

Seated before him on the white chaise longue, Miki Suzuki swivelled sideways, then leaned backwards and, in one dexterous movement, she folded her legs up over her head, bringing her knees either side of her ears.

The psychiatrist scribbled a line of scrawl in his notebook.

'What are you doing, Princess Tsune?'

'Princess? I am not a princess.'

'Then who are you?'

'I am a stone… a rock.'

Mesmer quickly recorded the conversation in his notes.

'What is your name, rock?'

'It is Tempest.'

'And what is your purpose?'

'To crush the people of Paris! To smash them until they are all dead, and then to grind their bones into dust!'

'And why would you want to do a thing like that?'

Miki scratched behind an ear with her foot:

'Because they are the children of the Devil,' she said.

60

FOR THREE DAYS, Miki was kept isolated from the other patients. She spent her time up in her room, plaiting and unplaiting her hair, and staring into space. She was offered pens and paper, and even books in Japanese to read, but she shunned them all.

It was true to say that she was not herself. But it was equally true to say that she was no one else in particular either. Clouding with indistinct thoughts and memories, her mind flickered through a multitude of emotions and personalities.

Some of the time she was Princess Tsune. And, some of the time she was the rock, called Tempest. But, as one day melted into the next, she became a kaleidoscope of other people and things.

On the fourth day, Dr. Mesmer received a call from the Japanese embassy. They had been informed that the now infamous Miki Suzuki had been admitted to the psychiatrist's care.

It was no great surprise.

For, over the previous decade, an ever-increasing number of their nationals had been sent to Mesmer, having been struck down by the mysterious Paris Syndrome. It was as though cases of the disorder were turning up thick and fast. But none, however disturbing, had so far caught the attention of the French public, nor of the Japanese back home, so acutely as that of Miki Suzuki.

'How would you describe her condition, doctor?' the first secretary asked on the phone.

'Advanced Paris Syndrome.'

'As advanced as you have witnessed before?'

'Yes… but I would say that in this case there are severe tendencies of indignation.'

'Is she a threat to society?'

The doctor swallowed hard.

'Possibly.'

'Is she fit to travel?'

'On an enclosed aeroplane – for many hours on a flight back to Japan?'

The first secretary grunted a yes.

'Absolutely not!' Mesmer exclaimed.

There was silence on the line, while the diplomat briefed his ambassador.

At length, he said:

'If you would permit me, doctor, I should like to pay a visit to see Miss Suzuki for myself.'

61

THE NEXT MORNING, shortly after six, Miki's delicate fingers pressed the red alarm button on the wall.

Nurse Polk sprinted upstairs and opened the door to room 14.

'What is the matter, Miki?' she asked, panting from the climb.

'I need a pencil.'

'*A pencil?*'

'Yes.'

'Do you want some paper as well?'

Miki shook her head.

'No. I don't need paper.'

'Then how are you going to write?'

Miki frowned.

'The pencil is not for writing,' she said.

Now it was the nurse's turn to frown.

'Then what is it for?'

'For a magic wand,' she said.

62

A LITTLE LATER that morning, Miki was permitted to join the other patients in the dining room. It was the first time she had seen them, and that they had seen her.

There were nine of them, both men and women. One was Chinese, two were Koreans, and three were Japanese. The others were a lugubrious Russian called Vladimir, who thought he was a Barbie doll; a South African called Bart who couldn't stop licking his lips; and a former ballet dancer from the Czech Republic, called Victoria.

'Good morning to you all,' said Dr. Mesmer over breakfast. 'I want to introduce the newest member of our family. Please all welcome Miki.'

The Japanese and Koreans stood up, bowed, and gave salutations. The Russian thrust out his bosom and blew a succulent kiss. The South African licked his lips and winked. Beside him was a small woman with perfect posture, scarlet hair, and a hard-to-place accent. The Czech ballet dancer, she clapped riotously, until Nurse Polk asked that she stop.

'If you like, I will show you my dresses,' said Vladimir gloomily. 'They're up in my room.'

Miki didn't say anything. She just sat down and looked at the shaft of the pencil she had been given. Unsharpened, it was blunt at both ends. Closing her eyes, she clenched her fists to her chest, and jabbed the little pink eraser in the direction of the Russian.

The Japanese and the Koreans gasped.

The woman with bright red hair clapped.

And the South African licked his lips.

63

AT TEN O'CLOCK precisely, Hideo Tottori, first secretary of the Japanese embassy, arrived. He was taller than Dr. Mesmer had expected, and had a pleasing face, the kind that makes one feel immediately at ease.

Until then, the hospital had only ever been visited by less senior diplomats. The arrival of a first secretary suggested the importance of Miki Suzuki's case.

Mesmer led the way into the surgery, and through to his private office. The walls were adorned with framed diplomas, and sombre-looking portraits of the founding fathers of psychiatric medicine. On the desk was a life-size model of the human brain and, beside it, an oversized jam jar filled with human teeth.

'I thought it best to have a little chat before I take you to see Miki,' said Mesmer.

'Please, tell me doctor, how is she today?'

'Well, as I told you on the phone, Miss Suzuki's condition is advanced.'

'Can you suggest what may have brought it on?'

'Hysteria… of the most acute nature.' The psychiatrist paused. He looked out of the window and allowed his eyes to focus on the mass of pink bougainvillea. 'It's always the same,' he said, distantly. 'I have seen it so often.'

'Seen what?'

'The same hysterical, manic reaction to the French capital. Most frequently it affects Japanese women – women like Miki, women in their mid-twenties.'

'Is there anything else common to them all?'

The doctor pressed his fingertips together.

'They all seem to be very passionate,' he said. 'They are women who have fallen deeply in love with the fantasy of a city they don't really know.'

Mr. Tottori found himself squinting at the jam jar on the desk.

'Miki Suzuki is an embarrassment to our country,' he said with a sigh. 'Her passion is not doing us favourable service. As you can imagine, the media are feasting on her story, at home in Japan, just as they are in France.' The first secretary glanced down at the teeth again. And, without looking up, he said: 'We want to get her back home as soon as we can.'

The doctor wagged a finger from side to side.

'Transporting her in this condition would be distinctly inadvisable,' he said.

'Couldn't she be sedated?'

Again the finger wagged.

'Even sedated she could pose a danger to others.' Mesmer breathed in sharply. 'Just use your imagination,' he said.

64

MIKI WAS SITTING on a bench in the garden with her fingers in her ears.

Perched down beside her, Vladimir was spouting a stream of beauty tips. Wearing big dangly earrings and a fuchsia-coloured dress, he had achieved a profuse cleavage by stuffing many pairs of socks down the front.

The nurse approached and invited Miki to the surgery, where the diplomat and Dr. Mesmer were waiting. Irritated by the Russian, Miki got to her feet. For a moment she half-imagined she heard the sound of a windmill, its immense sails turning in the breeze.

She shuffled in from the garden to the salon, and on to the surgery, without removing her fingers. And, as she went, she made the same dolphin *click-click-click* that she had produced at the police station, earlier in the week.

As soon as he saw her, the diplomat jumped up.

'*Hajimimashite dozo yoroshiku*, I am pleased to meet you,' he said.

Miki continued to click. While she did so, Dr. Mesmer scribbled half a line of ink in his notebook.

'Please tell me Miss Suzuki, how have you enjoyed Paris?' the first secretary asked, sitting once again.

Her fingers still in her ears, Miki went on clicking.

The psychiatrist encouraged her to sit on the white chaise longue. She did so. When seated, her eyes seemed to focus on a point in space six inches in front of her nose.

All of a sudden, Miki's expression changed. It was playful, light, and completely relaxed.

Her fingers flopped down into her lap, and wove themselves together. And the *click-click* of the dolphin stopped. It was replaced by a faint whimpering sound, like that of a little child.

The diplomat repeated his question.

After what seemed like an eternity, Miki looked at the first secretary, then blinked.

'*Paris?*' she said. 'No, no, I do not know Paris.'

'Tell me, then, what do you know?' the doctor enquired.

'Strawberries. I know strawberries. I love them. Give me some, will you? Please, please give me some strawberries!'

Mr. Tottori swallowed anxiously. He was trying to think of something to say. Before he could pose a question, Mesmer asked:

'Please do tell us, who are you?'

Miki's expression slipped from one of gentle composure to that of absolute angst.

'I am lost!' she cried. 'Lost in the forest!'

'And where is the forest?'

'In the mountains.'

'And where are the mountains?'

'In Hokkaido.'

The first secretary leaned forward in his chair.

'*My* family is from Hokkaido,' he said.

'Are you my father?' Miki asked, her eyes focussing again just in front of her nose.

'I do not think so.'

Miki began to sob, dabbing away the tears with her sleeve.

'Who are you?' the doctor repeated.

'I am Akiko.'

'And where are you from, Akiko?'

'From the edge of the forest. My father is chief of all the Ainu.'

'And your mother?'

'She is dead.'

'Do you have brothers and sisters?'

'Perhaps. I am not certain.'

'And why are you in the forest, all alone?'

Miki's gentle sobbing transformed into a tidal wave of tears, as she remembered where she was.

'Because I was searching for strawberries and I went far from home. And now it is dark and I can hear the wolves. Can't *you* hear them? I am frightened and cold and I don't know what to do. Will you help me? Will you take me to my village?'

Dr. Mesmer smiled warmly.

'Yes, Akiko, I promise that we will help you get back to your village,' he said.

65

SHORTLY BEFORE LUNCH, the Mercedes minibus rolled up to the front doors of the Hotel George V, and the group from Paradise Tours got down.

The chairman of the Angel Flower Beauty Company descended first. He was followed by the three housewives, by Pun-Pun, Noemi, and by Mr. Nakamura. The group exuded a sense of excitement and extreme pleasure, after their excursion to Mont St. Michel and the Loire.

But, beneath this jovial façade, all was not well.

From family and friends, the housewives had heard of how a rogue Japanese tourist had stormed through the hallowed halls of Louis Vuitton, Paris's grandest emporium of luxury. None of them had dared to admit that the woman, who had become such a sensation back home in Japan, had been sitting on their very tour bus just days before.

With gritted teeth, the chairman was counting the hours until the return flight to Narita. And he was praying. Praying that the media didn't manage to identify the woman as a former employee of the much-beleaguered Angel Flower.

As for Pun-Pun – he was seething.

During the journey back from Tours, he had visualized himself beating Miki with a cane fashioned from a strand of barbed willow. He imagined the pain he would cause her, and the delight that the pain would provide him. He saw scars and blood, tears, perspiration, and a small mouth pleading for him to stop.

Once inside the hotel, he strode over to the reception desk.

'I left a letter here for a colleague to collect,' he explained. 'Her name was Miss Suzuki... Miki Suzuki. Can you tell me whether she took it?'

The receptionist's fingers shuffled through a neatly squared pile of envelopes behind the desk.

'I believe she did indeed collect it, sir,' he replied. 'It does not appear to be here now.'

Although confrontation was not in his nature, Mr. Nakamura felt he had to say something. In private, he blamed Pun-Pun for pushing Miki over the edge. Now, his own emotions boiling over, he craved to admonish him publicly.

As the group waited for their room keys, the tour leader took advantage of the moment. He constructed a sentence in his mind – a cold, cruel, reproachful sentence, directed at Yamato-san.

'I would like to make an announcement,' he said, leaning forwards on his toes.

The group turned to face him, expecting details of the evening's programme. Nakamura-san breathed in forcefully and swallowed. As he did so, he rehearsed the sentence a second time.

It seemed even more reproachful than before.

'Yes, Mr. Nakamura,' the chairman said. 'We are ready for your message.'

The tour leader pressed his perspiring palms together. He moved the sentence from his brain, southwards towards his vocal cords. But the planned sentence was not the one that emerged from his mouth.

'I am guilty,' he said glumly.

The chairman winced.

'What are *you* guilty of, Nakamura-san?'

'Of not taking proper care of Miss Suzuki. She was *my* responsibility.'

Pun-Pun regarded the tour leader with a caustic glance.

'To Hell with her!' he said. 'She brought our company into disrepute.'

'She is a criminal,' Noemi added.

'She is not a good person,' said the trio of housewives all at once.

Nakamura-san leaned back a fraction, his forehead beading with sweat.

'Miki Suzuki has behaved imprudently,' he said.

66

IN THE DAY room of the hospital, the patients were enjoying a little leisure time.

Dr. Mesmer encouraged them to spend at least an hour each day making something with their hands. He was confident that physical creation was a way of venting anxiety, and of calming the tortured mind.

The two Korean patients – Mr. Kim and Mr. Park – were seated at a long table at the far end of the room. They were both digging their fingers into large balls of clay, shaping them into smaller balls. Mr. Park was cackling, as though the activity was bringing him great pleasure. Beside him, Mr. Kim was humming the theme tune from *Star Wars* as his fingers worked away.

In the middle of the room, three of the Japanese patients were making models using drinking straws. Two of them were women in their twenties – Mrs. Ito and Miss Fujimoto. The other was a plump lopsided man called Mr. Tanaka, who believed he was a turnip. As such, he was in constant fear of being chopped up and thrown in a cooking pot.

'We are not going to eat you, Tanaka-san,' one of the women said firmly, weaving straws together.

'But I can see the way you look at me when my back is turned.'

'And how do we look at you?' asked Miss Fujimoto.

'As if you can't wait to taste my tummy.'

There was the muffled sound of a bell, and Nurse Polk entered.

'It is time to put everything away,' she said.

'Is it time for us to dig the tunnel?' Bart, the South African asked, licking his lips. 'I want to get it started. If we don't begin today we'll never finish by Christmas.'

'No, it's not time for the tunnel.' The nurse touched a hand to her starched white cap. 'It is time for our exercises. And, as it is bright, I think we will do them outside.'

Vladimir led the way into the garden. The only patient permitted to wear street clothes, he was dressed like disco Barbie, in a sequinned miniskirt and extra-short tank top.

Victoria, the woman with scarlet hair, went next. And, after her, Mr. Chen, who was from Hong Kong.

He had been admitted to Dr. Mesmer's care after mistaking a woman in Neuilly for a postbox. The police had been called after Chen had chased her down the street, trapped her against a wall, and attempted to stuff a letter into her mouth.

Once the patients were outside, the nurse did a head count.

'We are missing someone,' she said.

'The new lady,' said Mrs. Ito. 'Miki Suzuki-san. She is not here.'

'Perhaps she has dug the tunnel already and escaped,' said Bart anxiously.

'Perhaps she has eaten herself,' said the turnip.

'No, no, I think she is still in the day room,' the nurse replied. She went inside and coaxed Miki out into the sunshine.

All limp and huddled over, the newest member of the group seemed sorrowful.

'Did you dig the tunnel?' asked Bart energetically. 'Please show me where it is. We'll escape together.' Licking his lips, he added: 'I can show you how to surf.'

Arranging themselves in two rows, the patients followed Nurse

Polk's lead. First they stretched their arms out to the side, then above their heads, before straining down to touch their toes.

None of them executed the moves perfectly, none except for Victoria. The rigorous training with the Czech National Ballet gave her an advantage. She had moved to the French capital three years before, where she planned to marry a man she had met on the internet.

Online, his profile had been one of abundant good looks and unending success. Six feet two, with a chiselled jaw, and piercing blue eyes, he claimed to be a Ferrari-driving millionaire and part-time mountaineer. In reality he was a squat, balding, foot fetishist, with delusions of grandeur and an unhealthy preoccupation with telling lies. Having built herself up for a whirlwind of romance and luxury in the French capital, the anticlimax had pushed Victoria over an emotional precipice.

There was nowhere to go but down.

Standing limp beside Victoria, Miki failed to respond to the nurse's lead. It was as though all the blood had been drained from her. With a wan complexion, and no energy to move, she just stood there – all hunched over and forlorn.

At the end of the session, the patients ambled off. Some were talking to themselves, or making bird sounds, or licking lips.

Nurse Polk approached Miki and gently led her back to the day room.

'Would you like some tea?' she asked.

Miki blinked.

'Is that a yes or a no?'

'I want to see him,' she whispered.

'See who, my dear?'

'The comte.'

Straightening her back, the nurse gave a quarter of a smile.

'Are you the princess?' she asked.

'No. I am not.'

'And who is your count – which one is he?'

A lone tear welled up in Miki's left eye and tumbled down her cheek.

'He is the kindest man in all the world,' she replied.

67

AT THE EXACT moment that the group from Paradise Tours were leaving the George V for the airport next day, a young reporter named Michi Kinjo was getting the scoop of his short career. Hailing from Okinawa, his timid disposition sat uneasily with his obsession with investigative journalism.

For days, the footage of the so-called 'Louis Vuitton Attack' had been played round the clock on Japanese TV. Every news editor in town was trying frantically to land the story and work out the identity of the attacker.

In Tokyo, at the headquarters of the *Asahi Shimbun* newspaper, Kinjo had worked his way through an extensive list of tour operators. He had called every Japanese travel firm with an office in Paris, and even some Parisian firms, too – using his satisfactory command of French. Most of them had heard of the Louis Vuitton Attack, but none knew anything about it.

Desperate to please his editor, Kinjo got down on his knees and said a prayer to his deceased grandfather. After all, the ojiichan's spirit had helped the fledgling journalist before – saving him from death by boredom at the local *Kagoshima Shinpo* paper, and transporting him to Japan's most prestigious daily in the national capital.

At that moment, the news desk's telephone rang.

The young journalist reached for the receiver.

'This is Kinjo of the *Asahi Shimbun*.'

'Are you a journalist?' asked an elderly woman on the other end.

'Yes. I am.'

'My name is Mrs. Suzuki and my family honourably requests your help.'

The reporter was about to mumble excuses and end the call, when something in the pit of his stomach told him to wait.

'I am listening to you,' he replied.

'My daughter has gone missing in Paris,' said the woman. 'We think that we saw her face in your newspaper.'

Michi Kinjo froze. He gulped. Then, very slowly, his heart pounding, he reached for his pen.

'Mrs. Suzuki, would you do me the honour of telling me your telephone number?'

Fifteen minutes later, Kinjo was on the bus to Narita airport.

Three hours after that, he was sitting in a cramped window seat on Air France flight 275, to Roissy Charles de Gaulle.

68

OF THE PATIENTS at Mesmer's hospital, almost all were suffering from some variety or other of Paris Syndrome. Somewhat unusually, there were a number of nationalities, as well as Japanese.

The only patient not being treated for the condition was Vladimir.

His affliction involved a deep-seated personality disorder related to Barbie dolls. His ultimate intention was to be surgically transformed to look like Mattel's classic – a condition known professionally as 'Barbie Syndrome'. Dr. Mesmer had invited him to the hospital for the simple reason that he was too intriguing to pass up.

As for the other patients, the doctor believed they were the tip of a psychiatric iceberg – as most sufferers of the condition were never accurately diagnosed. He had treated fifteen other cases of Paris Syndrome in the last year alone. The truth was, however, that there was very little he could do for them except to appease their frayed nerves and send them home.

Both Koreans, and the Japanese, were suffering from what Mesmer had suggested was Syndrome-A. Clearly defined, its symptoms included mania, chronic anxiety, clinical shock and varying levels of hallucination.

Victoria and Bart were affected by Syndrome-B – the chief variance of which involved an enduring sense of persecution, as though the entire world was pitted against them.

As for Chen, Mesmer felt certain that his condition was classic Syndrome-C – an almost exact facsimile of Stendhal Syndrome – one aroused by the physical beauty of the French capital.

Never a man to miss a professional opportunity, the psychiatrist decided to invite a handful of his peers to pay a visit. Having seen the footage from Louis Vuitton replayed time and again on French TV, they all jumped at the invitation. Rumours sweeping through psychiatric circles had suggested that Dr. Mesmer had been given charge of the woman responsible for *l'attaque LV*. There wasn't a psychiatrist in France who would have turned down the opportunity of meeting the attacker herself.

The next morning, five leading psychiatrists arrived by appointment, and found themselves in the surgery. They were shown to seats arranged in a line, opposite the white vinyl chaise longue. Dr. Mesmer asked Nurse Polk to bring in the patients at random.

She returned a moment later with Mr. Park.

Once he was seated on the sofa, Mesmer gave a line of background:

'Mr. Park is thirty-four years old,' he said, 'and is from the city of Busan in South Korea. He works as an office manager, and is unmarried.'

The doctor invited his colleagues to ask questions for themselves.

A suave psychiatrist from Bordeaux raised a finger.

'I would like to ask you to describe Paris for me,' he said.

Mr. Park cackled as he had done while playing with the clay. Then he pressed his fingertips up to his nose and sniffed them very hard.

Mesmer repeated the question. Mr. Park stopped sniffing.

'I went there,' he said.

'*To Paris?*'

'Yes.'

'What was it like?'

'It was very moist.'

The psychiatrists frowned. Some scribbled notes.

'Was it as you imagined it would be?' asked the first.

'Oh, yes,' Mr. Park responded. 'I knew it would be moist.'

'And how did you know that?'

'Because I had heard it in the trees.'

After a few more minutes of examination, Mr. Park was led out, and Miki was brought in. She was less limp than before. Her eyes were red from weeping.

Again, Dr. Mesmer made a brief introduction.

'Miki Suzuki is twenty-five, and is from Miyagi Prefecture, in Japan. She came to us earlier this week, after catching the attention of the media.'

The psychiatrist seated in the middle of the row held a hand in front of his face. He was tall, dressed in a grey handmade suit, with a pink polka-dot tie.

'Miss Suzuki, would you tell us where you are now?'

Miki squinted at the doctors. She rolled her eyes, then, with a capricious little laugh, she replied:

'They keep me here because of what I know.'

'And what is it that you know, Miss?'

'The Secret. The Great Secret.'

'*The Great Secret*?'

The doctor straightened his tie.

'Will you tell it to me?' he asked.

'But you will tell the others.'

'I promise not to.'

'Are you sure?'

'Yes, quite sure.'

Miki thought hard for a full minute, a knuckle touched up to her mouth.

'There are tigers in the labyrinth,' she said. 'Thousands of them.'

'*Tigers*?'

Miki nodded.

'And where is the labyrinth?'

She pointed to the floor.

'Down there.'

'Are you sure?' asked another of the psychiatrists.

'Oh, yes,' Miki replied. 'I have seen them, and I have heard them, too. They roar in the middle of the night.'

69

MICHI KINJO STEPPED off the aeroplane at Charles de Gaulle and was soon in a taxi en route into Paris. It may have been his first time in France, but he was keen to exercise his French. Until then, he had cursed his mother for forcing him to study it so diligently. But the language was suddenly a building block in the wall of journalistic preparation.

Back in Okinawa, the editor at the *Kagoshima Shinpo* had taught Kinjo well. The first rule of journalism, he had said, was to be prepared, just as in the Boy Scouts. That meant always keeping a passport and a small overnight case packed ready and waiting at the office.

As the taxi stop-started its way through heavy traffic, Michi Kinjo congratulated himself on hunting out the trail and being awarded the assignment. And, closing his eyes tight, he prayed to his grandfather again. He prayed that he would find Miki Suzuki, and get her story splashed across the front page of the inimitable *Asahi Shimbun*.

His first stop was the Japanese embassy.

Through a mixture of flattery and pleading, he had been admitted into the first secretary's office, where Hideo Tottori was having a very bad day.

The Louis Vuitton Attack had snowballed into a field day of French mockery, aimed squarely at the Japanese government. Spiralling quickly out of control, it had led to a series of misguided diplomatic and political remarks on both sides.

Incensed by French ridicule, a high-level Japanese trade commission had cancelled at the last minute. The French ambassador in Tokyo had been summoned by the Japanese authorities, in order to explain his nation's condemnation. And, in Paris, the Japanese ambassador had been called to the Élysée Palace for a dressing down.

'How can I help you?' the first secretary asked, with only half his attention.

The young journalist took a deep breath.

'I have come to find Miss Suzuki,' he said.

Tottori flinched.

'*Miss Suzuki?*'

'Of the Louis Vuitton Attack.'

'How… how… how do you know about her?'

Kinjo sniffed. He had picked up the scent.

'Because her mother called me,' he said. 'She asked me to help her, to find her daughter and bring her home.'

'But you are a journalist and not a diplomat, are you not?'

'Yes.'

'Then what assistance do you imagine you could provide?'

Michi Kinjo sniffed a second time.

'I can offer a helping hand in her moment of need.' He paused, his heart racing. 'Would you please tell me where she is being kept?'

The diplomat dabbed a handkerchief to his brow. He didn't like journalists, and certainly not young ones. They were always so presumptuous. Pressing a button on the underside of his desk, he called security.

'I regret to say that you were misinformed,' Tottori said frigidly. 'I can be of no assistance to you in this matter.'

70

THAT EVENING, WHEN all the other patients were asleep, Bart the South African escaped from his room.

For two full months, he had worked away at the bars on his window, chipping at the cement with a bent rusty nail. Using modelling clay snatched from the activity sessions, he had made it look as though things were normal until he was ready to flee.

Bart shared a room with the Barbie-fixated Russian, and almost invited him to go along. But, wetting his lips with his long raspy tongue, he decided against it at the very last moment.

Vladimir was far too insane to take anywhere.

Climbing nimbly from the second-floor window, the South African scaled the drainpipe. But, rather than climbing straight to the street, he made his way across a low flat roof, and down to the garden.

Once on the ground, he scampered into the bushes below the vines, and pulled a teaspoon from his pyjama pocket.

Then, with the full moon glinting above, he began digging his escape tunnel.

Shortly before dawn, Bart climbed back up to his window, slipped through into his room, replaced the bars, and sealed them in place with the modelling clay.

It was just a matter of time, he thought to himself.

Dig a few inches of soil each night, and it wouldn't be long until he was free.

71

MICHI KINJO TOOK a room in a one-star hotel a stone's throw from the Gare du Nord.

The establishment doubled as a *bordel*, and specialized in well-built ladies from Albania. Judging by the satisfied grins on the faces at breakfast, they had achieved a rare mastery in their art. Like the rest of the hotel, the restaurant was in a terrible shape, and had a deeply ingrained stench of low-grade cigarettes – even though smoking had been banned for years.

Over a bowl of tepid coffee, Kinjo tapped a fingertip to the table-top anxiously and struggled to come up with his next move. There was almost nothing he was not prepared to do in order to land the story. Before Kinjo's hurried departure from the *Asahi Shimbun* offices, the editor-in-chief had wished him luck and instructed him not to fail. It was not a request but an order.

But failure was foremost in Kinjo's mind.

Back in Okinawa, his editor at the *Kagoshima Shinpo* had imparted the first lesson of journalism: that the line between total success and all-out failure is no thicker than the width of a hair. To succeed, the editor had said, a journalist has to be wily like an Okinawan flying fox.

Michi Kinjo sat there, tapping, as he tried to construct a cunning plan. And, as he tapped, he said a prayer that his grandfather would send him a badly needed clue, one that might take him straight to Miki Suzuki.

The lone waitress was doing her best to serve lukewarm coffee and stale croissants to the exhausted customers. A picture of exhaustion herself, she had been up all night, and longed for her village in the Dinaric Alps.

She nudged a croissant onto Kinjo's placemat. It was cold, hard and, like everything else, it reeked of cigarettes.

'Television?' she asked. 'You want television?'

Before the Japanese reporter could reply, the waitress pressed a chipped fingernail to the remote control, and the large flat screen on the wall came to life.

Michi Kinjo tried to fight it. But his eyes inevitably crawled up the wall and onto the screen.

Seated on a studio sofa was a middle-aged man dressed in a white lab coat. His ice-blue eyes partially hidden behind rimless glasses, he had an air of authority. Across from him, in an armchair, was the voluptuous female presenter. She had big hair and far too much lipstick. The man's name appeared on the screen in little white letters – Dr. Georges Mesmer.

It was just another slot on a breakfast show that no one ever watched.

Michi Kinjo was about to take the last slurp of his coffee and leave, when the grainy portrait of a Japanese woman's face flashed up on the screen.

Miki Suzuki.

Leaping up, the young reporter hurried over to the TV, hands grasped together beneath his chin. Although not quite fluent in French, he understood enough to appreciate that the doctor and presenter were discussing Miki Suzuki and her condition... a condition described as *Syndrome de Paris*.

72

IN THE DAY room of the asylum, the patients were making things again.

Meandering between the tables, Nurse Polk offered suggestions and praise.

'That is excellent, Mr. Park,' she said tenderly. 'What is it?'

The Korean was massaging his hands into a gooey mess of dough, mixing the colours together.

'It is a spaceship,' he said.

Beside him, the other Korean man was stabbing chopsticks into a plastic bottle. His teeth were gritted, his eyes wide with delight.

'And what are you making, Mr. Kim?'

Kim did not reply at first.

Chewing on his tongue, he stabbed three more chopsticks through the plastic. Then he said:

'It's a little mouse. I think I shall call him *Gaa-Gaa*. Yes, that is his name. *Gaa-Gaa*. He is a very naughty little mouse. I think I shall beat him.'

'Does he eat cheese?' the nurse asked.

Mr. Kim clutched the bottle to his chest.

'No! No! No!' he exclaimed indignantly. '*Gaa-Gaa* does *not* eat cheese!'

'Then what does he eat?'

'He eats mice.'

'But I thought he *was* a mouse.'

'He's a cannibal mouse,' Mr. Kim said darkly. 'And that's why he's grown so strong.'

At the next table, Victoria was threading large beads onto a strand of yarn. Her hair now electric blue, she was completely immersed in the task at hand. All of a sudden, Vladimir stomped up. He was dressed as Cinderella Barbie, in a long flowing gown. Snatching the necklace, he threw it out of the window.

'That's rubbish!' he yelled, thrusting out his bust.

Before the Russian could react, Victoria had pinned him to the ground and was head-butting him.

Just then, Dr. Mesmer came in.

He didn't seem to show any surprise or interest in the brawl. While Nurse Polk did her best to break up the fight, he asked Miki to follow him through to the surgery. Putting down a Lego model of a legless cat that she had made, she shuffled obediently towards the next room.

'I would like to show you some pictures,' said the doctor when they were both seated. 'And all you have to do is to tell me what they make you think of. It's best if you answer in a single word, and as quickly as you can.'

Miki stared into space. The doctor smiled engagingly.

'Do you understand?'

'Yes.'

'Excellent, then we will begin.'

Mesmer held up a flashcard of the Eiffel Tower.

Miki scratched the end of her nose.

'Frog,' she said.

Without reacting, the psychiatrist held up the next card – a picture of a man holding a fresh-baked baguette.

'Night,' Miki grunted.

'And what about this?'

The third card showed a picture of a choux cream pastry.

Miki blinked. She opened her mouth to say something.

Then, leaping from the white vinyl chaise longue, she snatched the card, ripped it into pieces, and swallowed them.

Resuming her seat, she scratched the end of her nose again.

'Bad,' she said.

73

THE DIPLOMATIC RIFT between France and Japan continued.

Each hour it gathered a little more momentum, insults becoming less diplomatic and increasingly antagonistic.

Whipped up by their media, the French public began to boycott Japanese goods. Dozens of Toyota cars were vandalized in Paris and beyond. The Japanese embassy was attacked with paint bombs in the night; and a group of tourists from Osaka were thrown out of their hotel and chased down the street.

Speaking on national television, the Japanese foreign minister warned his concerned populace to steer well clear of France. The French were, he told them, baying for Japanese blood – all because a helpless Japanese girl reacted badly after being so aggressively attacked.

On Avenue Hoche, the paint-spattered embassy of Japan was surrounded by a sea of agitated protesters and guards.

Inside, Hideo Tottori sat in his office with his head in his hands.

There had been times of friction during his diplomatic career, but he had never seen anything like this.

The telephone on his desk rang. It was the ambassador, asking for the first secretary to come through at once.

Seated behind a great carved mahogany desk, the chief of mission was signing papers when Tottori entered. He didn't look up, not at first. Taking his time, he squared the papers, laid them down on the leather surface.

And, clearing his throat, he said:

'This is a dark moment for our nation, as it is for the nation of France. Five minutes ago I received a telephone call from Tokyo.' The ambassador drew breath. Then, his voice trembling, he held up a finger. 'I have been recalled,' he said.

Ramrod-straight like a guardsman, Tottori pushed his shoulders back and struggled to appear detached.

'I understand,' he said.

The ambassador took off his glasses and placed them on the papers.

'This situation is very difficult,' he replied. 'I have no choice but to leave you in charge.'

'I understand,' the first secretary said again, his cool expression masking inner turmoil.

'It is all because of that damned girl.'

'The one who attacked Louis Vuitton?'

'Yes.' The ambassador frowned. 'Where is she now?' he asked.

'She has been taken to an asylum… in Montmartre. I visited her there a few days ago.'

'What was her condition?'

Hideo Tottori sucked air in through the side of his mouth.

'She was not well,' he said.

74

FOR TWENTY EUROS, Michi Kinjo got himself a white lab coat, and a clipboard – the kind he imagined French psychiatrists carried around.

A few minutes' research on the internet had dredged up the details of Dr. Mesmer's hospital. Somewhat nervously the reporter had made the call, pretending to be a visiting psychiatrist from Tokyo.

To his surprise, he was put through to the doctor at once. And, to his delight, Mesmer not only spoke Japanese, but invited him to meet Miki Suzuki.

At the asylum, Mr. Chen had picked a fight with the South African, and both patients were being punished when Kinjo arrived. Forced to stand facing each other in the corridor, they had been encouraged to radiate affection rather than loathing.

But the exercise was not going well.

'You smell like rotten cabbage!' said Chen.

'And you smell like my arse!' replied Bart.

'You hair is ugly. It reminds me of a toilet brush.'

'At least I *have* hair!'

Welcoming Dr. Kinjo at the front door, Nurse Polk requested that he sign in, then lock any valuable or dangerous objects away in a secure drawer at the front desk.

'I have nothing with me,' the visitor said, 'just this clipboard and a pencil.'

The nurse was going to ask to see a piece of identification, but it slipped her mind. She led the way through the security door, past Bart and Chen, and on to Mesmer's office.

Straining to appear older and more mature than he actually was, the journalist introduced himself as Dr. Kinjo from the Psychiatric

Department of Tokyo University. He explained that he was in the French capital making a study of so-called 'Paris Syndrome'.

Mesmer took his seat behind the desk, and cracked his knuckles one by one.

'The Syndrome is, as you may know, my own speciality,' he said. 'I have published a number of papers on the condition.'

'I understand it is on the rise,' Kinjo replied.

Dr. Mesmer rubbed his eye with a thumb.

'Oh, yes, that's right.'

'Could you tell me, doctor, why you believe this to be the case?'

'The increase in cases?'

'Yes.'

'Some say it is because of better identification – that we are becoming more expert at recognizing it.'

'Is that what you believe?' asked Kinjo, well aware that small talk was the key to a successful interview.

'No,' Mesmer answered. 'Paris Syndrome is on an exponential rise. Each month the cases double. Given time, I believe it will reach epidemic proportions.'

'But why?'

'Because of the Oriental love affair with our capital. It began with the Japanese, as you know, but we are now identifying the condition in Koreans, Chinese, and even the occasional European. The only question is who will be next?'

Dr. Kinjo straightened the collar of his lab coat.

'Would you tell me about Miki Suzuki?' he asked.

Mesmer looked down at the jam jar filled with human teeth, his eyes glazing over.

'An extreme case if ever there was one,' he said deliberately. 'She is the classic victim. So classic that she is the stereotype... twenty-something, unmarried, passionate about Paris, naïve...'

'And her rampage through Louis Vuitton?'

'So terribly unfortunate,' the doctor muttered. 'It's sparked great problems for our two nations as you know.'

'Is she remorseful?'

Mesmer cracked his knuckles once again.

'I am not certain,' he said. 'As you may know, Paris Syndrome manifests itself in different ways. These depend on the individual, and what exactly has been the trigger. In Miki's case, the triggers were multiple. And, as a result, the reaction – the syndrome – is unusually complex. To insinuate that she is remorseful would perhaps be inaccurate. I would say that more than anything she is confused.'

'How exactly *is* her state of mind?' Kinjo asked, scribbling a note on the clipboard.

'Well, she does have moments of lucidity. But, at other times she exhibits a range of personalities...'

'*Personalities?*'

'Oh yes. She has been the Meiji Princess Tsune, and she has been a rock... and an Ainu child lost in the forest. And I fear that those manifestations are the tip of her dissociative identity disorder.'

The visiting psychiatrist swallowed hard, well aware he was out of his depth. As he did so, Dr. Mesmer looked up at him, half-wondering how old he could be. Just as he was about to enquire whether Dr. Seifu still headed the Psychiatric Department of Tokyo University, Dr. Kinjo lowered his head a fraction.

'Would you mind introducing me to Miki Suzuki?' he asked.

75

An EXERCISE OF damage limitation was well underway at the Angel Flower Beauty Company.

The *Japan Times* had finally linked the Louis Vuitton Attacker to the girl who had stood so famously in the icy realm of Shiba Park. The only surprise was that it had taken so long to put two and two together.

Outside the firm's headquarters, a string of satellite trucks were parked neatly against the kerb. And, clustered at the front door, was a throng of journalists, with notebooks, cameras, and cordless microphones.

All of them were anxious to get news of Miki Suzuki.

Up on the thirty-ninth floor, a group of senior executives were locked away in the conference room in closed session. Absolute silence prevailed. There was an unknown sense of urgency, as though an enemy had just declared all-out war.

At the head of the long table sat the chairman of Angel Flower.

Still suffering from jetlag, he looked fatigued, sullen, and possibly suicidal. Adjacent to him, angry rather than depressed, was his henchman, Pun-Pun.

The chairman let out a sigh.

'These are our bleakest days,' he said. 'I will not waste your time or mine by explaining how we arrived at this terrible situation. What is important is for everyone in this firm to help turn our predicament around.'

Dressed in grey suits, the forty executives present – all of them men – exuded an air of diehard allegiance to the firm. Salarymen through and through, each was as loyal to the cause as any foot soldier marching into battle.

None dared to speak, none except for Pun-Pun.

'We will make an example of Miss Suzuki!' he spat ferociously. 'We will not stop until she has been publicly humiliated and shamed!'

The chairman sighed a second time.

'I will have to speak to the media,' he said. 'They are down there, waiting.' Sniffing, he wiped his glasses clean. 'And I do not know what to tell them.'

Again, Pun-Pun spoke up:

'Perhaps, sir, you could level the blame on Suzuki-san's shoulders. After all, she alone is worthy of blame.'

The chairman gazed down the long conference table, anxious grey-suited executives perched on chairs at either side. His mind wandering, he got a flash of his formative days in the world of beauty products.

A young executive, back then he was in charge of a line in cut-price lipstick – a product that was found to be injurious to human health. The press had been camped out outside, and they were baying for executive blood. Taking the situation in his stride, the chairman of the firm had held an emergency meeting. 'We must do the unexpected!' he had boomed. 'Because surprise is the best form of attack!'

76

RATHER THAN INVITE Miki to come through to the surgery, Mesmer led Dr. Kinjo into the day room, where the patients had been given tin whistles to play. Bart was the only one making something that resembled music. He was playing his own version of *Amazing Grace*.

On the seat beside him, Victoria had used her whistle to hold her hair up. And, next to her, Tanaka-san was rubbing his instrument fast between his hands while shouting 'Turnip!' over and over.

The Koreans were both blowing in the wrong end of theirs.

And, Vladimir had stuffed his down the front of his dress.

Miki was seated at the far end of the group. She was holding her whistle in a clenched fist, as though about to stab someone with it.

Mesmer entered and introduced Dr. Kinjo.

The Japanese patients bowed their heads. At least one of them whooped.

'Can anyone here tell me what the river that runs through Paris is called?' the doctor asked.

'Thames,' said Mr. Park with certainty.

'No, no, it's the Gaa-Gaa River,' corrected Mr. Kim. 'I have seen it. It's all blue and squishy.'

'It is called La Seine,' Dr. Mesmer said.

He took a step towards the middle of the day room. Before he could utter another word, Mrs. Ito put down her tin whistle and, very calmly, shuffled over to a pool of sunlight near the window.

There were tears running down her cheeks.

Her fingers gnarled and tight, she held both hands in front of her face.

Kinjo, Mesmer and the patients watched.

As they did so, Mrs. Ito began to scream.

'The water is coming!' she wailed. 'Can't you see it? Look out there! The wall of water! Hurry, hurry or we will all be drowned!'

Leaping back from the window, she climbed up onto a chair and screamed again – even louder and more stridently than before.

Then, hands over eyes, she began to quiver. A moment after that she was shaking uncontrollably.

All of a sudden she fell off the chair and collapsed in a foetal ball on the floor.

Then the Koreans both shouted out.

Mr. Kim warned the others that a tsunami was coming; and Mr. Park put his fingers in his ears and jumped up and down.

As he did so, the nurse coaxed Mrs. Ito from the ground, and back onto the chair.

Paying no attention, Mesmer led Dr. Kinjo over to where Miki was sitting, the tin whistle still clenched in her fist. He introduced them to each other, and both the psychiatrists sat down. Miki didn't look up, not even when she heard a friendly voice in Japanese.

The three of them sat there in silence, the rest of the room still agitated after Mrs. Ito's outburst.

Miki was watching light playing through a screen of birch trees.

As she concentrated, her imagination focussed on one of them, the last one in the line. A single drop of dew was glistening on a fragment of its coarse papery bark. Turning her body to regard it from the side, Miki smiled.

Dr. Mesmer said something, but she didn't hear.

With great care, she held thumb and index finger out, pinching them together. In her mind, she was plucking a little pink berry from a bush near the tree. She could hear the fruit singing to her, a song of lost love.

Again, the doctor spoke:

'Would you tell our visitor where you are from, Miki?' he said.

'I heard you come from Sendai,' Dr. Kinjo prompted.

Miki plucked another berry. She plopped it in her mouth.

'*From?*'

'Where are you from?' Kinjo asked. 'From Sendai?'

'No, no,' Miki whispered, her voice the barest trace of sound. 'I am not from Sendai. I am from Kyoto.'

'And who are you?' Dr. Mesmer enquired.

Her eyes quite glassy, Miki tapped her feet on the floor.

'I am a unicorn,' she said.

At the far end of the day room, Tanaka-san had begun running frantically in circles. He was fearful that the Koreans had hatched a plan to throw him in a pot and cook him. Shouting 'Turnip!' over and over, his hands waved riotously above his head.

Mesmer strode over to quell the disturbance.

As he did so, Dr. Kinjo slipped Miki a tiny folded note.

77

THE QUESTION OF how exactly to achieve the unexpected, dominated the remainder of the meeting at Angel Flower.

Given the challenge by their chairman, the grey-suited executives scratched their heads, sucked air through their back teeth, squinted, gasped, and struggled to give the impression they were thinking very hard.

After a full thirty minutes of strenuous consideration, one of the younger managers, seated at the far end of the table, held a finger in front of his nose. He was profoundly fearful, as though giving the wrong answer would oblige him to commit *seppuku*.

'I have a small idea, sir,' he said, ducking his head down low. 'It is a stupid, worthless idea, and I am ashamed that it is all I can think of. Excuse me. I apologize. I am not worthy of the responsibility placed on my shoulders.'

Peering down the long table, the chairman grunted.

'What is it – your idea?'

The executive dabbed a handkerchief to his brow. His facial muscles almost paralysed with trepidation, he murmured:

'We could do the unexpected… and make Miki Suzuki a heroine.'

The silence that followed the remark was so absolute that the smoke alarm mounted high on the ceiling of the conference room could be heard recharging itself.

After more than a minute of the agonizing interlude, the chairman sat up. Eyes narrowed, his jagged teeth visible behind badly chapped lips, he emitted a long deep tone of sound...

A sound of extraordinary pleasure.

'A heroine,' he said. 'That's it! We shall make Suzuki-san a heroine!'

78

SITTING ON HER bed, Miki was imagining the little pink berries on the bush, and how she longed to eat every last one.

She could watch them for hours on end, marvelling at the way the light played over them. From time to time she would pick one, suck on it, and crush it with her molars.

Each one tasted different.

Some of the fruit tasted like watermelon, others like plums, or even like roast ham. The more she caressed them in her fingers, the more unexpected the taste appeared to be.

At seven o'clock an alarm sounded next door.

The Koreans were having an argument in their room, about the best colour in the world. Mr. Kim claimed it was red, and Mr. Park was insisting it was blue. The discussion had become so raucous that one of them had pushed the alarm button – so that Nurse Polk could adjudicate.

Lying down on her bed, Miki closed her eyes and found herself in the forest. Her hands and feet were hooves, and a long strand of ivory thrust out from her forehead into the night. Her silvery coat glinting with perspiration, she galloped between the trees.

As she raced ahead full kilter, Miki felt something in her pocket. It was small and sharp-edged. Charging through the forest, she picked the object from her pocket and held it.

A note.

A little note.

A little note folded half a dozen times.

Raising it to her nose, Miki sniffed it gently. And, sticking out her tongue, she gave it a lick. She frowned. *An odd little thing*, she thought. *Quite beautiful and mysterious, but not nearly as pleasing to a unicorn as berries on a bush.*

With the Koreans yelling at each other next door, Miki placed the folded paper on the post of her metal-framed bed.

Even before she climbed under the covers to go to sleep, it had fallen – lodged in a gap between the nightstand and the wall.

79

AT 9 A.M. the next day, the Angel Flower Beauty Company held a press conference in its central assembly hall.

It was the first such gathering in the firm's long and chequered history. Until then, the executive hierarchy had always believed it best to keep the media firmly at arm's length. But these were drastic times – times in which the much-tarnished name of Angel Flower was itself at stake.

And drastic times called for drastic measures.

Every national newspaper and television channel was represented.

Most of them had fielded reporters for days outside the company headquarters.

Filing into the assembly hall, the print journalists took their seats near the front. TV crews set up their lights and cameras, and attached a forest of microphones to the podium.

By 9.15 there were more than three hundred journalists at the ready.

Poised in the wings, the chairman chewed the inside of his cheek, and counselled himself to remain calm. He was not the kind of leader who enjoyed public gatherings. The very thought of them sent his heart racing, and drenched his thin grey hair in oily sweat.

As far as he was concerned, the media were a pack of wolves, dead set on tearing corporate flesh apart.

Giving the signal for the lights to be dimmed, he stepped anxiously onto the stage and made a beeline for the podium. Set squarely in the middle, it had the Angel Flower logo – a rose with a halo – glued lopsidedly to the front.

The microphones were switched from standby to ON. The TV cameras rolled. The rows of journalists flicked to fresh pages in their notebooks.

Complete silence.

Then, and only then, did the chairman clear his throat.

'My dear friends,' he said in a mellifluous voice. 'We are grateful to you for attending at such short notice. As you no doubt are aware, Angel Flower is much more than a company – it is a family. We regard all our employees as valued members of that family. Each one is special. Each one is like my own child.'

The chairman glanced down at the journalists. He could sense them baying for blood – for *his* blood.

'I know you all will have seen the footage of a woman, a *Japanese* woman, Miki Suzuki, in what has become known as the "Louis Vuitton

Attack". And, as you also know, this woman – this young spirited *innocent* woman – is an honourable employee… the Angel of Angel Flower.'

The chairman took a deep breath, dabbing the perspiration from his eyes. 'She is a member of our family,' he said. 'And even in these dark days of her illness, we regard her as a lost daughter – an angelic daughter we urgently want home.'

A reporter from NHK stood up.

Everyone in the room knew her by reputation as the Rottweiler, a sobriquet gained from her tendency to tear interviewees limb from limb.

'Where is Miki Suzuki now?' she asked icily.

'She is still in Paris.'

A radio reporter at the front held up a hand. He stood up, then bowed.

'We understand that she has been put in an asylum,' he said.

A wave of muttering rippled through the assembly hall. The chairman wiped his face with a starched handkerchief.

'This is not an ideal situation,' he responded. 'The French authorities detained Miss Suzuki. They insist that she is unwell.'

The Rottweiler leapt up again.

'Is Miki-san their prisoner?' she asked quizzically, her canine nostrils sensing blood.

The chairman dabbed his face a second time, then signalled to a technician at the back of the room. No sooner had he done so than a giant photograph unfurled itself behind him on the stage.

It was not the grainy ranting picture of Miki the Attacker, but the lovely serene image of a woman standing proud, in harmony with the forest.

'This is Miki Suzuki-san,' the chairman said, his words tempered with emotion. 'She is our sister, our daughter, our friend… our angel.'

He paused, swallowed, dabbed his face again. 'But above all, she is a woman lost behind enemy lines, a young woman who needs help from us all.'

80

THAT NIGHT, MIKI dreamed that she was galloping in a distant land, through a magical realm conjured from a child's fantasy. She felt free, as though her hooves had stumbled into a paradise for the senses.

Had she recognized the scrap of paper as a note, and opened it out, she might have known to expect the visitor who had climbed onto her window ledge.

His face drained from adrenalin and fear, Michi Kinjo had scaled the asylum's stone façade. In the name of journalism, and in honour of the *Asahi Shimbun*, he had come to Miki Suzuki's aid.

The young correspondent had worked out which window was the right one, from details tossed into the conversation by Dr. Mesmer. Cautioning himself to be brave, he had fought away his dread of vertigo.

Having said a final prayer to his grandfather, he tapped a fingernail gently on the pane of glass.

There was no reply.

He tapped harder.

Still no sign of life.

So he tapped much more forcefully – so hard that Nurse Polk turned on the light downstairs.

Clinging spreadeagled to the asylum's façade, Kinjo considered his options.

As he hung there, pondering, fingertips numb from holding on, he spied the shadow of a man climbing deftly from a nearby window.

Now paralysed with fear, Kinjo dared not utter a sound, even when the fellow climber was an inch or two away.

'Excuse me mate,' the other man said politely in a South African accent. 'Just need to squeeze by.'

The journalist watched in disbelief as the South African clambered over him and down towards the garden, a teaspoon gripped in his teeth.

When he was gone, Kinjo plucked up the courage to tap once again.

This time, he heard what sounded like footsteps in the room. Then he saw the silhouette of a woman.

As she moved towards the glass, he saw her face.

'Quickly!' he hissed. 'Open the window!'

Miki reached out a hand and placed her right palm square on the glass. It was as though she were still dreaming.

'Hugo,' she whispered at length. 'I have waited for you.'

'Miss Suzuki! I am a journalist with *Asahi Shimbun*,' Kinjo explained, an air of formality in his tone. Still clinging to the face of the building, he pleaded with Miki once again to open the window.

'I will take you to freedom!'

'The window is locked and barred, my dearest Hugo,' Miki replied.

'*Hugo?* No, no… I am *not* Hugo. I am a journalist with the *Asahi Shimbun*. You met me in the afternoon. I was pretending to be a doctor!'

Michi Kinjo grinned at his artifice.

'Please go downstairs and come with me!'

'Not Hugo?' Miki whimpered again, her right hand now pressed up against her cheek.

'No… not Hugo… *Michi*… I am Michi.'

Ten seconds of silence passed.

Then the alarm.

A riotous, screeching, jarring wall of sound.

Miki's right hand had moved from her cheek to the big red button on the wall.

81

By LUNCHTIME, THE photograph of Miki Suzuki had graced every television, smartphone and computer screen in Japan.

It had surged through social media networks, and had been printed onto T-shirts, badges, banners and mugs. And, each time it was shared and spread, it became less of a portrait and more of a symbol – an iconic symbol of a young woman in desperate need.

From Sapporo to Fukuoka, everyone had the same question:

When was Miki Suzuki coming home?

At Angel Flower, the throngs of former protesters were now all armed with hastily made placards. Bearing the face of Miki, the boards symbolized injustice, and the cold calculating hand of European domination. The legions of sales staff at Angel Flower had turned into foot soldiers with a new and important cause.

Upstairs in his office, the chairman was given a briefing.

'We may have a hope of redemption,' he said wearily to Pun-Pun. 'So long as no one discovers that it was we who quite happily abandoned Suzuki-san behind enemy lines.'

82

WITH THE RISE of Miki, model citizen and iconic symbol of Innocence and Peace, came the final break-up of relations between Japan and France. Her face now known to every man, woman and child, portraits of Miki Suzuki were saluted and hailed across the Japanese islands.

Heading his diplomatic outpost thousands of miles to the west, Hideo Tottori was doing his best to brave the offensive taking place outside the embassy on Avenue Hoche.

Vexed protesters had encircled the building. Most had turned up in the eager hope of a brawl. Setting fire to Japanese electronics, the national *Nisshoki* flags, and portraits of the emperor, they taunted the riot police, spoiling for a fight.

The first secretary was on the telephone to his ministry in Tokyo when, at 10.03 a.m., a Molotov cocktail was hurled at the embassy. As riot police charged at the perpetrator, Tottori's staff set to work to extinguish the flames.

Maintaining an impassive demeanour, the first secretary listened to the ministerial liaison on the other end.

'*The sound*, sir?' he said absently. 'Just a missile thrown by one of the demonstrators. *What kind of missile?* I believe it is a small petrol bomb. *The protesters…?*' Tottori glanced through the curtains. 'Yes it would be true to say they are becoming agitated, sir.'

At that moment a cognac bottle filled with petrol ripped through the office window and smashed against the back wall. Stuffed into the neck in place of a cork, its touch-paper was a burning rag.

Within a moment the room was ablaze.

'Forgive me sir,' said Tottori in an awkward voice as he bowed, the flames licking around him, 'I believe I must end the call.'

83

MOVING HELTER-SKELTER FROM the second-storey window to the ground, Michi Kinjo had used every muscle in his body, covering the vertical distance in five seconds flat. Dexterity and quick thinking had saved him from being captured.

The same, however, was not true for the lip-licking South African.

Unfortunately for Bart, he was ascending the drainpipe, teaspoon clenched between rows of white teeth, at the precise moment that Miki had raised the alarm.

Muddy and blinking in the nurse's lamplight, he was dragged inside and reprimanded for disturbing the peace.

As for the *Asahi Shimbun*'s finest newshound, he hobbled away and was soon back in the hotel room near Gare du Nord. His body and his pride bruised, he lay down on his bed.

Outside, a police car on call clattered by.

And, in the next room, the Albanian waitress lured her client into a state of ecstasy.

84

AT BREAKFAST NEXT morning, Tanaka-san the turnip was running about in a continuous figure eight.

Babbling, blinking, and flailing with his arms, he was annoying the other patients. Nurse Polk asked him to sit down and eat his eggs. But the instruction only caused him to speed up.

Eventually he did sit, slouching down next to Bart, who was still in disgrace.

A few minutes passed, and Miki shuffled into the dining room.

Her face was drawn and grey, her hands trembling as though she were frozen to the bone.

Mr. Chen pointed to her and mumbled something. Then Victoria reached out an arm and gave her half a hug.

'Miki looks like she's dead,' said Vladimir, who was painting his nails fire engine red.

The nurse glanced round.

'Didn't you sleep well?' she asked gently.

Miki dunked a croissant into a communal saucer of jam, and held it in front of her face.

'Mariko wants me to meet her across the street at noon,' she said.

'Who's Mariko?' asked Bart.

'Mariko is meeting me at noon,' Miki said again.

'*Mariko?*' the nurse asked.

'Mariko smells like strawberries.'

'Is she your friend?' Nurse Polk enquired.

'Yes. My friend.'

'How does she look?'

Miki stuffed the entire croissant into her mouth. She chewed once or twice, then swallowed.

'Mariko is tall… and Mariko is…'

'*Is?*'

'Mariko is green.'

Sitting at the next table, Mrs. Ito scratched her head.

'How can Mariko be green?' she asked.

'Of course she is green.'

'You've gone crazy,' said Vladimir, putting away his nail varnish.

'Why is Mariko green?' Nurse Polk enquired, waving a hand at the Russian, to silence him.

'Because she is a tree,' Miki said.

85

THAT AFTERNOON, A TV satellite van made its way up a deeply pitted lane a few miles from Sendai, and came to a halt outside a ramshackle house.

The curtains were all drawn closed, and the porch was piled up with junk. An old wheelchair was lying upside down, a litter of stray cats living inside. The home was so decrepit that the NHK film crew wondered whether they had the right address.

The first to get out of the vehicle was a mousy producer in a duffel coat. She was followed by a tall, confident woman, dressed from head to toe in black. Checking her makeup in a compact, she spat a line of instruction to the crew:

'Keep filming whatever happens,' she said in a sharp voice, '… even if they slam the door in our face. Remember, we will be going out live!'

The cameraman and sound engineer got their equipment ready and clambered out.

'Ready,' they both said at once.

A moment later, the heels of a pair of new black riding boots were marching up the steps to the front door, film crew in tow.

The thick skin of the Rottweiler's fingertip pressed down on the bell button.

A minute passed. The finger pressed again, longer and harder. Before the reporter had pulled her hand away, the door opened inwards.

An anxious, grey-haired woman was standing in the frame.

'*Yes?*'

'Are you Mrs. Suzuki?'

'Yes.'

'Mother of Miki Suzuki?'

'Yes.'

Instinctively, the Rottweiler stepped to the left so that the camera could get a close-up.

'We have come from NHK to talk to you,' she said.

The next thing Mrs. Suzuki knew, national TV was broadcasting live from her kitchen. The timid producer had cleared the table and was setting up equipment, while the Rottweiler got straight down to business.

'We want to know Miki as you know her,' she growled. 'We want to know everything about her, as if she were our daughter.'

Pinned to the kitchen's back wall, a bright light and camera lens pushed in her face, Mrs. Suzuki glanced down at the floor.

'All she ever wanted was to go to Paris,' she said. 'It was her dream... the only thing she ever spoke about... the only thing she cared about.'

Turning to give the viewers her good side, the Rottweiler struggled to exude humility.

'And how did it all begin?'

'With Ojiichan.'

'*Ojiichan?*'

'My father.'

Miki's mother led the lens and the light through to the sitting room, where an old man was dozing beneath a patchwork quilt on the couch. His teeth were in a glass on the coffee table. Beside them was a chamber pot half-filled with cold pee.

'You were telling us how it all began,' the Rottweiler probed.

'With Ojiichan's story... the story of his coin pouch, the one from Louis Vuitton.'

The reporter signalled sideways to the producer, and the camera took in a clutch of family photos on the wall. Then it swung back round, to find Ojiichan sitting up, with his teeth in, and the chamber pot gone.

Jabbing the old man with her boot, the Rottweiler urged him to begin his tale.

'I was a young man back then,' he said in a frail voice. 'It was so long ago that I have forgotten quite when. I was in Paris. It was heaven. I can see it clearly. The sunlight. The leafy trees. The sweet scent of perfume.'

'What about Louis Vuitton?!'

Ojiichan blew his nose and pushed his teeth back into place.

'Before leaving Paris, I looked in the window at Louis Vuitton. There were all kinds of treasures. But in the middle of them all was the most beautiful thing I had ever seen – a little leather coin pouch.'

'Did you buy it, Ojiichan?' the Rottweiler asked impatiently.

'Oh, no, no, no.'

'Why not?'

'Because it was a Sunday and the shop was closed. And so I came home to Sendai. But years later I gave that little coin pouch to Miki as a gift.'

'But you said that you didn't buy the coin pouch.'

'Yes.'

'So, how did you give it?' the Rottweiler demanded, tiring of the old man and a tale which didn't make sense.

'As a story,' he replied. 'I told the story to Miki... and that is what made her fall in love with Paris.'

86

WITH DIPLOMATIC RELATIONS worsening by the hour, the Japanese government again warned their nationals against travelling to France.

The announcement came as immigration officers at Roissy Charles de Gaulle dug their heels in deep. They refused entry to a flight packed with students from Osaka, that had been mid-air when the directive went out.

It was the last straw.

Hours later, a French cruise liner was turned away from the port of Yokohama. After that, a ship packed with crates of Bordeaux, bound for high-end restaurants in Tokyo, dumped its entire cargo over the side.

As the tit for tat reprisals spiralled out of control, Tottori-san and a handful of his staff held their ground. Barricaded in a small third-floor office, they spent their time shredding sensitive documents and extinguishing fires.

Out on the street, the protesters were becoming ever more belligerent. They were calling for ordinary Parisians to bring Japanese electronics, to fuel their immense bonfire.

At the same time that the NHK TV crew were touring the Suzuki family home, an effigy of Miki was being launched into the flames on Avenue Hoche.

As her head and torso caught fire, an army of protesters charged at the embassy, hurling a barrage of Molotov cocktails. Sensible to the fact they were out of their depth, and angry at being underpaid, the riot police stepped aside and let the demonstrators through.

Across Paris, shops selling Japanese electronics and other wares were targeted by vigilantes. Most of the city's sushi restaurants were attacked. A good many were burned to the ground – even the ones with Chinese owners. No amount of pleading by them could appease the anger of the mob.

SITTING IN HIS office, Dr. Mesmer watched the scenes online in horror and dread.

His expression sullen, he knew it was only a matter of time before the protesters would be breaking down the door of his little hospital. Miki Suzuki was the name on their lips, and it was her blood they were after.

Mesmer struggled to come up with a plan.

As he sat there, staring into space, Nurse Polk knocked.

'Have you heard what is happening, doctor… on Avenue Hoche?' she said, standing in the doorframe.

The psychiatrist blinked.

'Yes. I have seen,' he said.

'They are calling Miki's name.'

'I know.'

'They want to kill her – to tear her limb from limb.'

Again, Mesmer blinked.

'We are not safe,' he said.

'So what can we do?' Nurse Polk asked, a trace of hysteria in her voice.

Stepping forward into the office, she looked at her employer in a way that she had not regarded him before. For the first time in the twenty years she had worked for him, she felt that she had to speak out.

'We must escape,' she said.

'I cannot leave my patients,' Mesmer replied. 'They need me now more than they ever have.'

'We will take them.'

Gazing distractedly at the model of the human brain, the psychiatrist frowned.

'Where would we go?'
'To a place of refuge.'

88

WHEN THE LIVE interview with Ojiichan was at an end, a girl of twelve
went out of her home in Hiroshima and tied a red ribbon around a tree.
Then she took a picture with her phone and tweeted it to her friends.
Within an hour, red ribbons were appearing on trees all over
Chugoku province. By the next morning, the ribbons were popping
up in Osaka, Yokohama, and Tokyo. And, by noon, they were found in
every city, town, village and hamlet in Japan.

Ribbon manufacturers worked in overdrive to satiate the sudden
and massive demand for their product. As they did so, Miki Suzuki's
portrait was unveiled in public places. Surrounded by burning candles
on makeshift pavement shrines, or hanging in school auditoriums, and
stadiums, the picture represented everything that made Japan proud.

Recognizing the need to get aboard what could be the ultimate in
vote-winning bandwagons, the Prime Minister dispatched a secret
military aircraft to Paris. Ordered to leave at once, the crew received
their combat briefing once airborne.

On board was a unit of the much-respected Tokushu Sakusen Gun,
the elite Japanese Ground Defence Force. Their mission – codenamed
'Golden Swallow' – was to storm the asylum and to bring Miki home.

Having received confirmation that the covert strike force was en
route, the Prime Minister went on national TV.

'I give my assurance,' he said gravely, 'that the government of which
I am a part will not sleep until Miki Suzuki-san is safely home with us
in Japan!'

USING FOOTAGE FROM the family home near Sendai, the Rottweiler and her team edited together a one-hour documentary of Miki Suzuki's life, loves, and aspirations.

Miki's best friend, Ichiko, was interviewed, as was the sales clerk at Kinokuniya bookshop, who had suggested she visit the Musée Nissim de Camondo. And Miki's first-grade teacher gave her recollections, as did Saito-san, the French teacher in Hayama. Even the girl in Hiroshima, who had tied the first ribbon, was asked for her opinion.

But, most importantly of all, the Rottweiler spoke to the chairman of the Angel Flower Beauty Company.

From the first moment that the heels of her black leather riding boots crossed the firm's threshold, NHK's chief reporter sensed unease. Unsure quite why, her journalistic gut was telling her that Angel Flower was a hotbed of secrets and intrigue.

Once the lights had been set up and his face had been daubed with chalky foundation cream, the chairman got behind his desk. The camera's record LED began to flash. The soundman gave a thumbs up.

And the Rottweiler got down to work.

'Can you tell our viewers about Miki, the employee?' she asked.

Gazing into the middle distance, the chairman's expression was dim.

'She was a ray of light,' he said slowly. 'A blinding ray of the brightest light. In all my years in this business, I have never known a woman so committed, or so loved.'

'What is your most cherished memory of her?'

'Ah, I suppose it was in Paris,' said the chairman with a smile. 'She was so in love with the city.'

The Rottweiler's left nostril twitched.

'You were there in Paris, with Miki?'

'Yes, I was. Me and a team of others from Angel Flower. We toured the city together. And what a good time we had!'

The Rottweiler signalled for the camera to zoom in for a close up.

'Am I right that you and your associates left Miki in Paris, that you flew back *without* her?'

The chairman touched a hand to his brow.

'In a manner of speaking,' he said.

Her hackles rising, her sharp teeth glinting, the Rottweiler went in for the kill.

'And so, I put it to you Mr. Chairman, that the reason Miki Suzuki-san is lost – missing in action in an enemy land – is because *you* abandoned her, so far away from home, and from the family and friends that she so dearly loves.'

90

As THE NHK interview was being screened, an insider in the Paris gendarmerie slipped the protesters the information they longed for – the exact location of the LV Attacker.

Having burned the Japanese embassy to the ground, they pelted the last remaining staff with stones.

Then they hurried north to Montmartre.

Dr. Mesmer and Nurse Polk were rounding up the patients, urging them to come at once to the day room, bringing nothing more than a toothbrush.

The instruction had sparked a general state of hysteria.

Tanaka-san was doing figure eights again. This time he was hopping, shouting 'Turnip! Turnip! Turnip!'

The Koreans had got down on the floor and were pretending they were starfish.

Victoria was screaming.

The Japanese women were crying.

Bart was licking his foot.

Chen was whooping.

And Vladimir had packed up all his dresses and makeup, and was crouching down, whistling *Highway to Hell.*

As for Miki, she was sitting on a stool at one of the tables, drawing faces in a mound of sand.

'Please listen to me!' Dr. Mesmer called out in an unusually forceful voice. 'I need you all to listen!'

No one paid any attention.

Nurse Polk clapped her hands together. Rather than bringing silence, the action fanned the flames of frenzy.

Mesmer stood up on a chair.

'I have a surprise,' he said, in a whisper.

Silence instantly prevailed.

The patients fell into line. Some of them were trembling. Others were fidgeting, or were jumping up and down.

'Tell us! Oh, please tell us!' begged Tanaka the turnip.

'What is it?!' yelled Vladimir and Bart both at once.

'It's waiting outside,' said the psychiatrist.

'In the garden?' Victoria asked.

'No, not in the garden. Outside... on the street. In Rue Ravignan.'

Tanaka-san fell down on the floor. The sense of surprise was too much for him to take.

Mr. Park and Mr. Kim looked terrified.

'We are not allowed to go outside,' they said, one at a time.

'But this is a special occasion,' Dr. Mesmer said. 'And it *is* allowed because I shall be with you.'

'Why are we going outside?' asked Mrs. Ito.

'Because we are going on a journey,' said Mesmer.

'To see the queen?' blurted Chen.

'No... not to see the queen, but to visit the countryside.'

'Can I take my teaspoon?' Bart asked.

'Yes, of course you may,' the nurse replied.

Leading the way into the hall and out through the security doors, Dr. Mesmer stood poised on the doorstep. His face pale, his heart beating ferociously, he took a deep breath, and then waved a hand toward the minibus waiting at the kerb.

The driver got out and opened the sliding passenger door.

A minute later, all the patients were seated inside, and the doors were locked.

'Are we going to New York?' said Chen. 'I have always wanted to go to New York.'

Nurse Polk held a fingertip to her lips.

'We need to all be quiet,' she said, 'because being quiet is part of the surprise.'

Dr. Mesmer said something to the driver.

'*Oui, je connais bien la route,*' he replied.

'*On y va,*' the psychiatrist said, and the minibus began to move down Rue Ravignan.

91

HAVING BEEN AT the Japanese embassy when it was razed to the ground, the fearless reporter from the *Asahi Shimbun* had gleaned that Mesmer and his patients were in grave danger. After all, the protesters were yelling in one voice, demanding that Miki Suzuki be handed over to them without delay.

His taxi speeding up the hill towards the little asylum, Kinjo suddenly saw a line of familiar faces in the windows of a passing black Peugeot minibus. He pointed at the vehicle.

'Follow!' he exclaimed. 'Follow the bus!'

Spinning the wheel sharply through his hands, the driver did as requested.

As the taxi steered off Rue Ravignan, the first protesters arrived at the asylum.

Jeering, shouting, chanting insults and threats, they hammered at the door.

There was no answer.

'Let's break it down!' screamed a short woman at the front of the pack.

Ten seconds later, the door was hanging off its hinges and the protesters were flooding inside. While they ransacked the asylum, setting fire to furniture and bedding, the Japanese Ground Defence Force arrived.

Charged with adrenalin, and in full combat gear, the eight members of the elite unit attacked.

Donning gas masks, they hurled stun grenades into the building. Weapons at the ready, they charged inside – on a life or death mission to bring Miki Suzuki home.

92

THE ROTTWEILER'S PRIME-TIME documentary sent shock waves through Japanese society.

The programme had three main effects.

The first was that donations poured in from ordinary viewers, to enable the Suzuki family to travel to France.

The second was that all French products were removed from sale in Japanese stores.

And the third: pro-Miki demonstrators, who had rushed to Tokyo from all over the country, and had surrounded the headquarters of the Angel Flower Beauty Company, were demanding the chairman's head.

93

BATTERED, BRUISED, AND limping on a bloodied foot, Hideo Tottori made his way to a public phone across from the Arc de Triomphe.

He gave a number to the operator.

A minute after, he was put through to the emergency action hotline at the ministry in Tokyo. After identifying himself, he said:

'It is with extreme regret that I must inform my superiors… that our mission on Avenue Hoche, Paris, has been destroyed.'

On the other end of the line, a deep male voice sounded displeased.

'Casualties?' it asked indignantly.

Fighting back his tears, the first secretary replied:

'All staff accounted for.'

'Instruct immediate return to Japan.'

Hideo Tottori took half a step back from the telephone and bowed.

'Instruction understood, sir,' he said.

94

THE DRIVE THROUGH the Paris suburbs seemed to calm the patients. It was as though there was therapeutic advantage to forward movement.

All eyes were trained on the world outside.

Gradually, the ugly high rises and graffiti-strewn flyovers of the *banlieues* gave way to fields, planted with young crops of barley and wheat. There were tumbledown barns and scarecrows, too, and piercing church steeples, dairy cows, and swathes of endless forest, all luxuriant and green.

Vladimir tut-tutted all the way from Montmartre to the turning for Fontainebleau. His expression rancorous, and his hands twingeing, he regarded Nurse Polk with a spiteful stare.

'What is the matter, Vladimir?' she snapped, irritated.

'My dresses do not like to travel,' the Russian riposted tersely. 'And I don't have the outfit for Safari Barbie.'

'I am sure it will all be fine.'

'No, it will not! If I can't be Safari Barbie everyone will laugh at me!' Vladimir was nudged hard in the ribs by Bart, which silenced him.

'Are we going to New York?' said Chen, repeating himself. 'I hope we are going to New York. I want to see the Big Apple. And I want to take a big bite of it.'

'*No,*' Mesmer responded firmly. 'We are *not* going to America. We are going to Bourgogne.'

'To Barcelona?' Victoria asked.

'No, to *Bourgogne,*' said the psychiatrist, 'to my country house.'

95

FRENCH TELEVISION BROADCAST live shots of the protesters responsible for torching the Japanese embassy as they stormed north towards the Montmartre asylum.

Filming from a helicopter, France-24 captured the moment that the elegant stone building was breached – first by protesters, and then by the Ground Defence Force.

The discovery that a crack Japanese commando unit was on the scene enraged the French government, which had not been informed in advance of their presence. At the Elysée Palace, the covert mission was being regarded as nothing short of an open act of war.

Meanwhile, his team having stormed the Montmartre asylum, the unit commander relayed the unpopular news to his superior that Miki Suzuki was not to be found inside.

In Tokyo, this information was immediately regarded as proof that their national heroine was being held in a secret military installation by the French government.

As the hours passed, Paris, the suburbs, and beyond, were emptied of Asian visitors and even of diehard Asian Francophiles who had lived in France for decades. A great many resorted to disguise before travelling elsewhere, by car, bus, train or plane.

With tensions running so high, no one with even the faintest hint of almond eyes was safe. Vigilante groups and lone revolutionaries were out, hunting anyone who looked to them the least bit Japanese.

96

HAVING WATCHED THE pictures in real time, Dr. Maurice Flaubert, one of the psychiatrists who had visited Mesmer's hospital only days before, agreed to give an interview to the media.

A specialist in the psychiatric treatment of clinical addiction, Flaubert found himself in a news studio. Dazzled by the lights, and his mouth a little dry, the doctor listened as the newscaster gave a résumé of his considerable expertise, then asked:

'The whole of France has been preoccupied with the case of Miki Suzuki, and her rampage through Louis Vuitton. Could you describe to us her underlying psychiatric condition?'

Flaubert leaned back in his chair.

'I had the opportunity of making a cursory examination of this woman very recently,' he said. 'And I can say with a large degree of certainty that she is suffering from what we call "Paris Syndrome".'

The presenter touched a hand to her hair. It had been sprayed so copiously that nothing would have moved it.

'*Paris Syndrome?*' she repeated in bewilderment.

'A severe psychological condition... increasingly prevalent among Japanese and other Asians visiting our magnificent capital.'

'But what causes this syndrome, doctor?'

Again, Flaubert leaned back. Taking his time in responding, he allowed the camera to feast on his intellectual superiority.

'Obsession,' he said, mouthing the syllables thoughtfully. 'An extreme obsession with Paris. An intoxicated sense of awe at its architecture, its customs, and its general *joie de vivre*. Paris Syndrome is a manic inability to make sense of it all.'

The newscaster shrugged.

'But it sounds as though it would be harmless,' she said.

The comment was a red rag to a bull.

With the French nation watching, Dr. Maurice Flaubert erupted. '*Harmless?!*' he wailed. 'Do you have any idea what you are saying, you imbecilic creature? Paris Syndrome is among the most misunderstood and most dangerous of all psychological conditions. Did you not see the woman's rampage for yourself?!'

Up in the gallery, the news editor thrust a fist in the air.

'This guy's going to send our ratings off the charts!' he yelled.

97

HIS EXPRESSION AS taut as a poker-face, the taxi driver steered down the highway, stopping only at the toll booths.

Never once did he enquire why the Japanese passenger reclining on the back seat had wanted to follow what had seemed to be a random minibus. Nor did he ask where the journey might end.

Michi Kinjo might have been worried at how he would ever justify the expense of an extended taxi ride. But his gut was telling him to go where the story took him... and his mentor, the editor at the *Kagoshima Shinpo*, had insisted there was nothing as important as following a journalistic gut.

So, calmly, Kinjo watched the French landscape unfold.

A few dozen yards ahead, the Peugeot minibus was bursting with anticipation, fear, claustrophobia and general pandemonium. Both the nurse and the doctor were doing their level best to keep the passengers quiet, but they dared not stop. Their worst nightmare was that the patients would have a chance of mingling with the general populace.

As the minibus sped past the small picturesque town of Avallon, Vladimir took off his silky crimson dress, followed by his underwear.

He planned to change into his Barbie Swimsuit attire, in place of the safari costume.

While the other patients screamed and shrieked and laughed, Dr. Mesmer insisted that the Russian put the garments back on.

The only one who failed to show any interest or emotion was Miki. Sitting alone on the very last seat, hands in her lap, her eyes were focussed out on the road.

She was daydreaming of a journey made across an ocean in a cast iron bath, a bath with a mast, and a sail made from calico rags. Waves lapping up over the sides, she steered the vessel through the eye of a storm. After almost drowning a thousand times, her makeshift boat reached a desert island.

Approaching it, Miki jerked out the plug, and the bath was instantly marooned on a reef. And, as she waded through shallow water, and up onto the platinum-white sand, she heard what sounded like singing. Craning her head back, hand shading her eyes from the sun, Miki spied the silhouette of a giant bird, its feathers made from brass.

'Miki!' the metal bird called down, 'come with me and I shall take you to the treasure you seek.'

98

NEWS THAT THE Japanese embassy in Paris had been destroyed spread like wildfire through the diplomatic world.

Condemnation and reprisals followed incomprehension.

And, while ambassadors, ministers, and talk show guests debated the situation, the matter reached the General Assembly of the United Nations in New York.

Stepping up to the podium, the Japanese representative denounced the French government for seeking to gain political mileage for its own ends.

As he did so, far away on the edge of Sendai, Mrs. Suzuki was packing her overnight case. She took three changes of clothes, a pair of woollen mittens that she had knitted herself and, without quite knowing why, she packed her passport as well.

'I shall only be away for a few days,' she said to her husband. 'I do not like to leave you with Ojiichan, but I do not have a choice.'

Standing beside the window of the bedroom, Miki's father was even more subdued than usual.

'Please tell them in Tokyo that Miki has done nothing wrong,' he said.

'They know that. Everyone loves her,' Mrs. Suzuki replied.

'But the French people want to harm her.'

'And that is why I must go to Tokyo... to make sure they give us our daughter back.'

99

THE LONG SHADOWS of late afternoon shrouded a slim stretch of road, as it meandered through villages and up into the hills.

Having staved off the combined anxieties of his passengers, Dr. Mesmer found himself pondering a childhood spent in the forests and the vineyards of rustic Bourgogne.

He remembered lazy days down at the canal, scorching afternoons of straw hats and sawn-off shorts. Glimpsing back forty years, he thought of the long moonlit walks across muddy fields, to watch Céleste, the girl he loved, riding her horse at dawn.

He could still see her clearly.

Alabaster skin, a hint of pink on the cheeks, and posture so perfect that she was like a bronze figurine. He had never loved anyone half as much.

Mesmer got a sudden flash of a church, a hearse, and a lace veil in black. His stomach knotting, he still felt the pain, and could remember every detail of that morning – the morning his beloved Céleste left the mortal world.

100

As soon as Dr. Maurice Flaubert had left the studios of France-24, he was invited on three more news channels.

His apparent knowledge of Miki Suzuki's condition, and his explosive interview style, made him the perfect talk show guest. While he toured the media, a crew from TF1 crisscrossed the capital, trawling for vox-pop. Their aim was to get to the bottom of the Paris Syndrome, a condition that was suddenly on everyone's lips.

In Montparnasse, they marched into the popular bar Le Falstaff, and asked the barman what he knew. Rinsing a glass, his eyes little more than bloodshot pinpricks in a tired old face, he coughed.

'Paris Syndrome is a smokescreen,' he said under his breath. 'A Chinese smokescreen.'

'But the LV Attacker was *Japanese*,' the reporter explained.

'Of course she was,' the barman replied in a husky voice. 'And that my friend is why the Chinese are so sly.'

The crew spoke to a taxi driver next.

'We should hunt down all the Asians and chase them from France!' he cried, feeding the steering wheel listlessly through callused hands, as he turned right towards Concorde.

Then they asked a homeless man on Rue de Rivoli for his impression.

'Paris *what?*'

'*Syndrome,*' the reporter said fast.

'I blame the government.'

'The Japanese government?'

Rearranging his clutch of plastic bags, the drifter shook his head hard – left, right, left.

'The *French* government.'

'Why?'

'Because they didn't let the spaceships land,' he said.

101

THE MINIBUS SPED through a tunnel carved from a jagged outcrop of granite, through forests and fields, and finally reached the small village of Villars Fontaine.

'You turn left after the church,' Mesmer said to the driver. 'It's the little chateau on the right.'

A minute or two later, the vehicle was parked on a patch of grass across from a fine stone house. A picture of Burgundian simplicity, it dated back to the seventeenth century. The roofs were grey slate, the façade weatherworn and so perfectly serene.

The minibus's door slid open and the patients hurried out.

Tanaka started running about in figure eights.

Mr. Park and Mr. Kim got down on the grass and rolled around.

'Is this New York?' asked Mr. Chen.

'This is Chateau Lugny,' Mesmer replied. 'It's where I grew up.'

Unlocking the front door with a great iron key, he called the patients to follow him.

Miki was the last to go inside.

In her mind, she was pacing through a forest on the desert island. The brass bird had coaxed her to eat a magical fruit, known as *Limbu-Limbu*. It had turned Miki's skin a curious shade of violet, and made her head feel very contrary indeed.

'Do you want to dance?' Mr. Chen asked her when she crossed the threshold. 'I always like to dance when I am in New York.'

As if in a dream, Miki walked over to the far end of the great reception hall. She stood at the fireplace and warmed her hands on invisible flames, her eyes quite glazed over.

'I feel different,' she said in a voice so faint that no one heard it except for her.

Vladimir bounded over. He had changed into his sequinned miniskirt.

'The doctor is going to sell us,' he said. 'That's his plan. To sell us to gangsters.'

'I feel different,' Miki said again. 'I feel as if I am made of glass.'

The Russian peered into the grate where the invisible flames were warming them both.

'The gangsters won't like that,' he said.

A few hundred yards from where they were standing, Michi Kinjo got out of the taxi at the top of the lane, having paid the three-figure bill with the last of his cash. Instructing the driver to return to Paris, he asked him to tell no one of the journey.

Then, having worried for a moment about his hotel room near Gare du Nord, he ran down the lane in the direction of Chateau Lugny.

102

Mrs. Suzuki took the Sakura Shinkansen from Sendai to Tokyo, where she caught the subway to the NHK headquarters in Shibuya. By the time she reached her destination, she was fraught with worry.

All she had ever wanted was a quiet life, a life not visited by catastrophe or public attention – and now the entire national media was looming down on her family.

Slipping through the doors of the grim glass building, the quiet unassuming housewife made her way to the recption desk in the busy meeting hall.

'I have come to see Miss Sasaki – Noriko Sasaki-san,' she said.

'What is your name?'

'I am Mrs. Suzuki from near Sendai, in Miyagi Prefecture. I am the mother of Miki Suzuki and...'

Before she could utter another word, Mrs. Suzuki was being mobbed by dozens of people. They all had the same question:

Where is Miki?

As Mrs. Suzuki struggled to answer, a woman in black lurched forwards in a beeline from the elevators to the reception desk. Elbowing anyone in her way, she approached Miki's mother, welcomed her, spun her round, and led her back to the revolving door.

'We will go straight to the airport,' she said firmly. 'The crew is waiting for us outside. Every minute is precious.'

'*Airport?*' said the old woman. 'But where are we going?'

'To Paris!' the Rottweiler exclaimed. 'To get Miki back!'

103

CREEPING DOWN THE lane to Chateau Lugny, the *Asahi Shimbun*'s intrepid reporter made his way over to one of the windows.

He peered in.

Inside, in the great hall, there were numerous figures. Most of them appeared to be highly agitated – dancing about, running, ranting, or lying spreadeagled on the parquet floor. All of them were wearing matching white tunics, all but a large hirsute man who was dressed in a cheap shiny miniskirt.

To get a better view of the far end of the room, Kinjo changed windows. There, he saw Dr. Mesmer in the same dark wool suit he had been wearing when they met. Standing between him and the fireplace was a nurse. Next to them, a young woman was crying, hands up on her head.

It was Miki.

His heart racing, the reporter struggled frantically to come up with a viable plan. He couldn't just run in, snatch Miki, and run out. If he wasn't apprehended in the act of grabbing her, there was a danger that she herself would sound the alarm, as she had done back in Paris.

Then Kinjo caught a flash of memory – the editorial office at Okinawa's finest, the *Kagoshima Shinpo*.

Rubbing a hand to his scraggly beard, his mentor, the editor-in-chief, was reminding him yet again to be prepared.

So, retreating into the village, he found a quiet room for the night. It was a world away from the raucous Albanians at the hotel near Gare du Nord.

Back in the chateau, Nurse Polk emptied half a dozen assorted cans into a pot, and did her best to scrape them together into a meal. Mesmer was sitting quietly on a chair in a back room. Having forgotten to bring his mobile phone, which was back at the hospital, he now realized that the only way forward was to be out of touch.

As a consequence, he had no idea that the little asylum on Rue Ravignan, that he had founded and run for twenty years, was nothing more than a burned-out shell.

Nor was he aware that all over France ordinary people were hunting the Louis Vuitton Attacker – the woman they claimed had single-handedly led to the devastation of Japanese–French relations.

The motivation for the hunt was wounded national pride.

But it was financial as well.

Le Figaro had offered twenty thousand euros to anyone providing information that would lead to Miki's capture.

104

THAT EVENING, AS the patients sat down to their bread and canned stew, the President of France went on national TV. Speaking from the *Salon doré* at the Elysée Palace, his hands resting on the red leather table-top, he stared straight into the camera.

'Distinguished and honourable people of the great Republic of France,' he began, the text scrolling down on the Autocue, 'I address you at a precarious moment in the Republic's history.

'Our majestic nation finds itself embittered by circumstance, the lives of us all touched by enmity.'

The President took a sip of water, and focussed back on the Autocue's text:

'The reasons are various and intertwined. Like the roots of a tree, they sink down, layer through layer to the bedrock of our glorious past.

'I call upon every man, woman, and child to stand together as one, so that this proud and mighty nation may rise above its sordid detractors from the East.'

105

SPOONING A LUMP of meat into his mouth, the South African licked his lips. Then his face lurched round to the window, as he wondered where to dig. Just as he was about to stuff the precious teaspoon into his pocket, Dr. Mesmer stood up.

'I want to welcome you all to Chateau Lugny,' he said softly, 'the place that I love more than anywhere else on this earth. It was here that I learned to ride a bicycle, and how to dance and...' he said, his face warming with the moment, 'it's here that I had my first kiss.'

The patients burst out laughing. Some of them stamped their feet. Others waved their hands in the air.

Only Miki failed to react.

She sat at the end of the table, staring into space.

A little later, as darkness enveloped the chateau, the patients climbed into their beds. The doctor checked on them all before turning out the lights. He found himself answering a barrage of questions, about talking trees and dancing mice, starlit kisses and about New York.

The last room that he went to was the one where Miki was lying under the covers on an old mahogany bedstead.

'I'll tell you a secret,' Mesmer said tenderly. 'That bed in which you will sleep tonight was *my* bed when I was a child.'

Miki rearranged the pillow under her head.

'I am feeling different,' she said, 'and rather confused.'

'How so?'

'As if I had sailed away across an ocean to a distant land, a land where I was ordinary – just like everyone else.'

Dr. Mesmer touched a hand to the bedpost.

'It's because of the magic,' he said. 'The magic of Chateau Lugny.'

106

DAYS AND NIGHTS of demonstrations at the Angel Flower Beauty Company had exacted a heavy toll.

Most of the staff had fled in fear of their lives. Almost all the lower windows had been smashed, the building having been pelted with homemade missiles. Members of the public had flooded in from all over Japan in their droves, to hurl Angel Flower beauty products at the firm they regarded as the ultimate manifestation of evil.

Up on the executive floor, Pun-Pun sat huddled in a corner with Noemi. They were hugged together like survivors adrift on the high seas. With the electricity cut off, they were in total darkness.

Down below, whooping and hollering, were the mob.

In his own office, the chairman was seated straight-backed at his desk, as though he were about to dictate a memo. Weighed down by a sense of honour and duty to the firm, he was prepared to go down with the ship.

Even if he and the handful of others had wanted to escape, it was too late.

The protesters had sealed off all escape routes.

Enraged by the cold-hearted nature of the once celebrated Angel Flower, a frail white-haired woman from Fukuoka made her way around to the back of the office building. With granddaughters about the same age as Miki, she had been unable to sit at home and watch the demonstration from afar.

Travelling the long distance north to the capital by Shinkansen, she had brought with her nothing more than a nylon daypack. Having reached the south side of the building, shrouded in darkness and mist, she opened up the bag, and pulled out a bottle.

It was half-filled with clear liquid.

Stuffing a rag down the neck, as she had learned to do during the War, she lit it with a match. And, with all her strength she flung the projectile into a broken window.

Three minutes later, the south side of Angel Flower headquarters was ablaze.

Five minutes after that, the entire building was on fire.

As the flames licked the night, the white-haired woman grunted to herself, turned on her heel, and set off for home.

107

SHORTLY BEFORE DAWN, Miki woke with a start.

A soft voice was calling to her.

Sitting up in bed, she strained to listen.

'Come to the window,' it said. 'Come to the window where I am waiting.'

Climbing out of the mahogany bed, Miki went over to the window and scanned the darkness. There was nothing unusual – just moonlight and the silhouettes of the trees.

'Who are you?' she said.

The voice came again, a little louder than before.

'I am *you*, Miki,' it replied.

'What do you want?'

'For you to know that you are complete again.'

'I do not understand.'

The voice melted away and, after waiting for what seemed like an eternity, Miki slipped back into bed.

108

BEFORE THE PATIENTS were up next morning, Dr. Mesmer went into the village and bought supplies at the little grocer's on the corner. A time capsule of rural life, it hadn't changed in decades.

There were wooden tubs packed with vegetables, shelves stacked with canned food, glass jars filled with bonbons, and tattered cardboard displays from half a lifetime ago.

The shop was owned by Monsieur Leblonde. He was as old as time, the skin on his face made from elephant hide, his legs swollen, and the feet below them stuffed into a pair of fraying bedroom slippers.

Like everyone else, he was eager for first-hand news from Paris.

'I hear there's a second Revolution!' he exclaimed, wiping his face with a dishcloth. 'But this time it's against the damned Chinese.'

'*Japanese*,' Mesmer corrected. 'I understand it began with a woman from Japan.'

The grocer wiped again.

'They are all the same,' he said.

At the *boulangerie* next door, the doctor got chatting to the baker's wife. A customer ambled in and held the morning paper up between his thumbs.

'Have you seen?' he asked with a shrug. 'Paris has gone crazy. The protesters are smashing every Japanese car, and are demanding that Japanese wear special badges so that people don't confuse them with the Chinks.'

Dr. Mesmer shook his head in despair.

'Like the Germans did with the Jews?' he said.

109

AT THE CHATEAU, the patients had all clustered down in the kitchen and were waiting for breakfast.

They seemed far more subdued than usual.

Seated at the table, Mr. Park and Mr. Kim were having a conversation about politics. And, beside them, Victoria was telling Bart about a journey she had made to Moscow twenty years before. Tanaka-san was standing still, and was not doing figure eights. Rather, he was telling the pair of Japanese ladies about the taste of peach ice cream in Venice.

And, even though the Russian had not apparently suffered from Paris Syndrome, he was now quite normal, too. This led Dr. Mesmer to deduce that his behaviour had indeed been affected by another form of the condition.

Gone were the flamboyant dresses, the cheap paste jewellery and makeup. Instead, Vladimir was sitting on a stool near the stove, dressed in the standard white uniform like everyone else.

As for Miki, she was sitting outside on the lawn, her mind filled with memories of Miyagi Prefecture.

She saw her parents watching TV, and her ojiichan dozing in the corner, his teeth in his lap. It was as though she had been reunited with a world that had strayed from her grasp – as if she was home.

Nurse Polk greeted Mesmer as he entered with the provisions and fresh bread.

'It's astonishing,' she said.

'What is?'

'They are all at peace.'

The doctor glanced around the room, then out onto the grass. He put down the provisions.

'A good day for New York,' he said.

'*New York?*' replied Chen, confused. 'Are you planning a journey, doctor?'

Stepping through to the hall, the psychiatrist called out through the window.

'How are you feeling, Miki?'

Turning slowly, she smiled.

'I feel like a weight has been lifted from my shoulders,' she said.

110

WITH NO DIRECT flights between Japan and France, the NHK crew were forced to fly to Brussels and take the train from there to Paris.

Even then, they were met with a glacial reception by French border police. Refusing to give an inch, the Rottweiler cited the Geneva Convention of Human Rights. Then, charging through, she led Mrs. Suzuki and her film crew ahead.

In the French capital they were turned away from a string of leading hotels, the managements fearing reprisals for taking in Japanese. After much pleading, the general manager of The Bristol conceded, and gave them accommodation. And he only did so because the Rottweiler, half-joking, threatened to burn the establishment down herself if they were not taken in at once.

As soon as they had registered, they headed out in search of Miki.

The streets were strewn with the smouldering remains of Toyotas, Mazdas, Suzukis and Lexuses. Billboards advertising Japanese brands had been defaced and, every few blocks, there were great bonfires of melted and charred electronics.

Leading the way through backstreets to Avenue Hoche, the NHK leader found herself staring with blank horror at the remains of what had been a key diplomatic mission.

The cameraman was setting up his equipment, when a posse of protesters stormed angrily up.

'Are you Japanese?!' they demanded.

Cool as a cucumber, the Rottweiler waved a hand at the embassy remains dismissively.

'*Nihao!*' she said. 'No, we are from Shanghai... and we *hate* the Japanese. We spit on them – *pah!*'

The vigilantes grunted approval and continued on.

When they were gone, Miki's mother clutched her handbag to her chest and declared:

'French people are aggressive.'

'They do not like Japanese,' the soundman mumbled.

'They will regret the day they declared war on our culture!' the Rottweiler exclaimed with a snarl.

111

MICHI KINJO, TOO, was hiding beneath a cloak of borrowed Chinese identity.

The couple who owned the auberge where he had spent the night had asked for his passport. The journalist was fumbling for it in his money-belt when the woman held up a hand and said cautiously:

'You are not Japanese, of course?'

'Er, um, no, no,' Kinjo had lied, sucking in air noisily. 'No, no, I am... I am... am... Chinese... from Shintao.'

Slipping from the auberge, Kinjo then hurried through Villars Fontaine, until he reached the chateau. With the spring sun high in a clear sky, he crept along the wall until he reached a side window.

Nurse Polk was giving an exercise class in the hall. For the first time ever, the patients were following her lead.

Standing at the back of the room, Dr. Mesmer was making notes in his journal in miniature black script. He was about to go through to the kitchen, when he noticed the silhouette of a man hovering at the window outside.

He crept out through the front door, and walked around the house, approaching the Japanese reporter from behind.

Mesmer coughed.

Kinjo turned.

'Doctor Kin...'

'Jo... Kinjo.'

'Yes, of course... Dr. Kinjo... may I ask you what are you doing here in Villars Fontaine?' Mesmer asked in surprise.

'I, er, um,' Kinjo replied, sucking through both sides of his mouth at once. 'I am... er... well...'

'You are?'

Kinjo wove his fingers together and thrust them up to his head, wiping his perspiring brow.

'I am here to offer you my services,' he said.

Dr. Mesmer took a step back.

'But how did you know I was here... that *we* were here?'

The young reporter flexed his back muscles and, leaning forward, he bowed.

'It was a lucky guess,' he replied.

112

IN MORE NORMAL circumstances, Mesmer might have been more inquisitive. But he was so eager to share the morning's findings, that he led Kinjo by the arm inside and pointed at the patients.

They were in the middle of the exercise routine.

'Look at them!' the psychiatrist said. 'They were as mad as hatters a day or so ago. And now... well... now they are almost normal.'

Kinjo frowned.

'The Paris Syndrome is gone?'

'Yes. Vanished.'

'It's as though a spell has been broken.'

'How?'

Dr. Mesmer scribbled a detail in his journal, crossed it out, and scribbled again.

'The Syndrome is rooted in the mania, the fixation – by, with and for, Paris. Take them out of the capital and the mania subsides,' he said, adding: 'Of course I knew that had to be the case. But I believed it was necessary to begin to remedy their condition prior to them departing.'

Michi Kinjo motioned towards Miki, who was stretching her hands out to the sides.

'Is she cured as well?'

'It appears so. Although I will spend the next day or two conducting systematic interviews.' Mesmer smiled inquisitively. 'Perhaps you would help me,' he said.

113

AFTER FINDING THE embassy destroyed, the Rottweiler put her nose to the ground and got down to searching for a fresh scent.

'How ever will we find Miki?' Mrs. Suzuki moaned.

'We may never find her,' the soundman whimpered.

'I think she is in danger,' the cameraman broke in.

NHK's star reporter shook her head.

'I know what to do,' she said.

'What? What can we do?' asked Mrs. Suzuki.

'We will go on television,' the Rottweiler said.

114

THE FIRST PATIENT to be interviewed was Mr. Chen.

He had been under Mesmer's treatment for five months. And, in that time, he had exhibited increasingly eccentric symptoms. These had begun with the well-documented postbox episode, and had culminated in Chen pulling the heads and limbs off all Vladimir's

Barbie dolls, and attempting to chop the remains into little pieces with a sharpened spoon.

When asked why he had done such a dreadful thing, he replied: 'Because the dolls told me to do it.'

Seated in a back room, with Mesmer and Kinjo on the other side of a long dining table, Chen looked down at his lap.

'Did I go crazy?' he asked.

'*When?*'

'In Paris.'

The psychiatrist looked at him hard, taking in his horn-rim spectacles and the broken veins on his cheeks.

'It depends what you mean by "crazy",' he said. 'You were affected by Paris in a most fundamental way.'

'And now?'

'And now... I would say that you are as sane as anyone else.'

Mr. Chen gave a double thumbs up.

'Can I go home?' he asked.

'I don't see why not,' said Mesmer.

115

THE NEXT PATIENT to come in was Victoria.

Like Chen, she appeared tense, as though guilty of embarrassing behaviour at an office party of which she had no firm recollection.

Sitting gingerly on the straight-backed chair, she put her hands on the table-top, and splayed her fingers apart.

'I do not know what you did to me, doctor,' she said, 'but I feel as though I have been reborn.'

'The country air,' Mesmer replied. 'It has magical effects.'

116

Miki was the next to enter.

In one motion, she shuffled from the door and into the seat.

As she trundled in, Kinjo desperately tried to conceive a plan – one that would culminate in his rescuing Miki Suzuki in the name of the *Asahi Shimbun*.

'How are you feeling now, Miki?' Mesmer asked.

'As though I were a caged bird that has been set free into the forest,' she said.

'Are you thinking about your home in Sendai?' Dr. Kinjo enquired.

Miki Suzuki looked out of the window and blushed – the deepest reddest blush of her life.

'Yes, I am thinking of my family,' she answered. 'But there is something else I am thinking of, too. Or, rather, *someone*.'

'*Someone?*' Dr. Mesmer asked, scribbling.

'Someone I met in Paris. Before I was robbed. He was very kind to me.'

'What was his name?'

'He was called Hugo, and...'

'*And?*'

'And...' again Miki blushed. 'And I love him,' she said.

117

A career spent dominating the Japanese media had taught the Rottweiler how to tame what she regarded as no more than a circus act.

Fifteen minutes after leaving the ruins of the Japanese embassy, she had lined up a satellite truck and a prime-time slot on NHK's nightly news. Ten minutes after that, Mrs. Suzuki and the crew were standing outside the Eiffel Tower.

'What are we doing here?' Miki's mother asked, more than a little intimidated by the network's star correspondent.

The Rottweiler slipped in an earpiece, and barked an order into her lapel microphone to a controller back in Shibuya. Then, hurriedly, she brushed her hair, and applied a thick coat of cerise pink to her lips.

'We are going to turn this awful situation around,' she said.

The technician in the satellite truck signalled to the cameraman, who gave a thumbs up. Less than a minute later, Mrs. Suzuki and the Rottweiler were standing in glaring phosphorescent light, with the Eiffel Tower rising up behind them like an enlarged child's toy.

The soundman gave the countdown.

'Five, four, three, two, one...'

He nodded.

Turning into the camera, the Rottweiler greeted her viewers from Paris – the city of lights, the city of love, the city where Japanese were no longer welcome.

'I am standing here behind enemy lines with the bravest of women,' she said, cerise lips pouting. 'Mrs. Suzuki of Sendai knows the pain of losing a daughter to uncertainty in a foreign land, a *hostile* foreign land.'

Having reminded the viewers of Miki's story – not because they needed reminding, but because it added to the drama – the Rottweiler coaxed her tear glands to well forth.

And, tears rolling down her cheeks, she said:

'Arriving in Paris this morning, we heard distressing news. A French newspaper has offered twenty thousand euros – two hundred and fifty thousand yen – to anyone who can capture Miki, *dead or alive!*'

The reporter looked into the camera hard, tears still flowing.

'This is a moment of national honour for all Japanese people,' she said. 'It is a moment that we will remember all our lives, and one that will bring us joy in years to come – because we will know that we did what was courageous and right.'

Through the earpiece, a producer in NHK headquarters demanded that she come to the point.

'And for this reason,' the Rottweiler growled, 'I am asking you – ordinary Japanese people like me – to come to Miki's salvation. The newspaper *Le Figaro* may have offered twenty thousand euros for Miki to be trapped and handed over to them like a convict. But we hope to pledge twice that to anyone who can return Miki Suzuki to us alive and well. And...' the Rottweiler concluded, 'NHK proudly pledges five hundred thousand yen, to begin the campaign!'

There was the muffled squawk of a producer far away yelling down an earpiece.

'Please call in right away and make your pledges now!'

Before the Rottweiler could utter another word, the transmission was cut – the enraged station chief at headquarters having pressed the TERMINATE button himself.

118

IN THE LATE afternoon, Dr. Mesmer sat on the chateau's back porch, his mind lost in thought.

Since his earliest childhood, Lugny had been a realm touched with the greatest magic of all. He caught himself wondering whether the spell of Paris Syndrome had been broken by his ancestral home, or simply by taking the patients far from the French capital.

Perhaps it was a mixture of both.

The question now was how to proceed.

Mesmer smiled at the thought. The answer was simple. Why continue to treat patients in Paris – the one place that amplified their mania – when they could be brought down to Bourgogne to be treated in the calm serenity of Chateau Lugny?

Forcing his head into his hands, the psychiatrist cursed himself for not breaking loose from the capital before. It had been such an obvious move. But, then again, as he reasoned it, half the thrill was to observe the full spectrum of derangement manifested in patients kept at the Montmartre asylum.

119

LYING BACK ON the lawn at the other side of the house, Miki, too, was lost in thought.

She was thinking of Hugo de Montfried. Studying his face a fragment at a time, she lay there half-dreaming, as Kinjo approached.

'Excuse me, Miki-san,' he said, bowing, before lowering himself onto the grass. 'I wanted to thank you.'

'Thank me…?'

'For not revealing me to Dr. Mesmer.' The reporter swallowed nervously. 'I am not a doctor as you know.'

Miki frowned, as though she were trying to make sense of a faded dream.

'Who are you?'

Michi Kinjo stiffened his back.

'I am proud to be a correspondent with the *Asahi Shimbun*,' he said.

'You're a journalist?'

'Yes... and...' he mumbled. 'And... I am hoping that you will come with me.'

'Back to Tokyo... together?'

Miki's expression turned to one of fear.

'I am so confused,' she said.

'Please do not worry,' Kinjo said tenderly. 'I can help you.'

Miki got a flash of Hugo de Montfried.

'The days I spent in Paris are a blur,' she said. 'I remember colours and sounds, a mixture that doesn't make much sense. But there is one thing that I do remember very clearly indeed.'

'Louis Vuitton?' Kinjo prompted.

'No... not that. It is a face, a man's face... the face of Hugo de Montfried.'

120

NO SOONER HAD the Rottweiler's face vanished from their screens, than the people of Japan rushed to telephones and social media to pledge donations.

Some gave a few thousand yen. Others many times more. And, in what later became known as the single most generous act of spontaneous public charity in the history of the nation, a vast sum was amassed.

Within a day of the Rottweiler's plea, the equivalent of three million euros had been promised. And, as the hours ticked by, the donations continued to pour in thick and fast.

Grasping that the campaign to raise money for Miki's salvation was a ratings winner unlike any other, NHK cleared its schedules. They devoted themselves to providing a live minute-by-minute update of the fundraising crusade.

An oversized electronic board flashed the total, the digits no more than a blur as the pledges kept rolling in.

The crème de la crème of the channel's presenters spewed trivia about Miki and her life. Against stirring classical music, they held up photos from the Suzuki family album – Miki as a new-born baby, as a toddler, a high school girl, a graduate. And they interviewed teachers, friends, and even random strangers who could help glimpse into Miki the woman... and Miki the myth.

As the money flooded in, news of the campaign – and the astonishing total – was covered by media the world over.

And it wasn't just the Japanese who were lured by the reward.

French people hurried out into the streets, searching for a slightly built Japanese woman, the one previously known for her Louis Vuitton attack. They scoured local neighbourhoods, looking in supermarkets and bakeries, on park benches, at bus shelters and in public toilets.

With news spreading, people flocked to France from across Europe and far beyond. They came from the Americas and the furthest reaches of Africa, from Arabia and the Far East. As they came, the French economy was boosted by the sharp influx of visitors, all of them searching for Miki Suzuki.

The President of the Republic went on national television once again. This time his address was more conciliatory. Sidestepping what had become known as the 'Japan Issue', he encouraged tourists to France, whatever their motives.

With the Japanese jackpot mounting higher each moment, *Le Figaro* had no choice but to withdraw its own award, which had paled into insignificance. The newspaper tried changing tack, relaunching its prize as *l'Honneur français* – in direct competition with the

Japanese TV award. But they were hopelessly out-gunned by NHK's massive publicity machine.

Fuelled by raw avarice, the search for Miki continued.

As it did so, the posses of zealous anti-Japanese melted into the shadows.

They were replaced by a new breed of Miki-hunters.

Willing to go to any lengths to find their champion, they themselves began brawling with each other, scuffling and sabotaging – in a crazed scramble to find Miki Suzuki and to claim the prize.

121

AT DINNER, MR. Park and Mr. Kim announced that they planned to return to Korea as soon as arrangements could be made. They wanted to see their families again, they said.

Tanaka the turnip and Mrs. Ito echoed a similar ambition, as did Victoria and Mr. Chen. His tongue firmly back in his mouth, Bart let out a giggle – a squeal of melancholy more than it was an expression of joy.

'I don't have a family,' he said.

Vladimir leaned forward and, in an exhibition of fraternity previously unknown, he touched the South African's arm.

'*We* are your family, Bart,' he whispered.

And so it was decided right there and then that, whatever the trials and tribulations that were to come, those dining at the Chateau Lugny would be a family of their own.

Toasting them all with a glass of homemade cordial, Dr. Mesmer said:

'Who's to say who is sane and who is mad, who can see and who is blind? The only thing that is important is that we are honourable and true.'

All of a sudden Dr. Kinjo seemed overcome. Thrusting his head into his hands, he begged forgiveness.

'What is the matter, doctor?' Mesmer asked.

'I have a confession.'

Every eye in the room focussed on the would-be psychiatrist, ears alert.

Rising to his feet, Kinjo bowed acutely – the angle more extreme than any other of his life.

'I have dishonoured you all,' he said.

'What do you mean, Dr. Kinjo?' asked Nurse Polk.

'I must confess something... something terrible.'

'What?' everyone said as one.

Kinjo blushed. He squirmed, clucked and bowed all the more.

'I am not a doctor,' he said.

Mr. Chen put a hand to his mouth. Mrs. Ito screamed.

'Then would you do us the courtesy of introducing yourself?' Dr. Mesmer asked.

His face flushed beetroot-red, his clothing soaked in perspiration, Kinjo replied:

'Michi Kinjo, journalist of *Asahi Shimbun*, sent to France to interview Miki Suzuki and...' he broke off and seemed to freeze for a moment in utter terror. 'And to bring her back home to Japan.'

Miki's eyes welled with tears.

'But I do not want to go home,' she said.

122

THE SUAVE FIGURE of a man was standing beside a cedar bookcase in a palatial private library at the Maison Pastache.

He was holding a copy of *Le Figaro* into the light of an Art Deco lamp, turning it gently as he got towards the end of the front page. Dressed in an immaculate grey gabardine suit, he had an air of rare sophistication, reached through good breeding and much rugged travel to distant climes.

Seated in a deep leather chair a few feet away was a young woman. She was pretty in an obvious sort of way, her complexion so pale that it was almost blue.

'What is the latest news of the Japanese situation, Hugo?' she asked, suggesting that she was more interested than she actually was.

'Hmmm?'

'The Japanese... what are they up to now?'

Comte Hugo de Montfried disliked conversation for the sake of conversation. And nothing tired him more than when his little sister attempted to be worldly. But, most of all, he disliked having to speak in a moment of shock.

'I had not realized,' he muttered. 'That *she*... it was *her*.'

Delphine de Montfried glanced across the rows of shelves. Her mind was on what she would wear for the ball that evening.

'They all look the same to me,' she said listlessly.

'Hmmm?' the Count replied again.

'The Japanese, the Chinese... all those little yellow people. I can't tell them apart.'

Rising to the bait, Hugo de Montfried turned, swishing the now-folded newspaper through the air.

'Of course they do,' he said caustically, 'because you know nothing about them.'

'Well, I know that they make lots of clever little electric things,' Delphine said, 'and that they never stop taking photographs of each other.'

Slipping onto the seat of a davenport beside the window, de Montfried scribbled a message on a sheet of monogrammed letter-paper. Having stuffed it into an envelope, he pressed a button mounted on the wall.

A minute later, an elderly butler was standing to attention in the doorway. Dressed in a black tailcoat, his face was a study in discretion.

'Ah, Claude, I would be grateful if you could do me a little favour.'

'Yes, sir?'

'Could you please take this message across to Monsieur Jacques Pigalle? I think you will find him dining at the Interalliée.'

'Why don't you just call him?' Delphine asked with a sigh.

'Because, dearest sister, some matters are best handled with paper and ink.'

123

In Villars Fontaine, the innkeeper was taking a Pernod at the bar with the baker and the grocer.

They had been moaning about the weather and about their wives. After that, the talk had moved on to their shared condemnation of New World wine.

The conversation lulled, and the baker jabbed a thumb at the TV screen in the corner of the bar. It was streaming pictures of foreigners arriving by the plane-load – all of them joining the frenzied hunt for the Louis Vuitton Attacker.

'Seen that?' he said.

'*What?*' asked the grocer.

'The Japanese situation… the woman who attacked Louis Vuitton.'

'I heard the prize money is four million euros,' said the grocer, draining his glass.

The innkeeper touched a hand to his chin.

'There was an Asian man in the auberge,' he said. 'Eyes like almonds.'

The barmaid, who had overheard the conversation, leaned over.

'She's supposed to be deranged,' she said.

'Who is?' asked the baker.

'The LV Attacker. They say she went mad just by going to Paris!'

The trio of drinkers guffawed at such a thought.

Then the grocer rubbed his head.

'Georges Mesmer,' he said.

'What about him?' the innkeeper asked.

'Well, he's back in the village. He came in this morning to buy some canned food and noodles. Twenty packs of noodles and a lot of cans. Seems as though he has many guests at Chateau Lugny.' He sipped his Pernod. 'And everyone knows that Asians like nothing more than noodles,' he said.

The grocer glanced at the baker, and they both looked at the innkeeper. Then they all turned to the barmaid, who had whipped off her apron.

'Where are you going, Françoise?'

'Down to the chateau, to make myself rich!'

124

JACQUES PIGALLE WAS unusual in that his connections crisscrossed the worlds of politics, diplomacy, and commerce as well. A confidant to the President no less, he was regarded as nothing short of a kingmaker. So aged was he that he could remember Pétain's rule over Vichy France.

Stepping out of a taxi at 10.30 p.m. he was welcomed at once into the salon of Maison Pastache.

Comte de Montfried served his guest a brandy and a cigar.

'Jacques, there is a matter in which I desire your assistance,' he said, after words of pleasantry. 'A delicate matter.'

Pigalle moistened his lips with Calvados, the Coeur de Lion from '74. He breathed in, allowing the vapour to warm his chest.

'I am at your service, as always,' he replied.

'The Japanese trouble,' the Comte mused.

'The burning of cars... the destruction of relations between Paris and Tokyo?'

De Montfried rolled his eyes.

'All of that,' he said. 'And the cause of it all...'

'The Attack?'

'Louis Vuitton.'

Pigalle grinned.

'They are calling it "*Syndrome de Paris*",' he said.

'So I hear. And now there's a four million euro prize to find the girl.'

'I understand that it's gone up to five million.'

Hugo de Montfried pinched the end of his nose, then glanced down at the interlocking pattern of the Persian carpet, a silk one from Shiraz.

'Is that so?'

'It's hysteria, of course,' Pigalle said.

'I'd like you to find her for me, Jacques,' said de Montfried without looking up from the floor.

His old friend sipped, frowned, then narrowed his eyes.

'I wouldn't have imagined you needed the cash.'

The Comte forced back a smile.

'I met her,' he said.

'The LV Attacker?'

'Her name is Miki… Miki Suzuki.'

'Were you hunting her?'

De Montfried held the cut crystal glass to the light, inspecting the vintage Calvados.

'She was at the George V bar, and then again at the Musée Nissim de Camondo,' he replied. 'Providence was forcing us together. I could feel it more keenly than I have ever felt anything before.'

'What was she like?'

'All nervous and shy.'

'Was she… you know – *deranged*?'

'No, no. She was an angel.'

Jacques Pigalle looked into his host's eyes.

'Am I witnessing the rare delight of true love?' he asked.

Hugo de Montfried put down his glass and smoothed a hand back over his hair.

'Perhaps you are,' he said.

125

IN VILLARS FONTAINE there was no such thing as a secret.

By the time the three friends and the barmaid reached the lane in which Chateau Lugny was found, they had been joined by forty other villagers.

Among them there were farmers armed with riding crops and hoes, old widows in their aprons, carpenters and vintners, stable hands and drunkards, landlords and even the local postman.

Some of them were clutching torches, others hurricane lamps. A few stragglers were stumbling behind the main group. Streaming forward from their homes, the throng turned into a posse with its own momentum. Chanting, heckling, singing, the villagers were united by a rare sense of purpose, one that had the possibility of making them all rich.

At the front was the innkeeper.

A pressurized kerosene lamp in his hand delivered a sweeping arc of platinum light, waking the birds roosting in the trees. Banishing the shadows as it moved fitfully down the lane, it gave an almost ethereal dimension to the surging multitude.

By chance, Nurse Polk was at the kitchen window filling the kettle at the tap. Lost in her own world, she was thinking of an elderly aunt who had once given her a brooch in the shape of a mermaid. Her gaze drifting towards the darkness, she saw the silvery lamplight and the irregular silhouettes of people.

Rushing into the salon, she raised the alarm.

Dr. Mesmer was sitting there with Kinjo, a glass of Hautes-Côtes de Nuits in his hand, and a mild rebuke on his tongue.

He hurried through to the kitchen.

'Oh my God!' he roared. 'They've come for Miki!'

'Who have come?' Kinjo asked quickly.

'The villagers…'

Clutching his hands together, Mesmer thought for a fraction of a second.

'She will have to escape – right now! And *you* will have to go with her!'

Mesmer tore upstairs and snatched Miki from her bed.

'You have to leave! *Now!*'

Rubbing her eyes, Miki sat up.

'What time is it?' she asked distantly.

'Time to go! There are people – *bad people* – out there now. They are hunting you!'

'*Me?*'

'Yes!'

Miki stepped over to the window and saw a sea of shadows and silhouettes.

'*Them?*'

Mesmer led her downstairs by the arm. Within a minute they were at the back door with Kinjo.

'Where shall we go?' asked the journalist.

Again, the doctor paused to think. On the front side of the chateau the sound of the rabble was getting louder.

'Go through the forest and over the field,' he said quickly. 'Keep in a straight line until you come to the main road.'

'Which way do we go… on the road, which way?' Kinjo asked.

'Left. Go left. Take a bus. Hitchhike… *anything*. It'll take you to Dijon.' He pulled out his wallet and handed the journalist a wad of fifty-euro bills. 'From Dijon you take a train.'

'A train to where?' Miki asked.

'*Anywhere.* Go anywhere,' Mesmer exclaimed. 'Go anywhere – except Paris!'

126

IN HER ROOM at The Bristol, the Rottweiler spent much of the night on the phone to NHK headquarters.

The appeal for funds had exceeded anything the station had ever known – in both the amount of money and the publicity it had generated. And, savouring the moment, the ferocious reporter had wanted to make sure that the great and the good knew it had been her idea.

Towards the end of the conversation, a fearful executive on the other end of the line cooed praise. Then he spat out a number, the running total of money pledged. The evening had seen a sudden and unexpected surge – the grand total standing at two billion yen, almost fifteen million euros.

The Rottweiler punched a muscular fist in the air.

'Tomorrow afternoon we will hold a press conference here in Paris,' she said decisively. 'The world's media will all be invited. Think of the publicity it will give NHK!'

The executive began to ask about the plan.

'Don't bother me with details,' the Rottweiler snapped. 'I don't have time for details. Get someone junior to see to them.' The phone pressed to her ear, the reporter looked out across Rue du Faubourg Saint-Honoré. 'Send out a release… At the press conference we shall reveal a great secret… a secret about Miki Suzuki!'

127

TWO MINUTES AFTER Miki and Kinjo slipped into the forest, the villagers stormed Chateau Lugny.

'Where is she?!' they demanded. 'Give her up or we shall tear the place apart!'

Pulling the door back as calmly as he could, Dr. Mesmer managed a smile.

'Good evening,' he said. 'Whom exactly are you searching for?'

The baker pushed his way to the front.

'The LV Attacker! We know she's here!'

The baker was elbowed out of the way by the village bus driver.

'You're hoping to claim the reward for yourself, are you, Georges?!' he bawled.

'I don't understand what you are talking about,' the psychiatrist replied.

The grocer waved a fist in the air.

'You give us no choice but to search the house!' he bellowed, leading the posse inside.

128

A FEW HUNDRED yards from the chateau, Miki and Kinjo were running for their lives.

Stumbling through the forest, they struggled to make out a path that ran in zigzag between the trees. It was a moonless night, the sky veiled in cloud. Neither one said a word. They were too preoccupied with making headway before the posse worked out that they had escaped.

Forty minutes after leaving the chateau, they reached a great expanse of farmland, fields planted with wheat. Without stopping for a moment, they hurried as they had been instructed in a dead straight line.

'There!' Kinjo said after what seemed like an age, 'I can see head-lights!'

'The road,' Miki replied. 'It's not so far now.'

Fifteen minutes more, and their feet stepped from mud onto tarmac. With no other choice, they walked in silence for an hour in the direction of Dijon.

Not a single car passed them.

'It's almost one o'clock,' Kinjo said. 'Everyone must be asleep.'

'It's like Miyagi Prefecture,' Miki replied. 'Very quiet at night.'
'Are you homesick?' the journalist asked as they trudged.
'I miss my family, but…'
'But what?'
Miki wiped a hand to her nose.
'But I don't ever want to go back to Japan,' she said.

129

THE NEXT MORNING, Jacques Pigalle shared a hushed conversation at the Interalliée with the chief of the DGSE. The agency responsible for monitoring electronic communications, it was France's answer to Big Brother. There was not a single phone call, email or internet communication in the country that escaped their ears or their eyes.

Three hours after their breakfast meeting, Pigalle received the call he had been expecting.

'It seems as though the LV Attacker – Miki Suzuki – is with a Japanese journalist working for the *Asahi Shimbun*,' the DGSE chief reported. 'His name is Michi Kinjo. He telephoned his editors in Tokyo at 05.16 this morning from a public telephone box at Dijon Gare. He informed them that he had Suzuki in his care. The line dropped, and he has been unable to get through to the number again.'

'So they are en route to the airport?'

The intelligence chief conferred with his aide.

'No,' he said, 'Miki Suzuki's passport was apparently stolen. So she is en route to her embassy to apply for a new one.'

'The Japanese embassy on Avenue Hoche?'

'Yes.'

'But it was destroyed.'

'Precisely,' said the chief. 'But, as I understand it, neither of them are aware of that fact.'

'Where are they now?' Pigalle asked.

Again, the intelligence chief broke off to speak to his assistant.

'Kinjo made a second call at 08.42.'

'Where from?'

'We tracked his position to Gare de Lyon.'

Pigalle gave thanks.

'Please keep him in your sights,' he said.

130

TWO HOURS TRAMPING in the dark had been followed by a ride in the back of a passing milk truck. Then, after another long walk, Kinjo and Miki had reached Dijon Station.

From there they had taken the 05.29 slow train to Paris.

Miki's need for a passport outweighed Mesmer's warning for her not to return to the capital.

There was no other choice.

Still dressed in the hospital smock, she was dazed and confused, as if she had just woken from a coma. She didn't want to go home to Japan but, at the same time, she feared staying in France.

All of a sudden Miki thought of Hugo de Montfried. She imagined him standing in the library at the Musée Nissim de Camondo. Feasting on him, she saw herself watching from a distance as he stood beside the window, peering out. A thousand times she replayed the details she could remember, and the charming way he spoke her language. *Gaijin Nihongo* – foreigner's Japanese.

Then, as the train paused at some unknown station on the outskirts of Paris, Miki thought of her ojiichan. More usually, he was all hunched over and old, teeth in a glass, reclining in the sitting room of the family home.

But this time he was handsome and young, with a youthful sparkle in his eye.

Miki followed him as he strolled between the horse chestnut trees to the same café where she had imagined him before. Instead of a newspaper, this time he was holding chocolates, a box in the shape of a heart. No sooner had he sat down, than the young woman in the yellow sundress arrived.

Presenting the chocolates, Ojiichan received a kiss on his lips in return.

After they had shared a bottle of chilled Mâcon-Villages, the woman stood up. She leaned over, kissed Ojiichan again and, as she did so, she dropped something very small and round into the top pocket of his blazer.

Fixing him with a stern glance, she strode off in the direction of the Arc de Triomphe.

Without wasting a moment, Miki's grandfather paid the bill and went inside the café to use the toilet. Checking the other stalls were empty, he took the object from his pocket and opened it.

Inside was a roll of 16 mm microfilm.

Examining the first few frames, Ojiichan took off his right shoe, slid off the heel, stowed the film in the secret compartment, and clicked the heel back in place.

Five minutes later he was walking briskly down the Champs-Elysées towards La Concorde. Gone was his carefree attitude, replaced by a palpable unease.

From time to time he looked over his shoulder.

At Concorde, he passed the Hotel Crillon and kept going to Rue de Rivoli. There, he stopped, took out a full packet of cigarettes, lit one, and tossed the rest of the pack into a rubbish bin.

Glancing around again, as though almost fearful for his life, he made his way along Rivoli until he reached the Louvre Museum.

131

THE ENORMOUS FUND of prize money had changed French perceptions. All of a sudden the nation was more than willing to show clemency – even if only because they hoped for a share of the cash.

And, every hour that passed, the bounty increased.

By lunchtime on the morning Miki returned to Paris, the total stood at more than twenty-five million euros. NHK had secured for itself many times as much in free worldwide publicity but, better still, they had captured a moral high ground.

And their star reporter, Noriko Sasaki-san, a.k.a. the Rottweiler, was having the time of her life. The last thing she hoped for was for Miki to be located any time soon, even though publicly she shared in the communal sense of fear and angst.

'I am certain it will be no more than hours before Miki is found,' she lied to Mrs. Suzuki, as they made their way to the Hotel George V, where the press conference was to be held.

Miki's mother had been up most of the night, unable to sleep.

'I think something bad is going to happen,' she said.

'What?' asked the Rottweiler, icily.

Mrs. Suzuki forced back her tears.

'I do not know. But I can feel terrible danger,' she said.

132

FEARFUL OF BEING hunted by vigilantes, Kinjo had the idea of disguising Miki, at least until they were in the safety of the Japanese embassy.

Unfortunately, his call to the *Asahi Shimbun* editorial desk had dropped before he could learn either of the NHK prize or that his embassy had been razed to the ground.

Leaving Miki at a café in Gare de Lyon, Kinjo went out in search of a charity shop. He was soon back with an odd assortment of clothing – some a little too small and the rest very much too large. All of it stank of cats.

Miki put it all on and started sneezing.

Dolled up in a knitted dress, a tweed trench coat, a feather boa in white, and pink wellington boots, she put on the straw boater and, lastly, a pair of Jackie Onassis shades.

'We will go by taxi to the embassy,' said Kinjo.

'How long does it take to get a new passport?' Miki asked.

'Maybe they will give you one immediately,' Kinjo replied optimistically. 'Maybe they will think you are a movie star,' he said.

They climbed into a taxi and Miki found herself sitting on the back seat, her head bombarded with random memories.

She thought of a hailstorm in Sendai when she was seven – the hailstones the size of golf balls. Then she thought of the scent of cherry blossom at the festival of *Sakura* in spring. And, after that, she remembered how it felt to be hated by Pun-Pun and Noemi, and how they were each so bitter and unfulfilled.

The taxi rattled fast over cobbles, and was soon at La Concorde. Swerving to avoid a group of American tourists stranded in the road, the driver steered north-west up the Champs-Elysées, the early afternoon light yellower than on previous days.

Miki's head began streaming with an cascade of recollections.

She thought of her father's favourite necktie, and her old school shoes, of her first boyfriend and of his awful zits, of when she learned to skip, of the taste of quince jam, of a flock of purple butterflies, of a sandstorm at dawn, of a cat without all its paws, of dead reindeer lying in the snow, of a mummified pharaoh's gnarled face, and of a soup tureen filled with human blood.

'My head is feeling strange,' Miki said in a low voice.

'Do you want to stop?' Kinjo asked, adding, 'We are nearly at the embassy.'

Miki was about to say that she would wait when, out of the corner of her eye, she spotted something – something familiar, something important.

Across the street, standing proud and glorious in a monument to style, was the headquarters of Louis Vuitton.

'Stop!' she screamed with all her might. 'I *must* go there!'

Before Kinjo could protest, Miki had coaxed him to hand over his wallet and she had leapt out of the taxi. Crossing the Champs-Elysées without a care about the traffic, she made a beeline to the place where all her problems had begun...

Louis Vuitton.

133

A FEW HUNDRED yards from the boater, the boa, and the pink wellington boots, Miki's mother was seated on a stage in the ballroom of the George V.

Sitting beside her was the Rottweiler, a fresh coat of cerise on her lips. And, next to her, was the chief of the Parisian police. Below the stage was a squirming sea of journalists – hundreds of them. They were armed with video cameras and still cameras, recording devices and notebooks.

Sick of waiting for the simultaneous translator's cue, the Rottweiler tapped the microphone on the table before her.

'I am ready now,' she said assertively.

The house lights were dimmed, and the stage was floodlit.

Taking charge, the star reporter welcomed the press, before launching into a précis of the situation at hand.

'We are here today because of a brave young woman,' she said. 'A woman called Miki... a woman who has touched us all, by reminding us of the values of compassion, love and dignity.'

The Rottweiler took breath and, as she did so, a bulky female reporter dressed in Chanel, stood up in the darkness below and yelled out:

'She's not dignified, she's the scum of the earth!'

Through headphones, the statement was conveyed in Japanese to the Rottweiler's ears.

A stony silence followed, one in which the translator breathed quickly three times. Experience had taught her that such pauses tended to be the calm before the storm.

But the Rottweiler did not reply. Not verbally that is.

Her face contorted with a crazed expression of anguish and rage, she leapt down from the stage.

Screaming like a banshee escaped from the confines of Hell, she shoved her way through the media pack, her long fingernails gouging and tearing as she went.

The ballroom was paused freeze frame.

No one dared move, speak, or even think. The only movement was the blurred slow motion frenzy of NHK's star reporter.

Reaching her quarry – the thick-set representative from *Le Nouvel Observateur* – the Rottweiler attacked.

Looming down over the unfortunate journalist, she sank her teeth into the woman's neck.

134

AT THE SAME moment that the Rottweiler was drawing blood, the pink wellingtons were making their way fearlessly through the great portal of Louis Vuitton. A moment after that, they were scuffling swiftly into the central gallery, which was adorned with some of the finest leather accessories ever created by man.

All around, an army of prim serving staff were going through the motions – fawning, smiling, demonstrating. They showed off exquisite leather wallets and sumptuous buckskin shoes, handbags and belts, and all manner of accoutrements made from porcelain, gold, and silk.

Without any hint of discernible emotion, Miki paced through the hall to where the coin pouches lay displayed behind glass.

In her knitted dress, tweed trench coat, straw boater and pink wellington boots, she was regarded as a wealthy eccentric, rather than a newly released psychiatric patient.

As she progressed through the great hall, a medley of images haunted Miki with each stride she took.

She thought of a car crash with bodies splayed lifelessly on the cracked surface of the road; of a soldier gasping from poison gas; of a little child screaming out in the rain; of an addict freebasing crack cocaine... and of the crazed silhouette of a Japanese woman terrorizing the interior of a luxury store.

The pink wellingtons paused at the counter where small leather goods were sold.

Shuffling to the left through ninety degrees, Miki faced the counter. The index finger of her right hand extended.

The sales assistant stepped forward, white teeth behind rosebud lips.

'*Oui, Mademoiselle?*'

The fingertip tapped the glass.

'That one, that little coin pouch.'

'*Mais oui*, yes of course, *Mademoiselle*,' said the saleswoman. 'Would you be interested in the Epi range, or in the Mon Monogram?'

The fingertip tapped again.

As it did so, Miki thought of a man hanging from a noose. She could hear the creak of the rope as the knot tightened, and imagine every detail in the uproar of strangulation.

'That one,' she repeated.

With due reverence, the assistant removed a fine black leather pouch, and demonstrated how it opened, then closed.

'I would like to buy it,' Miki said. Taking half a step backwards, she thought of a man armed with a chainsaw, cutting off the head of a jogger in Ueno Park.

'Certainly. Would you be requiring anything else?'

Miki shook her head. She blinked and, in doing so, she glimpsed a waterfall of blood, all oily and warm.

The price was announced in a hushed voice.

Her face streaming with perspiration, and her Jackie O glasses steaming up, Miki handed over a fistful of cash.

Less than a minute later she was outside on the pavement, a little brown bag dangling on her wrist.

The thoughts were coming thick and fast now, each one more gruesome than the last:

Killing fields drenched in fresh blood.

Limbless torsos being pecked by crows.

Butchered babies.

A mound of infantile skulls, towering forty feet high.

Standing at the kerb, Miki found her vision veiled through a lens tinged with gore.

Hyperventilating, she rubbed thumbs to her eyes.

Across the street, Kinjo opened the taxi window and waved in Miki's direction. But she couldn't see him.

She couldn't see *anything*.

The journalist jumped out of the cab, and ran across the Champs-Elysées.

'Miki-chan, are you feeling OK?'

Her face contorting as though she was witnessing true terror, Miki replied:

'The children are all dead. Every last one of them.'

'*What?*' said Kinjo, bewildered.

'They were beheaded. We must run!'

'Miki, come with me back to the taxi. In five minutes we will be at the embassy. They will take care of you there.'

Holding Miki's elbow, Kinjo turned her towards the street.

As he did so, a dark blue van screeched up. It braked so hard that the air stank of burning rubber.

Two men leapt out from the back. They were wearing black balaclavas.

Without a word, they grabbed Miki and hurled her into the back of the van. Five seconds later, they were speeding away down a side street.

Michi Kinjo stood at the kerb in shock, unable to move. The passersby had assumed it was all part of a film shoot or a publicity stunt.

No one even turned.

The journalist from the *Asahi Shimbun* folded down onto the pavement. His masquerade of bravado gone, he broke down and wept.

Next to him, on its side, lay the little brown paper bag, the words 'Louis Vuitton' in raised black lettering on the front.

135

A LEATHER-BOUND FIRST edition of haiku by Kobayashi Issa was cupped in de Montfried's hand, the pages brittle and yellow.

Sitting in a straight-backed chair in his library, he was reading the *kanji* but his mind was not on the text.

All he could think about was Miki Suzuki.

Not one to fall easily in love, the Comte castigated himself, then struggled to turn his thoughts to other matters. But, through a web of random associations, they kept steering him back to Miki's face.

He couldn't quite say what made her different. It was a mixture of things – the way she had been so earnest and shy, so enthusiastic for his home city, and such an admirer of all things French.

As he sat there, pondering the information provided by Jacques Pigalle, the butler entered, coughed softly to gain his attention.

'*Oui, Claude?*'

'Excuse me, sir, but I have just attended the press conference, as instructed.'

Hugo de Montfried peered up from the book.

'*And?*'

'And, it appears that the appeal initiated by Japanese television has surpassed twenty-five million euros, sir.'

The Comte closed the book.

'And how was the mood?' he asked.

The butler raised an eyebrow.

'Electric, sir.'

'Journalists from all over France?'

'From all over the world, sir.'

De Montfried's gaze moved to the glow of coals in the brazier.

'That's good,' he said. 'Thank you.'

Lowering his head in a bow, Claude walked backwards to the door. Just before going out, he paused.

'Would you mind if I were to say something, sir?' he asked, respectfully.

The Comte looked over to where the manservant was standing.

'Of course not, what is it, Claude?'

'Well, sir, it occurred to me while attending the press conference on your behalf, that Mademoiselle Suzuki may be in considerable danger.'

'And what makes you think that?'

'Because, sir, such a large trophy is likely to lure the darkest of forces.'

De Montfried cocked his head sideways.

'Thank you, Claude,' he said.

136

THE DARK BLUE van sped fast through backstreets, over the Pont Alexandre III, and down the Boulevard Saint-Germain.

In the back, Miki lay outstretched on the floor. Her tweed coat ripped down the side, and her feather boa missing, she had been sedated with a rag drenched in chloroform. Before causing her to pass out, the sweet vapour had flushed her mind of tortured thoughts.

Either side of her was poised the monstrous outline of a man, the balaclavas now gone. Great hulking brutes of muscle, unshaven and scarred, they both reeked of Albanian cigarettes.

One was holding a crowbar, as a weapon not a tool.

'I'll tie the blindfold,' he said quickly in Romanian.

'Why bother?' his accomplice replied. 'She's unconscious. Won't see a thing.'

The driver called out from the front seat.

'Five minutes now,' he said. His accent was from Moldova, and he was mistrustful of the two in the back, both of them from Transylvania.

Heading straight down Boulevard Raspail, he veered down a side street, turning sharp left at the end.

As soon as the van stopped, Marius, the larger of the men at the back, jumped out. Pulling Miki out after him, he jerked her limp body up over his shoulder as if it were of no weight at all.

Shielded by the side of the vehicle, the Romanians opened a manhole cover and descended a narrow stone staircase into the ground.

The driver, whose name was Remus, led the way.

He had flicked on a torch, its lacklustre beam throwing shadows over the granite walls.

Down and down they went and, as they did so, the temperature plunged. After two hundred steps, they reached a tunnel. Cold, damp, and with a fusty, fetid smell, it was lined on either side floor to ceiling with human bones.

There were millions of them – skulls and femurs, arm bones and vertebrae. Stretching out for miles beneath the Paris streets, the tunnels crisscrossed the capital, with only part of the catacomb labyrinth open as a tourist trail.

For the Romanians, it was a perfect hideout, a place to keep their kidnapped victim out of sight.

Roused by the cold, Miki came to.

She was still hanging limp over a shoulder, but her mind strained to make sense of what her eyes were witnessing – an unending wall of skulls.

Screaming louder than she had ever screamed in her life, a fist to the side of her face silenced her, knocking her clean out.

137

WITH THE PRIZE money still mounting, the hysterical search for Japan's greatest heroine went on. All of a sudden there were Miki Suzuki look-alikes everywhere, and all manner of crooks and conmen trying to cash in.

The French capital was awash with foreign visitors – each one hunting high and low. There were so many of them that all the hotel rooms in town were booked – even the Albanian-run hovels around Gare du Nord.

The tourist boom had led to a renewed sense of *joie de vivre*. And the hatred of all things Japanese had transmuted inexplicably into a rich appreciation for Oriental culture.

Ordinary Parisians were gorging themselves once again on sushi, were happily driving Toyotas and Lexuses, and were more avidly hooked on Japanese high tech electronics than ever before.

At The Bristol, Miki's mother was sitting in the salon downstairs, giving an interview to *Le Nouvel Observateur*. The journalist conducting the interview was an overbearing matron of a woman, with a great bouffant of faux chestnut hair. Dressed head to toe in Chanel, she had been cajoled into dropping charges against the Rottweiler in return for an exclusive.

A silk scarf hiding the puncture wound on her neck, she had no interest in Japan, but recognized the value to circulation of a Miki Suzuki scoop.

'Would you please tell me,' she said through a translator, 'where do you believe Miki could be?'

Mrs. Suzuki's expression was bewildered and wan. She was missing home and a life of complete anonymity.

'I think that maybe my daughter is in danger,' she said in a slow pensive tone. 'She has dreamed of Paris all her life. But it is a dream that has become a nightmare.'

The journalist took down the answer word for word.

'And what kind of woman is Miki?' she asked.

Mrs. Suzuki sat up straight, as if she had sniffed smelling salts.

'Strong,' she said. 'Miki is strong. She is not fearful of anything at all.'

138

FOR FIFTEEN MINUTES after the kidnapping, Michi Kinjo had remained hunched in a kneeling position on the pavement outside Louis Vuitton. As he huddled there in shock, an Albanian pickpocket had grabbed the little brown bag and had run.

Eventually, one of the LV doormen had spotted Kinjo there, motionless against the blur of pedestrians. He hadn't actually seen the kidnapping, as he had been giving directions to an elderly American couple from Detroit.

'Are you in need of assistance, sir?' he asked, approaching gingerly.

'They took her,' Kinjo replied blankly. 'Just like that. They snatched her.'

The doorman took a step back and leaned down.

'Took *who*?'

'Miki Suzuki.'

'*The* Miki Suzuki...? The *LV Attacker*?'

Stumbling to his feet, Kinjo looked at the doorman, and sighed.

An hour later he had given a statement to the police, describing what had happened in full. Inspector du Lac had conducted the interview, the same officer who had processed Miki after the Louis Vuitton rampage.

'Every year millions of Japanese visit our capital,' he said, 'and we never hear a word out of most of them. They come and go in silence like little sheep... and so why is it that your friend, Mademoiselle Suzuki, has caused such uproar?'

Kinjo was about to give an answer, when the duty officer looked over.

'It's because of the prize,' he said in a thick accent. 'I heard it is now about thirty million euros.'

'The police prize?' Kinjo asked.

The officer shook his head.

'*Non, non*, the NHK prize.'

The journalist frowned.

'I don't know about that one,' he said.

139

THE SIDE OF her face swollen, and her arms black with bruises, Miki came to again and found herself alone in darkness. Huddled there in a foetal position, she was lying on what felt like grimy cement.

There was absolute silence, as though she were dead.

Death.

Miki blinked at the thought of it. As she did so, she was confronted by another flood of images.

The blood-flow from a traumatic leg amputation.

The sight of fifty soldiers charred by napalm.

An African man with a burning tyre around his neck.

A cannibal feasting on a child's rotting flesh.

Miki blinked again.

The images evaporated, and were replaced by the thought of a dove in a gilded cage. It was perfectly white and so serene, as though it had just fluttered in from Paradise.

Peering closer, Miki saw that the little creature's eyes were missing. And, as she watched, blood streamed from the ocular sockets. She swallowed, her neck tense. Then, moving her head a fraction, she remembered who she was.

But where was Alexa? She was all that mattered.

Very slowly, her balance faulty, Miki sat upright. Without even the slightest trace of light, she sat in a state of raw paralysis, her fingers interlaced.

Alexa, Alexa, Alexa.

Miki didn't understand. Alexa had been with her a moment before. There could be no excuse. How could she have gone?

Miki leaned back on the wall. It was uneven. Large rounded stones and smaller ones. So many of them. Twisting around, Miki fumbled along them. She wondered where she was. But then, why wonder? Because Alexa would explain it all, as she always did.

Miki called out:

'Alexa, I am here! Alexa, come and find me! It's me – it's Francine!'

An hour passed, and Miki called over and over – sometimes in her head, and sometimes out loud. She called so much that she had no idea which was which – the voice or the mind.

There was no reply.

All of a sudden she felt something very rough and very small between thumb and forefinger. The tiniest fragment of grit. Rolling it back and forth, she held it up to her face, even though she couldn't see.

'Alexa!' she said impishly, 'how naughty of you to run away! I have been searching for you everywhere. Ask the others and they will tell you!'

Sliding the grit into the middle of her palm, she wagged a finger at it, tut-tutting.

'If you run away again I shall have to spank you very hard,' she said. 'And Ginzu won't come and save you next time.' Tilting her head sideways she lowered it towards her palm. 'No, no, no!' she exclaimed. 'I am *not* going to listen to your excuses! If you give me any more trouble, I shall put you on my tongue and swallow you!'

Miki took a deep breath, closed her fist, and clutched it to her chest. She sat in silence for a long while. After an hour of timelessness, she made out the sound of feet striding hard down on grime.

Angry feet... big angry feet.

With the footsteps there came light.

It began as the faintest glimmer – less than light – more of a distant glow. But, within thirty seconds, it grew in luminescence, until it was utterly blinding.

Miki was about to cover her eyes with her hand when she managed to focus on a familiar shape... then another, and a hundred more.

The scream that followed the sight was piercing enough to wake the dead. As it permeated from the ossuary and down the endless tunnels, Remus strode up, a torch held high.

'Shut up or I'll beat you!' he blared. 'Then I'll leave you down here. And that'll be the end!'

Miki's scream telescoped into a whimper.

Her fist still furled inwards towards her chest, she protected Alexa, whispering words of comfort in her mind.

The Romanian took something silver and square out of his pocket. Then he threw a folded newspaper down onto the dirt.

'Hold that,' he said.

Dazed, Miki picked up the paper.

A camera flash popped, throwing out such a riot of light that both she and the Romanian kidnapper were blinded.

'Alexa,' Miki said in a soft slow voice. 'Don't worry... I'll never leave you.'

140

FIVE HOURS AFTER her abduction, a photograph was emailed to the Paris police through a proxy internet server. It showed a diminutive Japanese woman, eyes bleary and body cowering, holding that morning's *L'Express*.

Along with the picture was a demand for five million euros, to be delivered to a specific grid coordinate in the suburbs. Upon failure to deliver the money within twenty-four hours, a small Oriental nose would be mailed to the chief of police.

Within ten minutes, the picture had been circulated to all the senior officers, and printed out a thousand times. Sitting beside the window in his cramped office, Inspector du Lac held the A4 printout between his hands.

'It is her, isn't it, Inspector?' said Laurent, the Breton duty clerk.

'Yes. A little more battered and bruised than before, but it's definitely her.'

The Breton went out. And when he was gone, du Lac held the photo into the light. He squinted at it, observing the details. The flash had been so powerful that it had washed out most of the features. But something in the bottom edge caught the Inspector's eye.

Holding a magnifying glass over the page, he adjusted it until the picture was in sharp focus.

A skull.

Or, rather, a line of skulls.

And below them, a neat arrangement of femurs, all stacked up like firewood.

'Laurent!' the Inspector yelled at the top of his voice, 'get me the chief of police on the phone!'

141

STILL CUT OFF from the outside world, Dr. Mesmer made arrangements for the remaining patients to be given passage home.

In their last days at Chateau Lugny, he conducted a series of thorough interviews. These were complemented by a range of psychological tests – some of them from the textbook, and others of his own design.

On the final night, the psychiatrist held a special dinner in honour of the future. Seated down either side of the long mahogany dining table were Vladimir, Bart, Victoria, Miss Fujimoto, Mrs. Ito, Messrs. Chen, Kim and Park and, last but not least, Tanaka the former turnip.

Mesmer and Nurse Polk sat at either end.

Despite the extraordinary possibilities that lay ahead, the general mood was a little melancholic, the conversation uninspiring.

The doctor asked his patients about their aspirations for the future.

'I shall go to Transvaal,' said Bart, 'where I will get work in the gold mines. They need people who know how to dig a good hole.'

'I plan to visit my brother,' said Mr. Chen. 'He lives in Sydney and is very rich. He is *so* rich.'

'How rich?' asked Bart.

'Rich enough to have his own golf course. And he has a helicopter as well.'

'What about you, Mr. Tanaka?' asked Mesmer.

The former turnip thought for a moment, sucked air in through his teeth.

'I will go home to Tokyo,' he said. 'And I will find a nice young woman and I will ask her to marry me.'

Sitting beside the former turnip, Mrs. Ito giggled.

'And what about you?' Dr. Mesmer asked.

Bowing her head, Mrs. Ito seemed even more awkward than usual. After a long silence, she said:

'I think I will tell my husband that I do not want to be married to him any more. Then he can marry his mistress.'

Another long silence followed the statement. And, once it had become interminable, Mesmer asked Vladimir for his future plans.

'I will write a novel,' he said, 'and I will call it *The Crucifixion of Honesty.*'

'That's a stupid idea,' said Mr. Park.

'It's not as stupid as your face,' Vladimir replied.

'I think it's a wonderful idea!' Victoria exclaimed, her hair now a curious shade of pea green. 'And I think I will write a novel, too.'

'What would it be called?' Dr. Mesmer asked.

Victoria turned to face him. She smiled, the most alluring of smiles.

'*Paris Syndrome*,' she said.

142

HAVING TAKEN THE photograph, Remus the Romanian thug had gone back through the catacombs, to send the picture to the police.

Miki was alone again, her friend Alexa clutched safely in her fist. She lay down for a while. Then, her face aching where she had been struck, she sat up, and found that she was standing.

Lost in the folds of skin, Alexa was saying something.

Miki put her fist up to her ear, like a little girl imagining she were listening to the sound of the waves in a seashell.

She listened.

'Run... run far away!' the little bit of grit squeaked.

'But there is no light,' Miki replied. 'And even if there was, I don't know where I am.'

Again, Alexa spoke. This time her voice was more shrill, more demanding.

'If you do not run, they will chop you into little pieces and they will feed you to the wolves!'

So, with one hand clenched and the other feeling its way forward, Miki stumbled out of the ossuary, and into the catacombs.

143

INSPECTOR DU LAC was no stranger to kidnappings.

The year before he had presided over securing the safe release of an Israeli couple, snatched from outside the Ritz in Place Vendôme. The petrified tourists had been held for a week before a ransom of five million euros was paid. A year before that, he had managed to save a Danish businessman.

Unfortunately, the ransom was late in coming, and the victim's thumbs were rather clumsily excised and sent to his family. The grim trophies had speeded up the payment, and the businessman was eventually freed.

In both the Israeli and Danish cases, the kidnappers were thought to have been Romanians.

'It's them again,' said the Inspector, at the initial briefing with the police chief. 'I can feel it in my bones.'

'We can't allow them to start carving her up,' said the chief. 'This damn woman has already sparked riots and vigilante groups. Now they love her. I've never seen anything like it.'

'It's all about the money,' said du Lac, the tone of his voice disapproving. 'What I don't understand is how the gang could have known the whereabouts of Miki Suzuki,' he said.

'Luck...?'

The Inspector shrugged. As he did so he held up the ransom photograph. 'At least we know where she is.'

'The catacombs?'

Du Lac nodded.

'You know as well as I that they stretch from here to eternity,' he said.

'If we cover all the exits, then send in officers with night vision...'

Inspector du Lac held out his hand.

'Forgive me, sir,' he said, 'but I have first hand experience with these guys. If they smell an armed response, they'll start chopping off fingers.'

'So what do we do?'

'As much as I hate to suggest it,' said the Inspector, 'we pay the ransom from the prize money and hope that Miki Suzuki walks away alive. I am sure that in the circumstances NHK would authorize the release of the funds.'

144

AN HOUR AND a half after the ransom note and photograph had arrived at police headquarters, Jacques Pigalle was seated in the library at Maison Pastache. Across from him, his expression vacant, his hands trembling, was Hugo de Montfried.

'They believe she has been kidnapped by Romanian thugs,' said Pigalle, 'and that she's being held down in the catacombs.'

The Comte wiped a hand hard over his face.

'I don't believe it,' he said. 'One little Japanese lady caught up in such a whirlwind.'

'The plan is to pay her ransom with the prize fund,' Pigalle replied. 'And, the Inspector assures me that once paid, Romanian gangsters tend to release straight away. It's the only way they can be assured that they are taken seriously next time.'

'So there is some honour left in the underworld,' de Montfried replied.

'It appears so.'

Jacques Pigalle's composed air wavered.

'There's other news,' he said. 'Not so good.'

The Comte almost laughed.

'Worse than that Miki Suzuki has been kidnapped?'

'An added difficulty.'

'What?'

'In the rush to gain the funds, certain details seem to have been leaked.'

'*Details*? What details?'

'That Suzuki is being held down there, in the catacombs.'

'Does that really matter?' de Montfried asked quizzically.

'In a case with such unrivalled public interest, I believe it does,' Pigalle said. 'After all, there are plenty of people in Paris who are desperate to get their hands on the victim and cash her in themselves.'

145

BROKEN BY SHAME at losing his ward, Michi Kinjo put his journalistic ear to the ground in a way he had not done before.

After much thought he hit upon a devious ruse.

He telephoned NHK headquarters in Tokyo and pretended the *Asahi Shimbun* was planning on running a double-page spread on their star correspondent.

Before he knew it, he was sitting face to face with the Rottweiler in her suite at The Bristol.

Radiating respect and faux admiration, he did his best to fan the journalist's monumental ego. Only when she was putty in his hands did he make an oblique enquiry about the kidnappers.

'They sent a photograph this afternoon,' the Rottweiler said, passing over a printout.

Kinjo squinted at the background.

'Are those bones?' he asked in a slow, flat voice.

'The police told me that they believe Miki is being held in the catacombs, under the city.'

'How much is the ransom?'

'Five million euros.'

Kinjo's eyebrows rose.

'So much?'

'Miki is a celebrity,' the Rottweiler hissed. 'So of course the ransom is high.'

'But how could it ever be paid?'

'From the prize money.'

'When is the ransom due?'

NHK's star reporter glanced at her wristwatch.

'In seven hours from now,' she said.

146

MIKI MIGHT HAVE been terrified, but Alexa was there to comfort her.

'Keep going, Francine!' she said, over and over, 'and you *will* reach the light.'

'But my leg is hurting, dearest Alexa,' Miki whimpered, 'and I am so anxious that I'll drop you.'

The little grain of grit seemed to laugh.

'If you lose me then just pick me up again,' she said.

'But I'll never find you!'

Again, Alexa laughed, a little squeaky snickery laugh.

'I am every speck of dirt under your feet,' she said.

So, for three hours, Miki stumbled and fumbled, whimpered and moaned. Sometimes she screamed, and at other times she wept. But still she kept moving. Banging from side to side, she felt her way down the walls of skulls.

She was about to give up when she heard something.

A galumphing sound. Like the marching of feet…

'What shall I do?' she said fretfully without speaking.

'Quickly, go to the feet and you will be saved!' Alexa replied.

And so Miki scurried forwards towards the thumping, her hands jostling fast over the skulls.

All of a sudden she made out another faint glow of light, a glow that became a pinprick, and a pinprick that melded into a dazzling shaft of luminescence.

Squinting, cowering, hiding her face, she got down on all fours.

The light became so bright that Miki screamed. The next thing she knew, she was being dragged back down the tunnel by her hair.

On either side of the passageway, the lines of skulls seemed to watch, stacked neat and orderly like spectators in a grandstand.

'I've got a little surprise for you,' said Remus, a cigarette held in his teeth. 'Something a friend of mine knocked up. Something a little special.'

Again, Miki screamed. Not because she was frightened, nor from pain. But because she had dropped Alexa.

'I need to stop!' she wailed. 'I must stop to get my friend!'

The Romanian grabbed the collar of Miki's dress and dragged her back into the ossuary. Her outburst silenced, she furled up into the foetal position. Her muscles had gone stiff, as though she was in rigor mortis.

Remus plunged a hand down inside his jacket and pulled something out. The size of a large hardback book, it had coloured wires and four straps, and seemed to smell of marzipan. On the bottom edge there was what looked like a cheap mobile phone, hard-wired into the contraption.

Jerking Miki upright, he slapped her hard on the face. And then, with uncharacteristic care, he strapped the device onto Miki's body. She didn't flinch.

'I can hear you asking me what I am doing,' the Romanian said, with all the gusto of a James Bond villain. 'Well, it's a way of coaxing the people up there on the surface to be a little more generous.'

Once the explosive belt was fitted, Remus whipped out his camera and took another shot, drenching the ossuary in platinum light.

He chuckled, then grinned.

'Don't move a muscle,' he said. 'Because if you do...' the Romanian chuckled again... 'there'll be a big *KABOOM!*'

147

AT 5.15 P.M. the new photograph reached the police headquarters. It was studied by a special team, as was the explosive belt, the kind used by suicide bombers.

Five minutes after that, the first members of the public descended through a disused entrance into the catacombs in search of Miki Suzuki. There were three of them, all friends. They had come to the French capital six years earlier from Pau. Their leader had spent an entire winter on the streets, and in that time had sought refuge down in the catacombs. Unlike his associates, he had no fear of skeletons, or of the horror stories. The other two were terrified, but all thoughts of demonic retribution were quelled by the fantasy of the enormous reward.

An hour after the men from Pau entered the catacombs, ten others had descended through various entrances, and were mounting rescue expeditions of their own. By seven o'clock, there were forty-five members of the public hurrying through the tunnels, all of them in search of Miki, and all hopeful of claiming the reward.

By midnight, more than three hundred people were searching, some with night vision, others with nothing more than paraffin lamps.

During the night, the police patrolling the main entrances into the catacombs had put up makeshift barricades. But there were so many entrances into the tunnels that stopping all the treasure hunters was quite impossible.

As they flooded in, the media joined them.

At least three news channels dispatched their own TV crews into the subterranean labyrinth. News 24 hired an ex-commando from the elite Special Forces Command to lead them.

Perceiving the media interest, the Romanians suddenly increased their ransom demand from five to ten million euros, and then to twenty million. Failure to deliver the full amount on time would, they explained by email, result in a pair of Japanese thumbs being chopped off with a blunt carving knife.

148

SQUATTING IN COMPLETE darkness, knees pushed up against her chin, Miki was as still as a marble statue. Her feet were together, head cocked to one side, eyes wide open. Something inside was telling her not to move, and that if she did so, she would meet an immediate and spectacular end.

And so she crouched there, quiescent and still.

On the outside Miki may have been motionless, but inside the confines of her mind, she was on a wild rumpus of a rollercoaster ride.

All memory of her beloved Alexa was gone, as was her own incarnation, Francine.

Both of them had been replaced by a new and surreal extravaganza.

Poised on the surface of a fluorescent green planet, Miki was not her usual self – whatever usual had been. In the middle of her face there was a single eye. As wide as a soup bowl, it was almond-shaped and crimson in colour, the skin around it a peculiar shade of turquoise.

Above and below the eye was a pair of mouths. Small and rather dainty, they were filled with squat sharp teeth and had elongated tongues that would curl up in spirals when not in use.

There was no nose, or hair, but there was a neck. It led to an enormous pear-shaped body with eight arms and as many hands, three legs and six feet.

'I think I will eat a snarch,' said Miki to herself. 'I like to have a snarch when the sky is katternack. And when the sky is katternack I like to think of mufflebof and mungin.'

As Miki chatted away to herself, another creature – almost identical to her in form – lolloped up. The only discernible difference was that its eye was not crimson, but saffron-yellow.

'Nug-poh,' said Miki listlessly.

'Nug-poh,' replied the stranger.

'I am Zazap-3,' Miki said.

'And I am Aarw-6.'

Suddenly, both Miki's tongues lurched from their mouths and licked at a passing swarm of dragonflies. They snared half a dozen each.

'I am going to eat a snarch,' she said. 'Because I like to have a snarch when the sky is katternack.'

The stranger blinked.

'Snarch is reeklp.'

'Well I like snarch,' Miki replied crossly. 'I like the way it's all bungoz when I eat it.'

The creature with the yellow eye was going to say something about the way snarch writhed and wriggled as they were masticated. But, instead, it lowered its head and covered its eye with all its hands.

Miki looked round. Her own oversized eye focussed on the horizon.

Both her mouths choked.

In the distance, moving fast over fluorescent green sand, was an army – an army of small red troll-like creatures.

'Lorxids,' said Miki.

'What shall we do?!' squealed the stranger. 'Lorxids like to gobble up zugards and *we* are zugards.'

'We must not move,' Miki said. 'Because if we do not move a muscle the lorxids will run right past us.'

And so that's exactly what Zazap-3 and Aarw-6 did.

They didn't move. Not the faintest trace of motion.

The lorxids scampered past, streaming around them and between them as if they were smooth rocks in a stream. They were armed with cleavers and axes made from gnorl, and had faces so ferocious that their victims would often drop dead at the mere sight of them.

When the lorxids had gone, Aarw-6 advanced until it was close to Zazap-3.

'You are a drid-bo,' it said. 'You saved my zmigg.'

Zazap-3 blushed.

'Wakda-wakda,' she said.

149

THE FRENCH NEWS media may have put ex-special forces operatives on the payroll, but Michi Kinjo of the *Asahi Shimbun* had someone even more experienced as a guide – a cataphile.

In his time, Maurice Gromet had been addicted to almost every stimulant known to man. He'd been hooked on crack and smack, uppers and downers, and had taken LSD, MDMA, and black tar heroin in abundance. At one time he had even made a habit of glue. His scalp was bald and blistered, the skin on his face and arms badly jaundiced. Until that moment he had been regarded by society as an utter wastrel, as someone with less than no value at all.

But within a heartbeat, Gromet's luck had changed.

Having resided in the Paris catacombs for the best part of twenty years, he knew every twist and turn. Indeed, he had spent so much time down below that he preferred life there to the surface. As he would tell people, on the rare occasions that they asked, 'the dead make no judgements'.

Until then, Maurice Gromet may have been a down-and-out with no prospects. But, all of a sudden, he was the one man alive who had a real chance of locating Miki Suzuki.

His fortunes had changed when he bumped into Kinjo outside the Grand Palais. The reporter was standing there under a streetlamp, studying the ransom picture.

Gromet sidled up, hand outstretched for alms.

'The catacombs,' he said.

'Yes. But where in catacombs?'

'I will show you.'

'Really?'

The down-and-out looked hard at the picture, tilted it slightly, and nodded.

'That's a little room where I spend the winter nights.'

'Are you sure?'

The down-and-out grunted affirmatively.

'How much to show me?' Kinjo asked.

Maurice Gromet rubbed his hands over one another.

'Fifty euros,' he said.

150

DELPHINE DE MONTFRIED was taking breakfast in the little blue salon at Maison Pastache, when her brother burst in. A draught of cool air swathed him, as though he had run up the stairs. His cheeks were flushed, his forehead beaded with perspiration.

'Whatever is it, Hugo?' she asked, looking up from her toast.

'I can't bear it! I can't bear it any longer!'

'What can't you bear?'

'The tension.'

As if hoping for more information, Delphine shrugged.

'*Tension?*'

'Miki Suzuki... the LV Attacker... she has been kidnapped as you know,' said the Comte, his nostrils flaring. 'Now the kidnappers have strapped a suicide belt to her. One movement and she'll explode!'

Delphine spread strawberry jam evenly on a corner of her toast. She blinked hard, once and then again.

'Excuse me?' she said.

'As if it was not bad enough that she's in the catacombs, she's in a suicide belt. They've strapped explosives to her.'

'*Mon dieu!* That sounds exciting!'

Regarding his sister with vexed irritation, Comte Hugo de Montfried wished she would leave and go far away.

'I fail to see the excitement,' he replied. 'But I do see the distinct possibility of an innocent Japanese woman getting her body blown limb from limb.'

Delphine nibbled her toast.

'Am I missing something?' she asked curiously. 'This is the woman who caused a trade war and all-out revolution – is it not?'

'Unfavourable circumstances were against her,' the Comte replied as he strode over to the window. 'She is nothing more than a pawn but...'

'*But?*'

'But she is a pawn with whom I am hopelessly in love.'

151

SHORTLY AFTER 8 a.m., Unit AZ-1, the first of two special forces Hostile Rescue teams descended into the labyrinth. Red tape, political wrangling, and general confusion, had contributed to the delay in their deployment.

They were kitted out with thermal imaging gear and state-of-the-art night vision units. And they had with them a full arsenal of weaponry. Each man was armed with a Heckler & Koch MP5 submachine gun with laser aiming, and with a pair of stun grenades.

The hostage was now deemed to be in such danger that pre-emptive action was authorized. The directive was sanctioned by the President of the Republic himself. Like every other politician in France, he had perceived that a great deal more than a Japanese woman's life was hanging in the balance.

The case of Miki Suzuki was all about winning votes.

Despite being continually refused permission to accompany the special forces, the Rottweiler had not backed down. In the end, she and the NHK film crew were reluctantly permitted to tag along. The reason was that they had agreed to stump up their prize money in order to pay the ransom. And, the agreement to allow them to follow was only made after they had signed a raft of legal documents absolving the French government of any responsibility for what might happen to them.

Dressed in dark combat gear, with a blacked-out face and no hint of cerise, NHK's star reporter trailed after the elite unit. Scurrying a short distance behind her was the film crew, their powerful arc light illuminating the rats and the bones.

Up at street level, Miki's mother waited with the support crew.

There were ten fire engines, and twice as many ambulances, police units, and buses – each of them crammed full of trained negotiators, counsellors and translators. A police helicopter circled above and, as it did so, the onslaught of media trucks arrived.

Far below the street, the frail figure was still crouching in complete darkness.

The fluorescent landscape had vanished, replaced by a fresh dreamscape.

In place of Zazap-3 was a new incarnation.

And, this time, it was almost human.

She looked like Miki, and had a youthful complexion and deep trusting eyes. Her hair was shoulder-length, and her feet so nimble that she could walk very fast. She was dressed in a red duffel coat with gold buttons, and appeared to be very happy indeed. Poised on the edge of an extensive body of water, an inland sea, she was as still as a marble statue.

There were coconut palms close to the water's edge. Near to them, on the far side of a rocky outcrop, a group of brawny fishermen were hauling in a huge fish. Miki watched as they toiled. But her attention was not on the men and their muscles, but the fish.

It was rainbow-coloured.

And, as Miki watched, the scales changed their hue, as though a stream of coloured inks was being poured over them.

Unable to resist, she hurried over and asked what kind of fish it was. The leader of the fishermen was about to reply, but the fish called out to her:

'I am a shimmer fish, and have been caught by these evil men. They will cut me up and cook me. You must save me!'

Moved by the creature's plea and allured by its colours, Miki offered the fishermen her gold bracelet. Weighing the object in his hand, their leader accepted.

A moment later, the great coloured fish was back in the sea.

Miki turned to leave, but she heard a voice. It was the fish, calling to her again:

'You may not know it, but you are one of us,' it said. 'You are a shimmer fish in human form.'

'I don't understand,' Miki said, approaching the water's edge.

Raising its head out of the waves, the fish called for her to wade into the sea. When she had done so, the fish said:

'Dig your fingers into the skin above your breast-bone, and pull the flesh away.'

Without stopping to think, Miki did as the shimmer fish had instructed her to do. She dug her fingers through the soft skin and into the flesh. To her amazement there were scales beneath her skin.

Tearing away at the tissue, she revealed the form of a fish, in the way that a snake sloughs a dead skin.

All of a sudden, Miki heard a voice.

Not the voice of the shimmer fish.

But a voice in Japanese.

'I am here to save you,' it said. 'I am Kinjo.'

152

FAR AWAY IN Tokyo, Pun-Pun was sitting with Noemi at the back of the Bogart Bar in Shinjuku.

All the waitresses, and at least half the clientele, were dressed in raincoats and fedoras, as though they had just stepped off the set of *Casablanca*.

The couple had managed to escape the siege at Angel Flower headquarters by dressing as vigilantes and walking slowly backwards from the building. In the hubbub, the attackers had assumed they were part of their ranks.

A Humphrey Bogart waitress approached the table and served a second round of drinks. When she was gone, Pun-Pun's left hand rested on Noemi's thigh, his right reaching for a tumbler half-filled with single malt.

That morning, before the siege had got out of control, he had been discharged from the Angel Flower's employ with a generous severance package. Despite feigning sorrow in public, he had been privately thrilled. For more than a decade Pun-Pun had secreted away company funds.

Noemi fluttered her long curled eyelashes, until she had her lover's full attention.

'How will we ever be able to run away together if you do not have a job?' she asked, fretfully.

Sipping his whisky, Pun-Pun smiled. He was about to hint that he had secured extraneous funds, when something caught his attention.

A picture had been flashed up on the TV screen on the wall opposite the bar.

Miki's picture.

It was followed by the grainy indistinct image of a woman in full combat gear hurrying down a tunnel lined either side with bones.

153

AT THE SAME moment as the NHK newsflash, Dr. Mesmer was loading his patients back into the minibus.

After a great deal of logistical preparation and no insignificant cost, airline tickets had been purchased for everyone. The original plan was to drive the patients to Geneva and to fly them out from there, so as to avoid the French capital altogether. But the Koreans and the Russian didn't have Swiss visas. So Mesmer activated Plan B – to send them from Roissy Charles de Gaulle, reaching the airport by skirting around Paris in the widest possible arc.

Clambering onto the bus, Vladimir asked Victoria if she wanted to go with him to St. Petersburg.

'I thought you were a cross-dresser – a cross-dresser who thought he was a Barbie doll,' she said.

The Russian balked at the thought.

'That was the *old* me.'

'And who is the *new* you?'

Vladimir winked.

'A hundred per cent stud.'

Next onto the minibus was Tanaka-san. He was humming to himself. Nurse Polk, who was sitting at the front, asked him how he was feeling.

'Happy,' he said. 'Like a raindrop that has fallen onto the petal of a beautiful flower.'

'You don't feel like a turnip?'

Mr. Tanaka shook his head. Then he grunted.

'I hate turnips,' he said.

154

A CURIOUS FEATURE of the catacombs was that the bones formed a layer of perfect insulation, like the sound-proofing on the walls of a recording studio.

The result was that the Miki-hunters, the Hostile Rescue operatives, and the Japanese journalist from *Asahi Shimbun* and his cataphile guide, had no idea at all of each other's presence. The general narrowness, and the way in which the tunnels snaked so randomly beneath the capital, provided the ultimate terror environment.

You could have been ten feet from someone else and never have known it.

And, as if there were not already enough isolated groups capering through the catacombs, another one arrived.

Having caused terror at the Montmartre asylum, the elite Tokushu Sakusen Gun commando force had retreated and awaited further orders.

These eventually came through on a secure frequency, in the military's state-of-the-art X-59Z encryption system:

Golden Swallow believed to be prisoner in catacombs beneath Paris. Proceed to Monpartnasse Cemetery. Enter catacombs through concealed staircase at north-east corner. Locate and rescue Golden Swallow.

155

TRAINING THE BEAM of his torch low as he approached Miki, Kinjo called out words of comfort.

'You will be in a warm bath full of bubbles very soon!' he said, followed by: 'You look more lovely than a princess in a field of chrysanthemums!'

Bowing his head respectfully, the reporter was about to reach out and touch Miki on the shoulder, when Maurice Gromet pushed him down.

'Don't move,' he said.

'Why not?'

Gromet jerked a thumb down at the wires.

'I've seen that stuff before.'

'What is it?'

'A suicide vest.'

156

AS DIRECTED, THE Tokushu Sakusen Gun commandos made their way to Montparnasse Cemetery, and were soon clambering down the concealed iron staircase into the catacombs.

By a stroke of extreme coincidence – and what turned out to be misfortune – Unit AZ-2, the second French special forces team, were checking their coordinates at the foot of the same staircase.

Their night vision goggles revealing the silhouettes as targets that were clearly armed, they feared them to be the kidnappers.

Raising their Heckler & Koch submachine guns, the French commandos lay in wait.

As soon as the last of the Tokushu Sakusen Gun was down in the tunnel, they were ambushed – and all eight of them were dispatched.

157

RECITING A SHORT mumbled prayer, one he made up on the spur of the moment, Kinjo took out his Swiss Army penknife – the top of the range. He reached out, his hands quivering, then leaned forwards as Gromet kept the light steady.

Miki didn't react. Not one little bit.

Her eyes were still wide open, but she was a million miles from the ossuary. She was swimming through the waves of the inland sea, with the other shimmer fish.

With extraordinary care, Kinjo sliced the first strap.

He could hear his heart beating, and feel the pulse in his brow.

Very slowly, he cut away the second strap.

And then the third.

A professional bomb disposal expert might have been more circumspect, or have been wary of booby-traps. But, fortunately for Kinjo, the Romanian kidnappers were skinflints. They had bought the belt cheap from a Chechen freedom fighter holed up in St. Denis.

All they could afford was the basic model.

The main unit was suddenly in the journalist's hand, the plastic explosive a little heavier than he had imagined. Resting it softly on the floor of the ossuary, Kinjo bowed his head in thanks to his ancestors.

Then he led the hostage to freedom.

158

FIVE MINUTES AFTER Miki had vacated the chamber, the AZ-1 Hostile Rescue team arrived. In their wake lumbered the Rottweiler, the blackout on her face now smudged.

The cameraman panned around the chamber, a live feed broadcasting the images worldwide. He tilted up onto the star reporter's blackened face, for her piece-to-camera, the grittiest of her career and, as it turned out, her last.

The Rottweiler moved over to the back wall, the camera taking in the orderly rows of skulls. She began describing the ossuary. As she did so, the commander flicked a thumb to the switch on his radio, and called the support unit on ground level.

'AZ-1 to Base.'

'Go ahead AZ-1.'

'The Rabbit is…'

Before the commander could finish his sentence, the Rottweiler reached down and picked something up… the main unit from the suicide belt – a harmless curiosity to an investigative reporter.

An ounce of mercury in the tilt-switch slid down the short glass tube.

There was a massive explosion.

The live feed instantly went dead.

In the blink of an eye, the Rottweiler, her film crew, and four special forces commandos, were spattered across the ossuary's bone-covered walls.

159

As the explosion shook the entire area, Maurice Gromet led the way through a secret tunnel, and up steep steps to the surface.

Neither he, Kinjo, nor Miki made comment on the noise. It was as though they were too close to it, or a part of it.

They lumbered up the steps like shell-shocked soldiers home from war. Judging by the needles and the trash, the passage had recently been frequented by users.

Miki was lost in her own world.

'What's wrong with her?' Gromet asked after a long silence.

Kinjo sucked air through his teeth.

'Paris Syndrome,' he said, awkwardly.

'*Paris?*'

'*Syndrome.*'

'Is there a cure?'

Kinjo let out a cough.

'Thankfully there is,' he replied.

160

With late morning sunshine blazing in through the windows of the minibus, the former patients of Dr. Mesmer's asylum took it in turns to sing.

Bart went first.

He treated the others to his own version of The Beatles' *Yesterday*. The lyrics were lewd, and he had learned them while mining opals in the Transvaal.

When he was done, Mrs. Ito piped up with a lullaby she had heard as a child. It was unlike her to make such a spectacle. But the others enjoyed her singing and clapped when she had finished.

Then Vladimir began with a Siberian folk song.

As the Russian filled the vehicle with a raucous and high-pitched wall of noise, the minibus driver felt a migraine coming on. Pressing the ball of his hand to his temple, he rubbed very hard, but the pain only grew worse. In need of a break, he pulled off the autoroute, onto a smaller road.

Twisting and turning through the countryside, the minibus ran alongside the highway for a while, before being channelled southwards on a meandering D-road. Now that Mr. Tanaka was singing, the driver's migraine had eased, and so he tried in vain to get back onto the autoroute.

But each attempt was thwarted by oncoming traffic or by restrictions in the road layout.

And so he kept on going.

Mesmer and Nurse Polk had both fallen asleep, calmed into a dream state by the succession of songs.

It was late afternoon when the doctor opened his eyes.

'Aren't we there yet?' he asked sleepily.

The driver jerked his head towards the gridlocked traffic.

'Been stuck in this for an age,' he replied.

Mesmer rubbed his eyes and peered through the windscreen. Suddenly, he sat up straight, his face drained of blood.

'*Non!*' he exclaimed. '*Non, non, non, non!*'

'*Quoi?*'

'This is the... the... the...'

'The Périphérique,' the driver said absently. 'We went off course, but it's all going to be OK now.'

'But I told you!' the doctor yelled, his cheeks flushing, 'you must keep away from Paris!'

The driver's head lunged to the right.

'*That's* Paris over there,' he said. 'So as long as we do not turn to the right we will be fine, *non*?'

At that moment, the traffic slowed.

'It's an accident,' said Bart.

An ambulance sped at high speed down the hard shoulder, and was followed by a fire engine. The minibus stood still in gridlock for another hour and a half. Then, inching forwards, it took another hour to go a hundred feet.

The driver jerked his head at a slip road on the right.

'If we go down there, we will break free of the traffic,' he said.

Nurse Polk wondered out loud why no one else seemed tempted to venture down the lane.

'Because they don't know the shortcut,' the driver said.

Mesmer tut-tutted.

'It will lead us into Paris,' he said, his voice forceful.

'*Non*, it will be our saviour,' the driver explained. 'I have taken it a hundred times.'

'The very same road?'

The driver nodded eagerly.

'But of course,' he said.

161

THE FIRST HOSTILE Rescue team's fate was relayed to the surface by the second unit.

Having donned breathing apparatus, the second team entered the ossuary, weapons at the ready. A veteran of numerous African wars, Beirut and Afghanistan, their commander grimaced. He recognized the effects of detonated plastic explosive when he saw them – and would have known the stench of cooked flesh a mile away.

Surveying the fragmented body parts, he radioed back to base:

'No survivors. Repeat, *no* survivors.'

A crackled voice rang out through his earpiece:

'What about Miki Suzuki?'

'Negative. Repeat, negative. The Rabbit is dead.'

162

HUGO DE MONTFRIED was among the first to hear the news, relayed to him by Jacques Pigalle. He took the call in his Bentley, seated in the back. His contact's sigh said everything before he had said a word.

'I am so sorry,' he said with real sincerity. 'At least the end would have been very quick.'

The Comte whispered appreciation, terminated the call, and asked his chauffeur to pull over. In a daze, he got out and ambled across a slim patch of grass. There was no way for him to know it, but his feet were walking over the same narrow stretch of parkland that Miki had so enjoyed on Mr. Nakamura's city tour.

Pausing beneath one of the chestnut trees, Hugo de Montfried broke down in inconsolable grief.

163

'MY TUMMY IS feeling funny,' said Tanaka-san, as the minibus careened south towards the centre of town. 'It feels, well, it feels all turnipy.'

Dr. Mesmer lurched round, his eyes wide with horror.

'Get this God-damned vehicle back the other side of the God-damned Périphérique!'

The driver took a left, and then a right, and another left. But, as though luck were not on his side, the route kept taking him south.

Then Mesmer's worst nightmare occurred.

The minibus had a flat tyre.

'My tummy's still hurting,' Tanaka-san the turnip repeated.

'Well, no one cares about you,' said Vladimir. 'All they care about is what happened to Hiawatha.'

'*Hiawatha?*' asked the nurse.

'My Red Indian Barbie.'

Bart licked his lips fast.

'Hiawatha was a boy,' he said.

'Say that again, and I'll sock you,' said the Russian.

Bart repeated the line and found Vladimir's fist in his mouth. He licked his lips.

'Yowza!' he yelled.

164

MAURICE GROMET MAY not have understood Paris Syndrome, but he did understand psychological conditions, suffering from one or two himself.

Kinjo had explained that Miki was in a state of deep trauma, and that the only cure was to be rushed out of Paris.

On the down-and-out's suggestion, the reporter took Miki to the suburb of Pantin, which stood just beyond the Périphérique. Maurice Gromet said that his brother lived in the town, in a neat stone house filled with terriers. His name was Raphael.

'Will it be alright if we stay there for a day or so?' Kinjo had asked.

Maurice Gromet had shrugged.

'Why not?'

'Because we are strangers.'

'Do you like dogs?'

Kinjo had given a thumbs up and, the next thing he knew, he was knocking on the front door.

After a long wait and much barking, a light came on inside and the door was pulled back. A thickset bearded man with sores on his neck was standing in the frame.

'I am Michi Kinjo,' said the reporter, 'and this is Miki… Miki Suzuki.'

'*Bonsoir*,' the man replied, questioningly.

'I am a friend… an *acquaintance* of Maurice.'

'*Maurice?*'

'Your brother.'

Raphael Gromet took a step backwards, terriers swirling round his ankles.

'I have not spoken to him in…' he thought for a moment, sneezed, and then thought again. 'For fifteen years,' he said.

'Could we stay with you?' Kinjo asked blankly.

'*Here?*'

'Yes.'

'The house is small and damp. And I have many dogs.'

'I like dogs,' Kinjo replied.

'Would you not be more comfortable in a hotel?'

The *Asahi Shimbun*'s finest sucked air though his back teeth.

'Maybe not,' he replied.

News of Miki Suzuki's death was broadcast to the furthest reaches of the earth.

There were tributes from the President of the Fifth Republic, and from the Emperor of Japan. Three days of national mourning were announced in both nations. Fresh ribbons were tied around trees. This time they were not red, but white – signifying virtue and love.

At the Angel Flower Beauty Company, the chairman laid a special memorial wreath at the front of the ruined building. Then he announced that a new line in beauty products would be established – the Miki Suzuki line.

Meanwhile, still in Paris, Mrs. Suzuki led tributes to her daughter.

In public, she was stoical and brave, but in private the grief was too much to bear. On French TV she announced that Miki would want everyone to carry on as normal.

The chief of police explained to the Suzuki family that the bodies had been so obliterated, that there was no way of retrieving anything amounting to a body.

'Tissue had been removed for DNA-testing,' he said. 'But it will be some time before the results are received.'

'In due course we would like to take something,' Mrs. Suzuki replied tearfully, 'even if it is a small piece of Miki.'

The officer sniffed, and pinched the end of his nose.

'I'll see what I can get you,' he said.

As the French nation mourned Miki and its fallen commandos, NHK ran tributes to their own heroes – the TV crew and the Rottweiler.

Three days passed.

Having blown the fifty euros on crack, Maurice Gromet curled up in the catacombs and fell into a deep sleep. And, not wishing to be inhospitable, his brother invited the Japanese couple in, and found them to be tremendous company for both himself and the dogs.

Kinjo tried time and again to telephone the newspaper headquarters. After a day of rest, having regained her sanity and composure, Miki called her parents. But all the lines were blocked. Everyone in the world, it seemed, was calling Japan.

'I must go to Louis Vuitton,' said Miki on the morning of the fourth day. 'I need to get the coin pouch for my ojiichan.'

Kinjo swallowed hard.

'I think that would be imprudent,' he said.

'But I cannot return home without it.'

166

THE FORMER PATIENTS of the Montmartre asylum were patients once again, having slipped a second time under the Parisian spell.

As for Vladimir the Russian, the fact he had been as affected as the others caused Mesmer to conclude that his Barbie fixation was indeed linked to its own curious form of Paris Syndrome.

The psychiatrist had cajoled the ambulance service into driving the group back down to the Burgundian village of Villars Fontaine. His gut was telling him that one day he would look back on the absurdity of it all. And, his bones were telling him that there was undoubted professional glory to be gained.

Once the Périphérique was behind them, the patients felt a lot better. By the evening they were all safely ensconced back at Chateau Lugny. It was the one place of safety that Dr. Mesmer could count on.

Then, just before dinner, news of Miki's death arrived, it having been reported on the radio.

The psychiatrist told the patients at the evening meal. It saddened everyone profoundly.

'I would have married her,' Vladimir declared. 'She loved me, and I loved her.'

'I thought you were going to marry *me*,' Victoria said.

'I was,' the Russian mused. 'But you were my second choice.'

Mr. Kim and Mr. Park both made statements about Miki.

The first was that she had a good soul and nice eyes. The second was that her breath smelt of peanuts.

'I think Miki was a heroine,' Miss Fujimoto said.

And, at the remark, all the patients began to applaud. Dr. Mesmer and Nurse Polk joined them and, all of a sudden, Chateau Lugny was triumphant with noise.

167

ANOTHER DAY PASSED, and Raphael Gromet went out to buy dog food. At the supermarket checkout, he caught sight of *Paris Match*.

On the front cover was the photograph of a Japanese woman and, beneath it, were the words, 'The Saint of Saints'.

Gromet frowned, wiped a hand over his mouth, and frowned again.

Ten minutes later he was back with his terriers and his guests, the magazine open on the table.

'Oh,' Miki said. 'They think I am dead.'

'The country is mourning you,' said Raphael.

Kinjo looked worried.

'They will not be pleased,' he said.

'They will be angry,' Miki echoed. She gulped. 'I have done a shameful thing,' she said.

The Frenchman poured a packet of dog food into the kitchen's trough. He frowned again.

'Surviving is shameful?'

The Japanese guests looked at one another and then they nodded.

'I will kill myself,' Miki said. 'Because that is the honourable thing to do.'

'I will kill myself, too,' Kinjo whispered. 'Because I have been dishonourable as well.'

Gromet pulled out a chair and collapsed onto it, wiping a hand over the sores on his neck. An instant later there was a pair of terriers on his lap.

'This is not a moment for sacrifice!' he bawled. 'People will rejoice when they know Miki is alive!'

168

TWO HOURS AFTER Raphael Gromet had spotted the copy of *Paris Match*, the editor of the magazine herself was sitting at his kitchen table. She was dressed in Versace, a wirehaired terrier clinging to her knees. Kinjo relayed the story of how he had tracked down Miki, and how he had cut away the suicide belt.

'Are you both ready for the Press?' the editor asked, brushing the back of a hand over her chest.

'The Press?'

She nodded.

'Miki, you are more of a celebrity than almost anyone alive,' the editor said. 'And you, Kinjo… you can claim the reward money.'

Raphael Gromet looked up and strained to appear nonchalant.

'*Prize money?*'

'Yes.'

'May I ask how much it is – this prize?'

The editor wove the tips of her fingers together.

'About thirty million euros,' she said.

169

THREE DAYS LATER, *Paris Match* broke the scoop of the century.

Having been reunited with her mother, and honoured by the President of France, Miki was taken in an open-top limousine through the streets of Pantin. After all, it was far too risky to take her back into Paris. Accepting Mr. Gromet's kind hospitality, she remained at the house, along with Kinjo. They were joined by Miki's mother. She had been only too happy to swap the more lavish quarters of The Bristol for the suburban terrier-filled home.

Meanwhile, the world's media were camped outside. The sleepy suburb of Pantin had never experienced anything like it.

In the city, at Maison Pastache, the curtains were pulled open for the first time in days. Hugo de Montfried yelled so loudly with joy that the exclamation was heard three streets away.

Pushing past his sister, who was standing in the hallway, the Comte hurried out to his car. Half an hour later, he was in Pantin, standing outside the plain home of Raphael Gromet.

Kinjo looked down from an upper window.

'I think you had better come and see this,' he said.

Miki paced over to the window. She was wearing Givenchy, her hair having been done by Dessange. But inside she was the same Miki Suzuki as the one who had stood out in Shiba Park.

On tiptoes, she looked down at the street.

There was silence for a long time.

And then, a squeal. A high-pitched, frantic, unearthly squeal.

'Who is it?' Mrs. Suzuki asked.

'The man I love!' exclaimed Miki, before falling to the floor with a *thump*!

170

IN THE WEEK that followed, Remus and his gang of Romanian thugs were apprehended, tried and jailed, in what was the speediest conviction in French history.

Just as they were being dragged away to the cells, the Gromet brothers were being decorated for their parts in assisting Miki Suzuki in her time of need. In all the hysteria, Raphael Gromet secured himself a lucrative sponsorship deal for dog food. And even his brother came out a winner. He signed a contract to promote a leading addiction clinic, one favoured by partied-out Russian oligarchs and A-list celebrities.

The next week, Louis Vuitton's CEO travelled from the head-quarters on the Champs-Elysées, to meet with Miki. He was accompanied by a throng of executives and contract-people, designers and hangers-on.

Arriving at Pantin in three black Mercedes limousines, they parked outside the modest home of Raphael Gromet. Despite being offered any number of hotels outside the capital, Miki had decided to remain as Mr. Gromet's guest.

By the time the chief of Louis Vuitton returned to Paris, he had signed Miki up as the new face of Louis Vuitton. A brand ambassador extraordinaire, she was to have her own range, a personal assistant and stylist, and as many free products as she liked from the LV catalogue.

There was, however, only one item that interested her.

The day after the LV visit, Michi Kinjo was presented with a cheque for more than thirty-two million euros by the head of NHK. The channel's CEO had flown to France specially to bask in all the free publicity. The presentation was made in Paris, rather than Tokyo, because of the extra glamour the station's leader imagined it would attract.

Bowing, then blushing, the young reporter took the cheque and apologized.

'It was my duty to help Miki Suzuki-san,' he said, 'as a humble journalist from the *Asahi Shimbun.*'

'Thirty-two million euros is a lot of money… more than four billion yen,' the NHK chief explained anxiously. 'You could buy your own newspaper with it!' he said.

Kinjo looked up, blinked, then smiled.

'I do not want any reward money,' he whispered.

'*You do not…*'

'Want it. No, I do not want it.'

'*None* of it?'

'No. None of it. You can have the cheque back.'

'Then what *do* you want?'

Michi Kinjo bowed once again, a little deeper and more sincerely than before.

'I would like to have a desk beside the window at the *Asahi Shimbun,*' he said.

171

BUT THE BIGGEST news was not the fate of the Romanians, nor was it the Gromet brothers, nor the LV deal, nor the fact that Kinjo had turned down the massive prize.

It was the news of an engagement…

172

AT TWELVE NOON precisely on the last Saturday of the month, the bells of the Chateau de Cheverny began pealing in the early summer sun.

The seat of the de Montfried family for three centuries, Cheverny was regarded as one of the finest chateaux in all of the Loire.

The guests were all gathered in the chapel – a sea of flowers, morning suits and wide-brimmed chapeaux.

A great many of those invited were unfamiliar to the bride – statesmen, politicians, members of the nobility and the landed gentry.

But some of them she did recognize.

Seated on the hard oak pews were Mr. Park and Mr. Chen, Vladimir and Victoria and the lip-licking South African, Bart. Mrs. Ito and Miss Fujimoto were there as well, and Tanaka-san the turnip, as well as Dr. Mesmer and Nurse Polk.

Behind them, dressed in a tuxedo, sat Kinjo, along with the brothers Gromet – both of them in suits. And, newly arrived from Tokyo, was Ichiko, Miki's best friend, Saito-san her French teacher, and Mr. Nakamura from Paradise Tours.

The Angel Flower Beauty Company was conspicuous by its absence. No one from the firm had been invited. Miki had requested that they stay away. Although she could have shamed them publicly, she chose not to. As she saw it, revenge would have been too easy.

The front row was reserved for family.

On one side sat Delphine de Montfried, her aged mother, and a scattering of cousins, uncles and aunts. And, on the other, sat Mrs. Suzuki. Beside her, was Miki's beloved ojiichan. The French air had brought colour back to his cheeks, and he felt a great deal younger than he had in years.

Cupped in his hand was a little leather coin pouch from Louis Vuitton.

Standing at the front, a little nervous and a little shy, was Comte Hugo de Montfried.

The great bell chimed once, and the congregation rose to their feet.

Then, as the pipes of the organ filled with sound, the bride entered.

Dressed in a mass of snow-white silk, she walked forwards very slowly as if in a dream, on the arm of her father.

As her miniature feet advanced down the nave, the congregation turned one by one.

173

AT THE END of the marriage service, the Comte and Comtesse emerged into the dazzling sunshine, the birdsong drowned out by cheers.

Pausing to kiss his bride once again, de Montfried burst out laughing.

'I am the happiest man alive!' he bellowed.

All of a sudden, standing there with the cheers ringing out, Miki got a cascade of memory.

She thought of Pun-Pun and the chairman of Angel Flower, of Noemi and Shiba Park. Then she thought of the George V and the Belle Rose Travel Lodge, of the fake gold ring and Parc Monceau. She thought of Dr. Mesmer's hospital, of Vladimir and the Turnip, and of the taste of choux cream on her lips.

At the end of it all, she thought of herself squatting in the catacombs, a suicide belt strapped to her chest.

'I am feeling a little strange,' she said in a frail voice.

The Comte looked deep into his bride's eyes.

He sensed something fearful there.

A shiver ran down his spine.

He was about to offer a glass of water, a chair, or another declaration of his love.

But Miki smiled and, in an instant, the smile melted de Montfried's fears.

'I will be fine,' his bride whispered. 'But please promise me something.'

'I would promise you anything in the world.'

Miki blinked, the corners of her mouth a little taut.

'Promise me that I shall never have to set foot in Paris again,' she said.

A Request

If you enjoyed this book, please review it on Amazon and Goodreads.

Reviews are an author's best friend.

To stay in touch with Tahir Shah, and to hear about his upcoming releases before anyone else, please sign up for his mailing list:

 http://bit.ly/tahirshah

And to follow him on social media, please go to any of the following links:

 http://www.twitter.com/humanstew

 http://www.facebook.com/TahirShahAuthor

 http://www.youtube.com/user/tahirshah999

 http://www.pinterest.com/tahirshah

 http://www.goodreads.com/author/show/7102.Tahir_Shah

http://www.tahirshah.com

CPSIA information can be obtained at www.ICGtesting.com
Printed in the USA
LVOW04s1329101114

412893LV00001B/318/P